UNANTICIPATED CONNECTIONS

Mitch gave a soft snort. It was unfamiliar territory, this trust thing, because he certainly hadn't felt it where any of the other nannies were concerned. Maybe it was the age difference between her and the ones who'd seemed hardly old enough to look after themselves, never mind three children. He shook his head at himself. No, it was more than that. There was something else. A depth the others hadn't had. A compassion rooted in what felt like empathy rather than sympathy. Like there was more to Abigail's story than simply needing a job as a nanny.

He'd seen it in the haunted shadows in her eyes when she'd first arrived, and again when she'd informed him she would only stay for three months. He'd ignored the shadows because he had enough to worry about, he'd told himself, and because Abigail's business was her own. Which it was, except...

Except he couldn't help but wonder who was looking after Abby's problems while she looked after his.

ABIGAIL ALWAYS

An Ever After Romance

Linda Poitevin

Michem Publishing, Canada

Published by Michem Publishing, Canada

ABIGAIL ALWAYS

Cover art by Kanaxa
Interior Design by Clara Stone

ISBN: 978-1-9994980-8-5

For Heidi Leduc,
who was every inch the kind, gracious, generous soul
that I made her in these pages.
I miss you, my friend.

Acknowledgements

Writing a book is never truly a solo effort. Somewhere, behind every writer, stands a team of indispensable people who have helped along the way, and I would like to give special thanks to some of them for their support and help in the writing of **Abigail Always**.

First, to my husband and youngest daughter, who suffered through my absence as I scrambled to meet my deadlines over the Christmas holidays. I know I wasn't around very much for a couple of weeks, and I'm so very grateful that you hung around waiting for me to re-emerge from my office.

Next, to author 'Nathan Burgoine, for opening my eyes to the need to reflect the diverse tapestry of life in my novels—and for his valuable advice on how to do it right (I hope I did!).

To my team of beta readers, who performed above and beyond on this book, meeting an insane deadline and still managing to give invaluable feedback. Bridget Connors, Karen Tanruther, Olga Gontarczyk, and Emily Nord—you guys truly rock!

A big thank you to the Ottawa Humane Society, as well, for providing me with a behind-the-scenes tour and patiently answering my many questions--and for the amazing work you do for the critters who need you.

And last but never least, the people who have my

back when it comes to production: my editor, Laura Byrne Paquet, who fit me into her schedule mere days before a Mexican vacation(!); my cover designer Natalie, who continues to wow me with her vision and her ability to intuit my own; and my interior designer Clara Stone, who is just downright fantastic to work with.

You are all awesome. Period.

CHAPTER 1

"You must have *something* I can do." Abigail Jamieson tried to keep the desperation out of her voice, but the way the woman across from her peered over her wire-rimmed glasses, she didn't think she'd succeeded. Through sheer force of will, she kept her hands linked loosely in her business-suited lap and didn't bolt for the door.

On the other side of the desk, Estelle Gagnon set aside the single sheet of paper that served as Abigail's scant resume. She leaned back in her chair and steepled her fingers, touching the index tips to her lips.

"Why childcare?" she asked finally, her English tinged by a slight French accent. "Why not something in an office?"

Abigail reached deep inside, past nerves left raw by answering this same question too many times over the last two weeks, and dug up the humility she needed to answer again. Nannies to Go was the last nanny agency on the list in the entire city of Ottawa, and she would not, could not, go home to her sister Gwyn's with no prospects yet again. Not after the conversation she'd overhead this morning.

"I know she needs our support, Gwyn," Gareth's voice floated through the door of his and Gwyn's

bedroom as Abigail passed by in the hallway. "But it's been three and a half months. And yes, she's helping out with the house, but you need your space back. We need our space back. At least let me put her up in an apartment while she figures out what she wants to do."

"Are you going to be the one to tell her she's overstayed her welcome?" Gwyn retorted. "She's my sister, Gareth, and her husband and daughter died. There is no way I'm turfing her out on her ear right now. She needs more time."

"She's already been here almost three months. How much more time does she need? Another month? Three—"

"Mrs. Jamieson?"

The recruiter's voice jolted Abigail back to the present, and she pushed away the memory of her sister's disagreement with her husband. Over her. She crossed her ankles and tucked her feet under her chair, sitting up straighter. "I've been out of the workforce for a number of years," she said, with rehearsed calm. "And I don't have any office skills to speak of, beyond being able to use a computer."

"You don't have any childcare skills to speak of, either," Ms. Gagnon replied. "Most clients these days are looking for someone with a background in early childhood education at the very least. I'm afraid one semester of a psychology undergrad degree isn't quite the same, even if you did plan on going into child psychology. Without some kind of hands-on experience, there's nothing I can—"

"I had a daughter." The words spilled from Abby

before she realized they'd even formed, surprising her as much as they obviously surprised Ms. Gagnon. The recruiter stared at her, eyebrows raised, waiting for more. Abby curled her hands into fists on her lap. It was the first time she'd told that to a stranger in more than a year. Or maybe it had been an eternity. "I had a daughter," she repeated, needing to say it again. Needing to hear it again. "She died."

Tears burned in the back of her eyes. Rapidly, she blinked them back as Ms. Gagnon stood up from her chair and crossed the office to a bookshelf under a window. She poured a glass of water from a pitcher there and returned to pass it to Abby. Then she leaned back against the desk. "When?" she asked, all trace of professionalism gone from her quiet voice.

"Just under a year ago," Abby said. "It was a car accident. She was eleven. She and my husband were both killed."

"I'm so sorry," said Ms. Gagnon. "Do you need a tissue?"

Abby gritted her teeth and shook her head. "Thank you, but I'm fine. Really."

"*Bon.*" Good. The recruiter went around the desk to retake her chair. She looked down at the resumé on the desk for a moment, then peered at Abby over her glasses again. "You're certain you want a job caring for children? It will not be too difficult for you?"

"I can manage," she said. "I've thought it through, and it really is all I'm qualified for. To be honest, I've never even waitressed or worked in retail, and I would much rather work at something I know I can do."

Ms. Gagnon tapped a pen against the resumé. "There might be something, but..."

Abigail's hopes leapt. Oh, to go home and tell Gwyn she'd found something! "But?"

"You would have to live in, and there would be some housekeeping involved as well."

She clutched the glass tighter, needing an anchor in the sudden swirl of hope even as the irony made her want to laugh. Or cry. Or both. Oh, how William would love this, if he knew. All those fights over her desire for independence, for stimulation outside the home, and now look at her. Heading back into the kitchen to which he'd kept her tied for so many years. But... she'd get to move out of Gwyn and Gareth's house and actually stand—more or less—on her own two feet for the first time in a very, very long time.

Make that for the first time ever.

"I can definitely do that," she told Ms. Gagnon. "I was a stay-at-home..." She trailed off, the word *wife* stuck in her throat, and *mom* still too raw. She compromised with, "I stayed home for twelve years."

Something flashed in the recruiter's eyes—sympathy? pity?—but she moved the conversation along. "There are three girls: a five-year-old, a nine-year-old, and a thirteen-year-old. Their mother passed away just over a year ago—cancer—and their father is... struggling."

"Struggling?"

"He runs his own construction firm, and his hours can be irregular. He's trying his best, but honestly, he's losing ground every time I talk to him."

Abby frowned. "Every time you talk to him? How long has he been trying to find someone?"

Ms. Gagnon hesitated. Then she sighed. "I'm going to be honest with you, Mrs. Jamieson. This isn't an easy job. Frankly, I'm not even sure it's a doable job. If you take it, you'll be the twelfth woman to attempt it in the last nine months."

"Oh? What's the problem?"

"My client's hours. His unwillingness to back up the nannies on discipline issues. Discipline issues, period." Ms. Gagnon leaned back in her chair and sighed again. "My understanding is that the older girl resents having anyone tell her what to do. Part of the problem is the father's distraction, of course, and part of it may be the age of the nannies themselves. Most women who are coming out of early childhood education programs are young, and I'm not sure they have the air of authority that's needed here. You, on the other hand..."

Great. Now she was being offered a job because she was old? Abby tried not to grimace. She couldn't afford to be proud right now. Heck, she couldn't afford much of anything. She lifted her chin and took a deep breath.

"I'll take it," she said.

"Excellent. You can start as soon as your police check clears. I'll ask a friend to rush it."

Abigail stepped around her sister as Gwyn bounced a fussy Julianne against one shoulder, patting the baby's back with her free hand. She felt Gwyn's gaze on her, following her from bureau to closet to open suitcase on the bed. Studiously, she avoided meeting it.

"You're sure about this," Gwyn said for the fortieth time in the week since Abby had delivered her news. "I mean, a live-in *nanny?*"

Abby tried not to bristle at what sounded like criticism. Truth be told, if Gwyn *was* questioning her ability with children, she had good reason, because Abby had done her level best to avoid her nieces and nephew ever since her August arrival. At first, she'd told herself that it was because she couldn't handle being so close to what was obviously a happy family when she had lost so much. However, after three months, she'd begun to think it went deeper than that—into territory that included guilt and resentment and a whole lot of other baggage she didn't care to examine. That made it all the more important that she leave now, before the toxicity brewing deep in her gut found its way out and poisoned her relationship with her sister even more than it already had been for years. She took a pair of pants from a hanger and folded them into the suitcase.

"I'm sure," she replied, also for the fortieth time. "I need to move on with my life, Gwyn. I can't camp out here forever. Katie needs her room back." She glanced at the stuffed unicorns piled on a shelf and the *Anne of Green Gables* series piled on the bedside table. *And I need not to be waking up every day in a room that could have been my own daughter's.*

"Katie is fine sharing with Maggie. This is about you." Gwyn wiped a trickle of drool from Julianne's chin, expertly following her daughter's twists and dodges and ignoring the squawks of protest. "I get that you want to move on, but raising someone else's children? What happened to that psychology degree you were studying for? Can't you do something with that instead?"

Abby closed her eyes. There was another thing she'd avoided since arriving here: any kind of conversation with Gwyn that touched on her life with William. For the same reasons she'd stopped writing to her sister about that life. Stopped confiding in her at all. Her cheeks grew hot, and she looked down at the floor. "I didn't finish," she answered, silently begging Gwyn not to pursue the subject.

"Oh," said her sister. Then, her voice hesitant, "Abby..."

"Don't." Abby shoved the last of her clothes, hangers and all, into the suitcase and slammed the lid down. She zipped it shut, then leaned on it, blinking back tears she didn't want to share. Didn't have the right to share, after she'd refused to be there when Gwyn had needed her—no matter what her reasons at the time. She straightened and turned, a tight smile pasted to her face. "I'm a big girl, Gwyn. I know what I'm doing."

"I'm not saying you don't. I'm just saying you don't have to do it. Stay. Please. Let us help."

Abby's resolve wavered in the face of the offer. Even after that conversation she'd overheard between Gwyn and Gareth last week, it would still be so much easier to remain here under their roof and their protection. So much safer. Except she'd lived her whole life sheltered from risk of any kind—first by her parents and then by William—only to discover there was no such thing as safe. Life didn't care whether she actively participated in it or not; it happened regardless. With all of its pain and its grief and its loss... and its devastation. Again, Abby blinked back tears. Then she straightened her spine and shook her head. "Thank you, but no. I need to do this. I need to look after myself."

Gwyn gave a small, hesitant shrug. "All right," she said. "But you know you can come back, right? Anytime."

"I know."

"And, Abby... one day, when you're ready? Let's talk. Just the two of us. Please?"

Her eyes blurring and her throat refusing to allow words, Abby looked away from the sister she'd once adored. She didn't see how they would ever overcome the chasm that had grown between them, but she nodded anyway. Because, in a perfect world, she thought she'd like that.

If only a perfect world existed.

"Auntie Abby!" her nephew, Nicholas, hollered up the stairs. "Your taxi's here!"

CHAPTER 2

Mitch Abrams pulled his head and shoulders out of the disaster that was the front hall closet and, sitting back on his heels, ran both hands over his close-cropped hair. He locked his fingers behind his head. Then he regarded the solemn, five-year-old girl at eye level to him, stuffed plush rabbit under one arm and one Wonder Woman running shoe clutched in her other hand. One, because the other was missing.

"You're *sure* you put both of them in the closet after school yesterday?" he asked.

Kiana nodded, her lopsided puff ponytails bobbing.

"Maybe you can wear a different pair today."

Her gaze dropped to the floor, and she shook her head, shifting from foot to foot. Mitch's innards cringed at the telltale agitation. He unlinked his fingers and pushed himself to his feet. Eyes closed, he pinched the bridge of his nose and breathed deeply. He was already ten minutes late for a meeting with the crew on the new build, and if he triggered one of his daughter's infamous meltdowns, he might as well cancel it altogether.

"Dad! Daddy!" a voice hollered from the kitchen at the back of the house. "The pancakes are burning!"

The shriek of a smoke alarm confirmed the announcement. Face scrunched tight, Kiana dropped the running shoe and slapped her hands over her ears. Then she turned tail and bolted up the stairs, heading for the safety of her bedroom. Mitch groaned. Great. There went another hour of his morning.

"Daddy!" Louder this time. And shriller.

"Coming," he called back. He loped down the hallway to where his two other daughters, Brittany and Rachel, flapped tea towels at the smoke billowing across the room to the island where they sat. Thirteen-year-old Rachel delivered a withering look as he reached up to pull the smoke alarm from its housing inside the doorway and stuffed it in a drawer to muffle its noise.

"Again?" she asked.

"You could have flipped them," Mitch retorted. "Or at least turned the pan off." He switched off the stove and grabbed the skillet, pulling back with a hiss when he connected with red-hot metal. Scowling, he picked up a tea towel and wrapped it around the pan's handle, then carried it and its blackened contents over to the patio doors and tossed the entire works out into the snow. *Shit, shit, shit.* He slammed the glass door shut again, so hard that it bounced half out of its track, reminding him that he still hadn't repaired the thing. He scowled at the offending, lopsided glass panel. For six years, he'd promised Eve he'd fix it, and—

The doorbell rang.

"Oh, for—" Mitch scowled, then headed back down the hallway. Rachel trailed after him.

"You know that was our last frying pan, right?" she asked. "You threw the other one out last week."

Mitch ignored the accusatory tone. And the fact

she was right. He kicked a path through the contents of the closet, strewn across the front hall floor. How in hell had that much stuff fit in there in the first place?

"And what are we supposed to do about breakfast, now?" she continued. "Starve?"

"Madame Sonia says that breakfast is the most important meal of the day," nine-year-old Brittany offered, joining them in the chaos that had become a reflection of their lives. "She says—"

"Oh, stuff Madame Sonia," Rachel snapped. "She's not God, you know."

"Enough!" Mitch barked, his last nerve fraying as he reached for the door knob. "Brittany, Madame Sonia is right, but now is not the time. Rachel, apologize to your sister. Kiana! Kiana, *please* come downstairs. Daddy has to go to work, goddammit!" He wrenched open the door and bellowed, "What?"

He registered the smoky blue eyes first, the fur trim of a hood surrounding a pale face second, and the lazily drifting snowflakes third. He didn't recognize the first two, but he knew without a doubt that the last observation had just killed all hope of making it into work that day. There was no army on the planet that could get Kiana into winter boots or a snowsuit without a week of advance warning, and with him not having so much as checked the forecast for the last several days, that opportunity had passed him by.

"Shit," he said, staring morosely out at the four inches of white fluff already piled up on the lawn. He recalled an image of the blackened frying pan landing in more of the stuff just moments before—he'd just been too distracted to pay attention. His gaze went back to the uninvited guest on his doorstep, traveling from head to toe. A woman, wearing a bright red jacket, pleated slacks, and the kind of furry boots Rachel had whined about for the last three Christmases and he had deemed ridiculous. He looked up again. A tiny frown had appeared between the smoky blue eyes.

"Mr. Abrams?"

He scowled. How in heck was he going to talk Kiana into anything halfway suitable for going to school? "Who wants to know?"

A white-mittened hand extended. "I'm Abigail Jamieson."

He stared at the hand.

"From the agency?" she prompted.

He stared at her.

"The nanny agency. Nannies to Go? I left you a voicemail message on Friday telling you I'd be here at 8:00 this morning."

"Daddy? Who's that?" Brittany wedged herself between Mitch's hip and the doorframe.

Smoky Eyes smiled down at her and again held out the hand Mitch had refused to shake. "My name is Abigail," she said. "But you can call me Abby. And I'm guessing you must be Brittany."

Brittany eyed the offered mitten for a second, then she accepted it and gave it a hearty pump. "Pleased to meet you," she said. "Are you really our new nanny?"

"I am," the woman said.

"No. She's not," Mitch overrode her words. He ran a hand over his chinstrap beard. The scrape of stubble against his palm outside the normal confines reminded him he had yet to tidy it this morning. Or shower. He held back the choice epithets growling through his brain. Maybe he should just give up and see if he could talk Derek into handling the meeting for him. Hell, maybe he should just give up on the whole blasted—

He cut the thought short and waved a hand in half-hearted apology. "Look, I'm sorry, but I haven't checked my voicemail all week, I know nothing about a new nanny, and I don't have time to interview anyone right now. Tell the agency to call me again next week, and we'll set something up."

His hand on Brittany's shoulder, he stepped back and started to close the door.

"Wait!" The white mitten shot through the opening and fastened around the edge. "I'm not here for an interview. I'm here to work."

Mitch pulled the door open a fraction again and peered around it. For the first time, he noticed the pile of luggage on the snow-covered sidewalk behind her. One large roll-along suitcase, one medium-sized one, and an overnight bag. He raised an eyebrow. Met the blue gaze. Raised the other eyebrow. "Work?" he echoed. "As in *move in?*"

The fur-framed face went even paler as the woman's expression wobbled, then tightened. Her voice dropped to barely a whisper. "I thought—I was told—Estelle said—"

"Estelle?"

"Ms. Gagnon. At Nannies to Go." The woman bit her bottom lip. "She said it was a live-in position."

"Not without a freaking interview, it isn't." Mitch looked her up and down again. "Do you really think I'd let someone move in with my children without meeting them first? Seeing their references? What the hel—heck kind of a parent would that make me?"

The blue gaze traveled past him to the shambles that was his front hall, and Mitch was pretty certain the words "a desperate one" hovered on her lips. He bristled, but to her credit, she kept the comment to herself as she squared her shoulders and nodded.

"Of course. I should have—I'm sorry. I'll let Est— Ms. Gagnon know. We can do an interview whenever you're ready." She waved her mitten at the luggage. "I'll need a cab, if you wouldn't mind calling one for me?"

His gaze went to the driveway, empty of any vehicle but his own pickup. Great. Now he was turning her away in the snow and cold? His conscience twinged, but sheer practicality overruled it. He was in no way prepared to take in a new nanny without any kind of warning, he knew nothing about this particular wannabe, he was growing later by the second for that meeting, and he still had three girls to crowbar and/or cajole out of the house. He firmed his jaw. "Of course," he said. "And we'll set up something for later this week. Maybe Thursday evening?" Then, because he'd been rather shorter with her than was needed, he added, "I'm sorry for the mix-up."

Horror filled him as the blue eyes turned shiny. Oh hell, no. She wasn't going to cry, was she? Could this morning possibly get any worse? As he debated closing the door on her—admittedly not his most stellar moment as a human being—a car horn tooted curbside and a cheery voice called out, "Morning, Mitch! The girls ready to go?"

Rachel shoved him aside and waved to her best friend's mother, a woman as comfortable with her generous curves as she was with her status as a divorcée.

"We'll be there in a minute, Jessica!" she called. Then, ignoring the woman standing on the porch, she crossed her arms and scowled up at Mitch. "You forgot that you asked Mandy's mom to pick us up for school starting this week, didn't you?"

"I—"

"And we still haven't had breakfast. What are we supposed to do, starve?"

Mitch bit back the uncharitable *yes* that hovered and instead said, "Just get ready. I'll get some granola bars from the kitchen." He turned back to the open door. "Ms. Jamieson, was it? I'm sorry, but I really ha—" He stopped mid-sentence as Jessica Perkins danced up onto the porch to join the wannabe nanny. Hell.

"Oh dear." Jessica pulled a face as her gaze went to the hallway behind him. "Rough morning? You really should take me up on my offer to get you guys organized, Mitch, my friend. A couple of weeks and you won't even recognize the place."

The air wheezed from Mitch. Oh, he'd seen Jessica's house, all right. The woman had invited the girls to go swimming in her pool in August, and then insisted on giving him the grand tour while wearing the skimpiest bikini he'd ever tried not to lay eyes on. He all but broke out in a cold sweat at the memory of how many times he'd had to extricate himself from various corners of that place. He didn't think the woman had any serious designs on him, but she had made it abundantly clear that she thought two lonely people could—and should—find solace in one another's company. She was right—her corners had been organized. He just had no intention of putting himself in a similar situation again.

"Thanks, Jessica, but—"

"Oh, pooh," Jessica waved away the objection. "You know it's no trouble. I'm happy to help. Why don't Mandy and I come over tomorrow after school? The girls can hang out, and I can get a start on things. We'll order pizza for dinner. It will be fun!" Without waiting for a response, she turned to the other woman. "I'm so sorry. How rude of me not to introduce myself. I'm Jessica Perkins, a family friend."

"Abigail Jamieson," Smoky Eyes murmured.

Was it Mitch's imagination, or was she trying not to laugh?

"I see," Jessica said, when no further information was offered. She nodded at the luggage pile she'd skirted on her way up the sidewalk. "And you're here... for a visit?"

"I'm—"

"She's moving in with us!" Brittany poked her head past Mitch, her voice muffled by the scarf she'd wound around her face. "She's our new nanny."

"Oh?" Jessica looked over her shoulder at Mitch. "Rachel didn't mention you'd found someone new."

Mitch opened his mouth to explain, then closed it

as an image of Jessica Perkins organizing his house popped into his head. Another one followed of her wearing a bikini while doing so.

On the porch, Abigail Jamieson steadfastly refused to meet his gaze.

Abigail Jamieson, his unexpected—and unsuspecting—lifeline.

"It was a last-minute thing," he heard himself reply.

"I see." Jessica's narrow gaze traveled between Mitch and Abigail Jamieson, who stared down at a hole she'd made in the snow with the toe of her furry boot. Then Jessica's expression cleared, becoming cheerful again and leaving Mitch wondering what she saw.

"Well then," she said, "Welcome, Abigail Jamieson. I'll leave you to get settled in, but make sure Mitch leaves you my number in case you need anything while he's at work. I'm happy to help if I can. Come on, girls, we're running late."

With a cheery wave, she trotted back down the driveway to the car she'd left idling. The snow swallowing the sound of her door closing as Rachel shoved past him, Brittany on her heels.

"Bye, Daddy!" Brittany sang over her shoulder. "Bye, Abby! See you after school!"

"Wait," Mitch called after them. "Granola bars!"

Rachel waved a handful of wrapped bars aloft as she trudged across the lawn. She didn't deign to look back. Seconds later, Jessica's car disappeared down the road, and silence fell over the yard, as thick and muffled as the flakes descending now in earnest. On the porch,

Abigail Jamieson stamped her ridiculous boots and wrapped her arms around herself.

Mitch sighed. Now that he'd made it past the knee-jerk reaction to her arrival, maybe giving her a try wouldn't be such a bad idea. Because the look she'd given his hallway was right. He was desperate. And he'd run through so many nannies in the last year that he'd been blacklisted by just about every agency in town. And Estelle Gagnon had assured him that every nanny she sent out had already passed a police check. And if he didn't find help soon, a lot more than the house was going to go south in his life. And—

He held the door wide. "I assume you have references?" he asked.

CHAPTER 3

Abigail didn't want to stare at the giant of a man standing in the middle of a pile of running shoes, backpacks, coats, and various other sundries—was that really a sparkly purple tutu sticking out from under his slipper?—but when he took up as much space as he did, it was hard not to. He had to be at least six-two, and he had shoulders on him like a linebacker, and, holy Hannah, did he have to keep glowering like that? She raised her chin in an attempt to look one part more confident and one part taller. The glower deepened.

Abigail shifted from one foot to the other amid her pile of luggage. Two pull-along suitcases and an overnight bag that represented all her worldly possessions except for the contents of a cardboard box left in Gwyn's care. Contents that made her breath hitch just at the thought of them, so she kept her attention on the scowl instead. It was an impressive one. She hoped at least part of it was attributable to the... interesting... Jessica Perkins, who for some reason seemed to strike a kind of terror into Mitch Abrams's heart.

And speaking of terror...

She summoned a determined smile to hide—she hoped—the utter panic roiling in her belly and tugged off her mitten. Once again, she held out her hand to her new employer. *This will work,* she assured herself. *It has to work.* "Abigail Jamieson," she said, as if for the first time. "And I'm so sorry we got off on the wrong foot."

The tall man with dark skin, surprising pale green eyes, and short-cropped, graying-at-the-temples hair still looked undecided about her presence in his house, but he let out a long exhale and reached to accept the handshake, his hand engulfing hers. "Mitchell Abrams," he replied. "And I'm sorry, too." He pulled his hand back and scratched at the strip of beard along his jaw. "It's been a challenging morning."

Abigail surveyed the catastrophe of a hallway. "I can see that."

"Coffee?" he asked. "I think there's some made, unless I forgot to turn on the pot."

She shook her head. "Thank you, but I already had some. Maybe my room, so I can get this"—she waved a hand at the suitcases surrounding her feet—"out of the way?"

"Of course. Except..." Mitchell Abrams grimaced. "I'm afraid it's not ready. I really haven't checked my voicemail lately. I'd given up on—I didn't think anyone —" He sighed. "In the interests of full disclosure, you do know we've had difficulty retaining someone, right?"

Abby nodded. "Estelle mentioned something, yes."

"Eleven in nine months. You're number twelve."

"I know." Darned good thing she wasn't superstitious, now that she thought about it.

"And yet you still took the job." He crossed his arms and leaned against the wall, green eyes narrowed. "Why?"

"You need a nanny. I need a job."

"That's not much of an answer."

She shrugged. "I have experience and I'm good at managing a house."

His gaze grew hooded as he studied her. "Still not much of an answer," he said finally, "but I suppose beggars can't be choosers."

Again, deliberately, Abby surveyed the chaos surrounding them, then she looked up at him, one eyebrow lifted just enough to underline her words. "No," she said. "I suppose we can't."

Her new employer gave a surprised bark of laughter and straightened up from his leaning post. "Touché. So, trial run? Three months."

Her feet itching to flee the madness that had become her life, Abby took a deep breath. "Trial run," she agreed.

"Good. I'll call my business partner while you take off your coat and boots, and then I'll meet you in the kitchen"—he pointed down the hall toward the back of the house—"in five." With those directions issued, Mitchell Abrams unhooked a cell phone from his belt, stepped into a room to the left of the stairs leading to the second floor, and closed an opaque French door.

Abby wasted four and a half of the allotted five minutes standing in befuddled, unmoving bemusement, wondering how her life had become so surreal in so short a time. She stared down at the entry's ceramic tile floor, almost buried beneath an avalanche of boots and shoes and balls and bags. At the warm white walls smudged by fingerprints and life, the stairs rising to the second floor, the hallway stretching to the kitchen. Into the living room to the right of the hallway, where enough light filtered between the drapes to outline a loveseat on one side of a coffee table and two over-stuffed armchairs on the other. And finally, at the luggage heaped by her feet and the mitten she'd removed, still gripped in her other hand.

If she'd had anywhere else she could have gone in those four and a half minutes, she would have turned tail and run. But she didn't, and so in the final few seconds, she slipped off her boots and parka, wedging the latter into the closet between a bright yellow child's raincoat and the worn, roughened jacket of a working man. And then she stepped across the avalanche and went to wait in the kitchen.

When the five minutes became ten, and then fifteen, she dug through the dishes piled in the sink until she found a mug. She washed and dried it, then poured coffee from the pot that Mitchell Abrams had indeed remembered to turn on. A quick perusal of the fridge turned up neither cream nor milk, but she'd learned to do without over the last year of rarely remembering to buy any herself, and so, black coffee in hand, she idly toured the room, closing dark wood cabinet doors as she went. A half-open dishwasher sat filled with more dirty dishes, but her search for deter-gent was unsuccessful. She closed the appliance and, using the pen hanging from a notepad stuck to the fridge door, added 'DW det' to the list already started there. Then she did another trip around the perimeter.

By the time she'd finished her third circuit of the room, she'd stacked papers and school books into a neat pile on the white table in the eating nook, cleared the island, run a sink of hot soapy water to soak dishes that appeared to have held a spaghetti dinner, wiped the newly liberated counters, and discovered the blackened remains of a frying pan half buried in the snow outside the sliding glass doors. She stared at the pan for a long moment, watching as the clean, falling flakes buried the mistakes it contained. Wishing life could be like those flakes but knowing it couldn't. With the back of her hand, she wiped away the tears gathering on her lower lashes.

She really, really had to stop crying every time she turned around.

Really.

Something scraped against the floor behind her, and she blinked, drawing herself tall and pasting the fake bright smile on her face again before she turned. But instead of finding Mitch Abrams there, she found a little girl seated on a stool at the island, black hair drawn up into two lopsided puff ponytails and a dingy stuffed rabbit hugged against her pink t-shirt. Solemn dark eyes regarded Abby.

"Well, hello there," Abby said in a voice that matched her smile. She winced and toned it down a few hundred notches. "You must be Kiana."

A cautious nod.

Abby crossed the room to join her, setting the now-empty mug on the counter. "I'm Abby." She held out her hand, and after a long hesitation, Kiana slipped a much smaller one into it, just for an instant. Abby waved at the sink. "We should do some of these dishes, don't you think? You want to wash or dry?"

"Wash." No hesitation there.

Abby smiled a real smile this time. Small, but real. "I thought you might choose that. Why don't you leave your bunny on the counter and pull one of the chairs from the table over to the sink?"

She tugged open a drawer where she'd already discovered aprons alongside the tea towels—and a smoke alarm—and pulled out a frilly blue one. When Kiana arrived with the chair, Abby helped her position it in front of the sink of water and then, with a detachment underscored by her determination to succeed at this job, she wrapped the apron around the little girl at chest height. Twice. And only had to swallow hard once.

See? She could totally handle this.

Kiana was tall for her age and didn't need to stand on the chair, only kneel. Abby tested the water temperature, handed the little girl a dishcloth, and said, "Go for it," as she took a clean tea towel from the drawer for drying.

They worked together in silence, with Kiana proving to be a slow but thorough washer of even the gummiest plates. As the clean dishes accumulated on the countertop, Abby cleared her throat. "So how come you're not in school today?"

"I lost a shoe. It's Wonder Woman."

"Ah. Somewhere in the front closet, I'm guessing?"

Kiana nodded. "Daddy got mad when he couldn't find it. Then the smoke alarm yelled."

Abby's gaze strayed to the almost-buried frying pan outside. "I'll bet it did." She frowned. "Hey, have you had breakfast yet?"

"Daddy was making pancakes. I think he burned them again."

"Again? Does he do that regularly?"

Another nod. "He's not very good at cooking. He keeps forgetting things."

"I see." And Abby did see. Between the disaster in the front hall, the condition of the kitchen, the forlorn frying pan, and the fact that Mitchell Abrams hadn't checked his voicemail in the last week, she was beginning to get a good idea of why her eleven predecessors hadn't been able to stick it out for more than a few weeks each. This family didn't need a nanny; it needed a small army to keep it in line. Or a mother. Abby's heart squeezed so hard at the thought that the air left her lungs in a tiny whimper and, in a blinding flash of panic, she saw her mistake. Understood it. And watched it loom over her as if it would devour her whole.

She couldn't do this. She'd been insane to consider it. Olivia and William were too fresh, too new. They would always be too fresh and new. Always be with her. And she could no more fit in with another family than she could bring back her own. *That* was why she'd had such a hard time fitting in at Gwyn's. Her hand shaking, she set the tea towel on the counter by the sink. "You keep washing," she told Kiana in a voice as brittle as she felt. "I just need to—"

"Sorry I took so long. I needed to—" The deep male voice behind them broke off, and Abigail whirled to find her new employer—correction, her about-to-be-former new employer—staring at his kitchen in shock.

"Mr. Abrams—"

"Mitch," he said absently. "Please." He stuck the fingers of one hand into his front jeans pocket and rubbed the other hand over his hair. "Wow. I don't think I've seen the place this clean in months. You've worked a minor miracle, Miss Jamieson."

Mrs., she thought. *I'm still Mrs.* "I—" she said.

Mitch Abrams swooped past her, scooping his daughter off the chair and swinging her around in a bear hug. "You! Did you help do all this?"

Giggling, Kiana wrapped her wet arms around her father's neck as they twirled around again. The knife that had sliced through Abby's heart laid open her soul, too. She pressed the backs of her knuckles to her lips and forced herself to look away. *I can't stay,* she coached herself. *I can't stay because I—*

"Are you all right?"

She jolted back to the moment and found father and daughter both watching her in concern. Mitch Abrams's gaze narrowed, seeing far more than she wanted him to see. She made her hand drop to her side. "Mr. Ab—"

"Mitch."

"M—M—" She gave up. "This was a mistake," she

said instead. "I don't think I'm right for the position after all."

He stared. The pale green eyes turned cold. "You can't be serious."

"I—"

He set Kiana on the ground, untied her apron, and handed her a tea towel. "Dry your hands," he said, "and then you can go watch cartoons for a while."

"But it's not a weekend."

"We'll pretend for today."

The little girl nodded and retrieved her stuffed rabbit from the island.

"Wait—" The word left Abby's lips unbidden, and Mitch fixed another cold look on her. She swallowed hard. "She hasn't had breakfast yet," she said, pointing toward the sliding doors and the now-invisible frying pan beyond.

Wordlessly, Mitch took down a bowl and a box of cereal.

"Umm," said Abby, "you're out of milk."

Mitch opened another cupboard and took out a carton of almond milk. "Milk allergies," he growled by way of explanation. "Gluten sensitivity, too." He poured cereal into the bowl, added milk and a spoon, and handed the meal to the waiting child. "No running."

"No, Daddy." Kiana cradled the bowl in her hands as she might a fragile treasure and headed toward the kitchen door. As soon as she was out of the room, Mitch folded his arms across his chest and scowled at Abby.

"Now," he said, "exactly what the *hell* are you playing at?"

CHAPTER 4

Mitch didn't wait for his new nanny's response. He was too angry. "I just spent half an hour on the phone apologizing to my partner and a client for being late and promising I'd get there as soon as I got you settled in. And then I called Kiana's school to tell them she'd be staying home today. And now you tell me you've changed your mind? Are you freaking kidding me? What happened to needing a job?"

Abigail flinched from his words—or from his anger—or maybe from both, but he didn't care. Not when his life was unraveling at its seams. His partner, Derek Simmons, had never been a particularly patient person to begin with, and these last few months had exhausted any goodwill that had remained after Eve's long illness and death. If Mitch didn't start to pull his weight in their construction firm soon, Derek had warned this morning, they'd have to start talking about Mitch buying him out, or alternatively, finding someone else to take over Derek's half of the company.

"I'm getting too old to be working sixteen-hour days, my man," Derek's voice echoed in Mitch's memory, fresh from their conversation. *"Paul is making noises about me not being around enough, and the hunting*

cabin is starting to look awfully good right now. On a permanent basis."

"I hear you, Derek, and I swear I can make this work. Just give me a week to get this new nanny settled in, and then I can put my full focus on the company again."

Derek snorted. "I've heard that before, remember? I've lost count of how many times."

"I know," Mitch said. "And I'm asking for one last chance here. You know I can't afford to buy you out right now, man. And the last thing I need is some new guy throwing his weight around."

"One month," Derek replied after a long silence, his voice heavy. "If you aren't fully up to speed—and I mean fully, Mitch, as in pre-Eve-getting-sick up to speed—I'm done."

"One month," Mitch agreed, because he had no choice. "You have my word."

It was a promise that had him scowling some more at Abigail Jamieson. "Well?"

"I'm not playing at anything," Abigail said quietly. "I just think I might not be the best fit for you after all."

Hands on hips, Mitch tipped his head back and closed his eyes while he weighed his options. He saw only two immediate ones. Leave Kiana—who was obviously *not* going to make it to school today—in the care of a stranger who didn't want to be here? Or call Derek to say he wasn't going to make it in after all and risk losing the company by the end of the week?

Bottom line, he needed to put food on the table and keep a roof over their heads. And the agency, one of the most reputable in Ottawa, would have done a thorough background check, he assured himself, so at least he knew this particular stranger was a safe one.

He shook his head. "I'm sorry," he said. And given the haunted shadow that overlaid the blue eyes and the fragile, porcelain-doll air about her, he really was—at least a little. Just not enough to risk his livelihood and the security of his children. "I need you to stay. I made commitments to my business partner based on the agreement you and I made in the hallway just minutes ago. If it makes you happy, I'll keep my file open at the agency, but if no one else turns up, I need you to stay for the three-month trial period."

"But—"

"Miss Jamieson, I don't have time to discuss this. I need to be at a meeting in"—he glanced at the impact-resistant watch on his wrist—"twenty minutes. Kiana will need to stay home with you today. I'll get your room cleared out tonight when I get home. We can talk more then."

"M-Mitch—"

"Mr. Abrams might be best after all."

His reluctant new nanny flushed brick red to the roots of her severely pulled-back hair and swallowed hard. "You don't understand," she whispered.

"Save it," he said. "My decision is made. And, Miss Jamieson, if you walk out on the job, I'll will do my level best to make sure you never find work with an agency in this city again. Now, Rachel and Brittany will be home at three. They'll need a snack. My cell phone number is on the fridge for emergencies. Don't hold dinner for me."

Abby didn't know how long she stared at the space vacated by Mitch—*Mr. Abrams*—before the sound of the front door roused her from her shocked stupor. Even then, she wasn't capable of doing more than letting her gaze travel an empty kitchen that suddenly felt more like a prison than a workplace. Dear Lord, what had she gotten herself into? And how was she going to get out of it again? Maybe she could call Estelle Gagnon and—but wait, the head of the agency had made it clear that if Abby didn't work out for the Abrams family, they would drop him as a client. There had been a hint of desperation underlining Mitch's anger that made Abby wonder whether that might be the final straw for him. Her shoulders sagged. Truth be told, as bad a shape as she was in, Mitch and his family seemed to be in equally dire straits. Could she really, in all good conscience, turn her back on them?

She rested her elbows on the newly cleaned island, buried her face in her hands, and groaned. How had her life taken such a dark, awful path? She'd lost so much—had so much taken away from her—why was she even bothering to continue standing? It would be so much easier to give up. To curl into a ball in a corner somewhere and hide. Quit. Just... stop. Her mouth twisted.

She'd already tried that, she reminded herself, and life had found her anyway, in the form of a sheriff with a court order requiring her to vacate her home eight months after the accident. *"Probate... estate being contested... need to leave..."* The sheriff's words had all run together, making little to no sense to a woman who hadn't left the house or spoken to another soul for more than a month. A woman who had subsisted on cans of tomato soup and stale crackers for two weeks because she'd run out of everything else and hadn't been able to summon the energy to get groceries. A woman whose friends—all of them William's friends, really—had stopped inviting her out after the first few weeks and stopped calling altogether after a few months.

In numbed silence and under the sheriff's grim supervision, she had packed her things into two pull-along suitcases, an overnight bag, and a single cardboard box. Personal items only. Clothing, a few pictures, Olivia's baby album. No jewelry, no books, nothing deemed of value to an estate locked in probate because William had died without a will, his sister had hired a fancy law firm to contest the estate, and the courts had been too bogged down to even look at the case.

And because William's sister's name had been on the house deed—God, how that woman had resented William marrying her—Abby had found herself standing on the sidewalk on a glorious, unrepentantly sunny day, homeless and waiting for a taxi to take her to a cheap motel on the outskirts of the city, with her neighbors studiously avoiding her gaze. Or maybe she'd avoided theirs. She couldn't remember, and it didn't seem to matter. All she knew was that she'd had enough in her meager private savings account for an economy-class ticket to the only person who might take her in —Gwyn.

But life had followed her to Gwyn's house, too, and now it had given her this—a family almost as broken as she was.

Another groan escaped her because, dear Lord, what in heaven's name was she supposed to do with it?

"Did you hurt yourself?" a voice inquired.

Abby lifted her head to find Kiana beside her, watching with her head tipped to one side like a bird, making her ponytails seem even more lopsided.

"You're making the same noise Brittany did when she broke her arm. Should I call an ambulance?"

A smile tugged at the corner of Abby's mouth. "No, I don't need an ambulance, thank you. I'm just…"

"Hurting inside?" Kiana offered when she trailed off. The little girl nodded at her own suggestion. "Daddy used to sound like that when Mommy was sick. He didn't know I heard. She died, you know."

Abby blinked back tears and swallowed hard, not sure if she was more taken aback by the way the words seemed to scrape her skin, by the image of tall, strong Mitch Abrams brought low by that same pain, or by Kiana's simple matter-of-factness. She cleared her throat. "I do know, yes. You must miss her."

"I miss the way she smelled. Daddy gave me one of her t-shirts, but her smell is gone now. She's been dead for a long time. Did you have someone die, too? Is that why you're hurting inside?"

Abby's insides felt like they might unravel altogether. This child was going to be the death of her. On her first day of the job. She took a deep breath to try to still her quiver. It didn't work. "I did, yes," she said. "But it was a long time ago, too."

"Do you miss their smell?"

"I do. Very much."

Kiana thought about this and then said, "We should probably change the subject. Grandma makes Daddy do that when he gets too sad."

"Your grandma sounds like a very wise lady."

The little girl nodded. "She came to live with us for a while after Mommy died, but she's old. She said she can't keep up with us youngsters. And she had to go home because Grandpa was all alone. Daddy told her we could manage on our own, but I don't think we're doing a very good job. Are you going to help manage us? You could be like Mary Poppins, but without the penguins and the umbrella and the flying and stuff. I like Mary Poppins, but I don't think those are very real, do you?"

"Probably not."

"So are you?"

"Am I what? Like Mary Poppins?"

Dark eyes rolled. "Going to help manage us."

"I... I don't know." Abby mentally scanned her innards and found them behaving much like innards were supposed to, for a change. In fact, she felt... not normal, but less fragile than she had in a very long time. Huh. Perhaps Kiana and her grandma were onto something with this distraction idea. Perhaps living here for a few weeks wouldn't be as bad as she'd imagined. She could do a lot in three months, and if she focused on getting Mitch and his daughters organized enough to look after themselves, and they all understood the arrangement wasn't permanent...

She regarded the little girl. "Maybe," she replied to the question. "But just for a little while, until your daddy is better at it."

Kiana looked skeptical. "You're going to have your hands full with that one," she said, shaking her head.

Abby swallowed a snort. "How old are you, exactly?"

"Five," Kiana confirmed what the agency had told Abby. "But Grandma says I'm going on eighty."

Another smile. "Grandma might be right," she agreed. "So. Any ideas about what to manage first?"

"My Wonder Woman shoe?"

"An excellent start. Lead the way, young lady."

White teeth flashed in a grin that somehow managed to warm Abby's heart even as it twisted the familiar knife in it at the same time, and for the first time in what felt like a very dark eternity, a tiny bit of color sparkled again in the world. She *could* do this, she told herself as she followed the bobbing puffs down the hallway. It was only for a little while, and it would give her time to come up with another plan, so she didn't have to go crawling back to Gwyn again.

She could totally do this.

Right?

CHAPTER 5

"You're still here."

Abigail looked up from stirring a pot of soup on the stove that she'd cobbled together from the odds and ends she'd found in the fridge and cupboards. The eldest girl, Rachel, stood in the kitchen doorway, still wearing her winter wear, including—Abigail winced—snow-covered boots. And her scowl matched her words.

Abigail decided to ignore both tone and boots. "Of course," she said cheerfully. "Where else would I be?" Not giving the girl a chance for a snarky comeback, she opened the oven door to peek at the biscuits browning inside and continued, "How was school today?"

"None of your business," Rachel retorted. "You're the hired help, not my mother. And what is that god-awful smell?"

Abigail counted to three. She really didn't want to get into an argument with the girl on her first day—and certainly not before she found out what her parameters were as far as setting and enforcing rules. She closed the oven door. "Soup," she said. "And biscuits. For dinner. And if you're hungry now—"

Rachel *tsked* an interruption, rolling her eyes. "It's Wednesday," she said, emphasizing the words as if speaking to someone having difficulty understanding. "That means it's pizza night."

Stirring the pot (unnecessary for the soup, but necessary for her temper), Abby counted to five this time. "Wonderful. I love pizza. I'll just put this in the fridge for tomorrow. What time should I order, and what does everyone like?" Wow, but it was hard to sound pleasant through clenched teeth.

"It's *my* job to order. That's why Dad—my father—trusted *me* with his credit card. I take care of a lot of things around here, just so you know." A straightening of Rachel's spine accompanied the words as she drew herself as tall as possible. Abby's heart contracted in response, but her understanding blossomed.

A territory dispute. *That's* what this was. A thirteen-year-old girl who'd found herself playing mother to two sisters for a year—probably more, given how ill Mrs. Abrams had been—having to deal with the intrusion of a total stranger in her home who seemed intent on taking control. No wonder this family had gone through eleven nannies in the last year. It was unlikely that a young woman, fresh out of childcare training, would see this as anything more than outright obnoxious rebellion on Rachel's part. But Abby had weathered a territory dispute of her own when she'd married a man whose sister had cared for him until her arrival—and she still bore the scars from it.

"Excellent," she said. "Then I'll leave that in your capable hands with thanks. But your dad said he'd be late tonight, so I imagine he'll eat out."

Rachel stared at her, seeming nonplussed by the

response, ready for a battle and not quite sure how to respond to an olive branch.

Abby returned to stirring the soup. "Kiana and I made muffins today." She switched off the stove and moved the pot to a trivet on the counter. "They're on the island if you're hungry. And she helped me make up a grocery list, but maybe you can go over it to make sure I have everything you need on there. It's on the fridge."

"I'm *not* hungry," Rachel growled, "and I already gave my father a list. I just have to remind him to get the stuff."

Abby decided no further response was required. She took the tray of perfectly golden biscuits from the oven, set them on a wire rack to cool, then rummaged in a cupboard for a storage container for the soup. The silence between her and Rachel stretched, and she was pretty sure there were invisible daggers being sent in her direction. But she was well used to cold silences—

Not going there, Abby.

And she was an expert at playing the waiting game—

Really, Abigail?

Rachel huffed from the doorway. "This is stupid," she muttered. "I have homework. I'll be in my room."

Eyes closed and arms crossed, Abby leaned back against the counter and waited for her stomach to unknot itself and her breathing to even out. As far as distractions went, Rachel Abrams was going to be a doozy.

"Don't worry about her. She's like that with everyone," a new voice said, and Abby opened her eyes to find Brittany on the other side of the island, stripped of her winter garments and eying the plate of muffins. "Are these for us?" she asked hopefully.

"They are. Your dad said you'd be hungry after school."

"I'm *starving*." Brittany swung her backpack onto the island, hitched herself up onto a stool, and took a muffin from the plate. She peeled back the paper liner, bit into the treat, and closed her eyes in ecstasy. "Mm... they're still warm. And I love raisins."

Abby smiled. At least someone appreciated her efforts. "Kiana told me."

"They're gluten-free for her, right? She can't have wheat. Mommy used to say it messes up her brain."

"I found gluten-free flour in the cupboard and used that for the muffins and the biscuits."

"The biscuits smell good, too." Brittany offered, words muffled around another bite. "And so does the soup. We can skip pizza tonight, if you'd like."

And wouldn't that go over like the proverbial lead balloon? Abby shook her head. "It's okay. They'll keep until tomorrow, and pizza sounds good."

"Yeah. You're right. Rachel wouldn't be happy." Brittany's hand hovered over the muffins. Abby nodded, and she snatched up a second one. "Is it okay if I do my homework in here?"

"Of course. I'm going to go shovel the driveway, now that it's stopped snowing, but you can call me if you need help. If Rachel orders pizza before I come back in, tell her I like anything except anchovies."

~

Unseasonable as it was for Ottawa in early November, it had snowed a *lot* since Abby's arrival that morning, and the double-width driveway sat well hidden beneath mounds of white stuff, with a ridge two feet high piled at the end where the plow had been by. She found a snowblower in the garage but had zero inkling how to use it, and so she settled for the wide aluminum shovel beside it. Kiana accompanied her, taking a child-sized shovel down from a hook on the wall, but she lost interest in helping after a few minutes and opted for building a snowman instead. The snow was perfect for the purpose—which made it less than perfect for shoveling. Twenty minutes into the task, an overheated Abby abandoned scarf and hat, grinning when Kiana pounced on them for use on her creation in progress. Five minutes more, and her gloves followed suit.

Grunting as she shoved and lifted, twisted and swung, Abby wondered whether she would even be able to move in the morning. This was way more exercise than she—

The shovel caught on something beneath the snow, driving the handle into her belly with enough force to make her wheeze. She stopped to catch her breath, leaning on the shovel and watching a snow-suited Kiana roll a lumpy ball of snow across the front lawn toward another, bigger one. The off-key strains of *Do You Want to Build a Snowman* drifted through the muffled, late afternoon silence, punctuated by the little girl's grunts every time she heaved the growing lump another few inches. Abby smiled at the picture-perfect winter moment.

Olivia had loved playing in the snow.

The thought blindsided her, the injustice of it twisting through her. But before she could recover enough to push it away as she was learning to do, a second thought followed on its heels.

Mitch's wife would have loved to watch her daughter.

Halfway across the yard, Kiana looked over and waved, grinning at her in the fading afternoon light. Abby forced a return smile and wave around the pain holding her immobile. She made herself inhale slowly, carefully, a part of her surprised that her lungs didn't shatter, so fragile did they feel. She'd never imagined she was alone in her grief, but neither had she been this aware of another's. Mrs. Abrams's, Mitch's, their daughters'. It felt as if a curtain between Abby and the world had been ripped aside, blinding her with an illumination she'd tried to hide from.

"Abby, can you help me?" Kiana called.

So much grief. So much loss. For all of us.

Abby took another breath and forced her muscles to life. There was a lot to unpack from behind the curtain, but not now. Now, she needed distraction again. Time to let the unexpected realization settle into her. "Coming," she called back.

By the time she was done shoveling and assisting with snowman building—Kiana had assembled a small army of them at the base of the one wearing Abby's hat and scarf—darkness had fallen over the neighborhood, and she was alone outside. One of the neighbors had come by with his snowblower and offered to do the last bit of the driveway just as the pizza delivery had arrived and Kiana had gone inside, but Abby had declined. The physical labor made her feel more alive than she had in months, and she found herself enjoying it.

Plus, she reflected wryly as she put the shovels back in the garage, she could pretty much guarantee she would sleep better than she had in those same months, too. She reached to turn off the light, and her gaze lingered on an SUV parked on the far side of the garage. Coated in a fine film of dust, it didn't look as though it had moved in a long time, but if it still ran, maybe she could ask her new employer for the keys tomorrow.

That assumed he wouldn't suspect her of wanting to run away with it, after her moment of panic this morning. She grimaced as she pressed the button to close the garage door. Between Mitch not wanting her here, then changing his mind, then *her* not wanting to be here... well, suffice it to say neither one of them had gotten off to a good start. However, they were both adults, and once they'd hammered out a firm agreement, things were bound to improve.

The giant door rumbled down and settled into place with a thud.

Abby stamped her feet on the mat in front of the door leading from the garage into the laundry/mudroom, then twisted the door knob. It didn't move so much as a fraction.

Locked. Of course it was locked, undoubtedly by

the oh-so-friendly Rachel. Abby leaned her forehead against the window in the door. At least now she knew why the girl had been so helpful in her offer to get Kiana out of her wet snow gear while Abby finished shoveling. With a sigh, she straightened again and knocked on the window insert. Seconds ticked past. The room on the other side of the glass remained dark. Abby's lips drew tight. Using her side of her fist this time, she banged again. And again. And again.

At last the inside light went on, and she saw Rachel pick her way through the puddles and wet clothing to the door—moving, of course, with excruciating slowness. Their gazes met and held, then Rachel unlocked the door but didn't open it, turned, and left again. Sudden exhaustion settled over Abby, and the chill of sweat-drenched clothing seeped into her bones. She pushed open the door and stepped inside. Things with Mitch Abrams might improve with their agreement, but she suspected it would be a whole other matter with his eldest daughter.

She stripped off her coat and hung it on a hook beside a bench, then stooped to pick up Kiana's wet things and hang them, too, because of course Rachel had left them for—what had she called her? Oh yes. The hired help. Abby rolled her eyes and stepped across the puddles before taking off her boots, making a mental note to ask Mitch whether there was a carpet to go on the floor for the winter weather. Then, too tired to do more, she turned off the mudroom light, closed the door behind her, and went into the kitchen.

The three girls were seated at the table, each with a

small pizza box in front of her, their contents half gone. A delicious aroma permeated the room, and Abby's stomach rumbled. Unfortunately, no other boxes appeared to exist. She sent Rachel a pointed look, one eyebrow raised. "None for me?"

Darned if the girl didn't look uncomfortable in the slightest.

"I'm sorry," Rachel said in a tone that begged to differ. "I'm not used to having someone else here. I didn't think to get you one."

Abby stared at her, hoping her silence communicated the "horse pucky" she didn't want to utter. Rachel didn't so much as blink.

"You can have some of mine," Brittany offered. "It has pineapple and green peppers."

"Mine, too," said Kiana. "It's gluten-free and vegetable-arian, and it has fake cheese."

"You need the leftovers for lunch tomorrow," Rachel said. "There's nothing for sandwiches until our father does the shopping."

"Thank you, girls," Abby replied, her steady gaze still holding their sister's, who undoubtedly thought using "our father" instead of "Daddy" made her sound more grown up. "But I'll just have some of the soup and a biscuit tonight, and tomorrow *I* will do the shopping."

Rachel stood, closed the pizza boxes, and stalked past Abby to put them in the fridge. At the doorway to the hall, she looked over her shoulder at her sisters. "Make sure you brush your teeth when you're done," she ordered. "Dad will be late tonight, so I'll tuck you in. Be ready at eight."

CHAPTER 6

Mitch turned off the ignition and pressed the button on the remote control attached to the visor. The garage door ground to a close behind him. Wearily, he gathered up gloves, coat, and a roll of blueprints from the passenger seat. He felt guilty as hell for coming home this late, but he just hadn't been able to face dealing with Rachel. Or, for that matter, the Abigail Jamieson problem.

He still couldn't believe he'd walked out on her like that, demanding that she stay and care for Kiana. And then he'd told her he wouldn't be home for dinner and essentially ordered her to feed his children? Groaning, he let his head fall back against the headrest. He was lucky the woman hadn't called Child Services on him. He had no doubt she was waiting for him in the front hall, dressed to go, suitcases at her feet, ready to make her escape the second she heard him come into the house. Because there was no way she'd want to take the position now. Hell, *he* wouldn't want to take the position after the way he'd behaved to her. Which meant—

He rubbed his free hand over his eyes. It meant he was back to square one, trying—and failing miserably—to keep his daughters semi-clean and healthy while trying—and failing equally miserably—not to lose the livelihood that made the rest of it possible. Freaking hell. What was he going to tell Derek? His partner had made it clear he wouldn't stick around if Mitch didn't start pulling his own weight in the company. Derek would walk before Mitch even got to the explanation, and there was no way any bank would consider him an acceptable risk on his own. Not with the company having had to scale back the way it had since Eve died. He'd gone over it and over it in his head all day, and he hadn't been able to come up with a solution because there was none. He had three young daughters depending on him, and he was screwed.

Sitting in a dark garage, however, wouldn't make it better. *Time to face the music, Abrams.* With a heavy sigh mingled with another groan, he pushed open the truck door, slid out, and headed into the mudroom. There, he paused to listen for a moment, mostly for the closing of the front door now that Abigail knew he was home, but the house stayed silent. Mitch slipped his feet out of their steel-toed boots, set his gloves on the bench, and reached to hang his coat on a hook. He blinked.

A bright red jacket hung beside Kiana's snowsuit, both still showing patches of damp. Two thoughts, equally monumental, crowded into his mind. First, if Abigail Jamieson's coat was here, it wasn't on her. Which meant she was also here, and maybe—just maybe—he stood a chance of apologizing and convincing her to stay. Second, she had somehow, impossibly, managed to talk Kiana not only into the hated snowsuit and winter boots, but also into going outside. Which meant the woman was a bloody miracle worker and he *had* to convince her to stay. Setting his jaw, he draped his coat over the hook beside the red jacket and headed into the hallway.

A light glowed in the kitchen to his right, so he headed there first but found the room empty of anything except what belonged in it. Clean counters, gleaming appliances, bare table with chairs pushed in, and a tidy stack of books on the island beside a bowl that had been empty of its intended fruit for two weeks or more, which reminded Mitch that he'd forgotten to stop for groceries. Again. About to turn and leave, he paused as a paper propped against the books caught his eye. He picked it up and read,

Mr. Abrams,
I'm assuming you've eaten dinner, but if not, there's
soup in the fridge and biscuits on the counter by the
stove. I've made a bed for myself on the loveseat in the
living room and set the coffee machine for 6:30 a.m.
I would appreciate a meeting with you at that time.
Abigail Jamieson

This time, a dozen different thoughts crowded in. She'd stayed. She'd made a decent dinner for his kids, with leftovers for him despite his earlier behavior. She could cook. And bake. And the idea of a meeting sounded positive, didn't it?

A bed on the loveseat.

Freaking hell. He'd walked out in such a temper this morning that he'd forgotten she would have nowhere to sleep tonight. Forgotten he had to come home early enough to clear the disaster area that had taken over the spare room. Forgotten, in his blind panic, to be a decent human being to the stranger he so needed in his daughters' lives right now, and so she was sleeping on a loveseat that wasn't nearly long enough to accommodate her.

Never mind apologizing. He had some serious groveling to do at that meeting.

Mitch read the note again, and his stomach rumbled at the thought of food. As it happened, he hadn't had time for dinner and had forgotten about it until now. His gaze strayed to the glowing blue 12:20 displayed on the stove clock. After the day he'd had, 6:30 was going to come awfully early, but he would most likely sleep better on a full stomach. He set the paper on the counter again and pulled open the fridge.

Stripped of all the spoiled food he'd been intending to clear out, the interior glowed bright enough to make him squint. His mouth pulled tight as he stared at the emptiness facing him. Damn. He really did need to get those groceries, didn't he? He reached for the single storage container on the top shelf, pausing when he noticed the three pizza boxes stacked below it. Right. Wednesday was pizza night. He should have mentioned that to Abigail this morning—along with a whole lot of other things—and told her to order one for herself, too.

God, the poor woman must really wonder what kind of a monster he was at this point.

He took the container from the fridge and five

minutes later, tiptoed past the dark, silent living room, steaming mug of soup in one hand and biscuit in the other as he headed up the stairs. At the top, he set his meal down on the table in the hallway and made his ritual rounds of his daughters' rooms, putting Kiana's plush rabbit back into the bed with her, tucking Brittany's covers over her shoulders, lifting Rachel's book from her chest and turning out her light, kissing each of them gently on the forehead. Eve's presence followed him, sad and accusatory, and he slumped against the wall when he was done.

"I know, I know," he muttered. "I told you I'd look after them, and I will. I'll figure it out, sweetheart. I promise."

And he would, somehow. His gaze strayed to the spare room door at the opposite end of the hall. He'd start there, first thing in the morning. Set the alarm for five, work quietly enough not to wake the kids, and have a proper room with a bed to offer Abigail at their meeting. With a plan—of sorts—in place, he gave a satisfied nod, picked up his dinner, and went into his room. Oddly, it felt even emptier than it usually did, and he paused in the doorway. Then he grinned. Then he chuckled. Then he shook his head at the bed, devoid of its cozy, flannel-wrapped duvet, which was without doubt now wrapped around the nanny on the living room loveseat.

"Touché, Abigail Jamieson," he said to the room. "Touché."

· · ·

Wide awake in her makeshift bed, Abby tracked Mitch Abrams's movements from the time the garage door opened and the vehicle pulled in. Footsteps from mudroom to kitchen. The sound of the fridge opening. The beep of the microwave finishing its heating cycle. More footsteps from kitchen to second floor. Movement overhead from room to room, with doors softly opening and closing. A pause. And then a soft chuckle followed by words she couldn't make out.

Had he discovered the missing duvet? Was that what made him laugh? She hadn't meant it to be funny, but she supposed it might be. She'd embarked on a fruitless search for bedding, but when closet after closet had yielded nothing and she'd seen the warm cover on the only remaining bed in the house, she hadn't even hesitated—partly because she'd been too tired to keep searching, but mostly because she'd been royally ticked. Him missing dinner on her first day here was one thing, but staying out so late that she had to sleep on a loveseat she couldn't even fully stretch out on? The jerk deserved to freeze his butt off tonight.

Of course, she'd regretted her spiteful theft the instant the duvet's soft, heavy weight had settled over her and a foreign male scent had wrapped around her. She'd even tried getting up to change the cover on it, but her limbs had turned to lead the second she'd lain down, and the effort had simply been beyond her. Besides, she couldn't remember seeing spare covers in the all-but-empty linen closet, and she suspected that most everything the family owned was a part of the mountain of laundry she'd edged past in the mudroom.

And she certainly didn't have the energy to tackle that tonight.

The second-floor hall light went out, plunging the stairs beside the living room into complete darkness. A second later, one last door closed softly. Abby rolled onto her side, pulled the duvet up to her chin, and dropped into a deep, exhausted sleep.

CHAPTER 7

Abby was already in the kitchen, sitting at the table in the nook and sipping her second cup of coffee, when Mitch entered. With his fingertips tucked into the front pockets of blue jeans and a gray long-sleeved t-shirt hugging his well-muscled arms and chest, he looked every inch the hunky suburban dad. No wonder Jessica Perkins wanted to clean his closets.

The rogue thought came out of left field, jolting through her and through her coffee mug, and making hot liquid slosh onto her lap. She yelped and grabbed for the tea towel on the table beside her, dabbing at the spreading stain on her own jeans.

"You okay?" Mitch asked.

She thought she heard a note of concern in his deep tones, but she didn't dare look up to confirm it. She settled for a nod, discovering that mortification had stolen her voice. Where in heaven's name had *that* sprung from? She had no business thinking that way about her employer, especially when they were going to be sharing a house.

Mitch set a steaming mug of coffee on the table and settled into the chair opposite her. Abby put aside the tea towel. An awkward silence stretched. Then he stretched a hand across to her.

"Mitch Abrams," he said. "Pleased to meet you."

Abby raised her gaze to the wry amusement in his green eyes. She gave a small half smile and accepted the gesture of peace. "Abigail Jamieson," she replied. "You can call me Abby."

Mitch released her hand from his warm grip. "And you really can call me Mitch," he said, leaning back in his seat. "I'm sorry about yesterday. What I said—my behavior was unacceptable. If we can, I'd like to start over."

"So would I."

His expression turned to one of guarded hope. "Then you'll stay? You'll give us a try for the three months?"

She had the distinct impression the man held his breath while she formulated her reply. "I will," she agreed, holding up a hand when sheer relief flashed across his face. "But only for the three months."

"I don't understand."

"I'm willing to stay for three months as the full term of my employment, not as a trial."

Mitch's eyebrows twitched together. "You sound pretty definite about that. May I ask why?"

"I am. And no."

His gaze narrowed. "Is this about yesterday?"

Yes, but not in the way he thought. She shook her head. "No. It's personal."

"Did you know you only intended to stay that long when you took the job?"

"No. I thought—I wanted—it just—" Abby gave up and fell silent.

He scowled when she didn't continue. "So, what? At the end of the three months, I'm just supposed to start all over again with someone new? Hell, I've been through every agency in town, Ms. Jamieson. I'm not sure I can *get* anyone."

She winced at the return to formality. One step forward, two back.

"I've been thinking about that. I want to get you and the girls organized enough to run things on your own, so that you don't need a full-time nanny. Maybe a housekeeper once or twice a week for the cleaning, and someone for the girls after school until you get home, but that's it. And I think your girls might actually prefer it that way."

The lines between Mitch Abrams's brows deepened to furrows. "You've been here exactly one day. How in hell would you know better than me what my daughters want?"

"*How* many nannies have you been through in the last year?"

Mitch's mouth opened, then snapped shut. After a long, drawn-out silence, he sighed, visibly deflating as he hunched over his coffee mug. "Point taken," he muttered. "But that doesn't mean you're right."

"It doesn't mean I'm wrong, either, and it doesn't change your situation. If Ms. Gagnon is to be believed, you've worn out your welcome at all the agencies in town, at least for the moment. Your only option is to get your act together. I can stay for three months to help you do that, and I can give you a reference that might help you get back into the agencies' good books."

He stared at her, his gaze both haunted and hunted in the way of someone who'd been hovering on the brink of disaster for too long. Abby recognized the look from the reflection she saw in the mirror every day. Sympathy stirred in her.

"That's really as long as you'll stay?" he asked, defeat edging out hope in his voice. "There's no way I can convince you otherwise? If it's a matter of money…"

"It's not about money," she said, thinking back to her realization yesterday that being a nanny for this family meant slipping into the role of pseudo wife and mother. Her chest tightened again at the idea, and she swallowed a bubble of hysteria. She'd be lucky to survive three months, and if she didn't consider Mitch's family straits even more dire than her own, she would walk away now. "Three months, Mr. Abrams. That's all I can do."

He sighed again. "Then you'd better tell me what you have in mind."

Abby's shoulders sagged in relief. She'd been so afraid her proposal would meet with more resistance than that. Or that Mitch would turf her out on her butt and she'd have to go crawling back to Gwyn and Gareth. She curled her fingers around her mug, clinging to it as she might a life preserver as she chose her words. He was willing to listen, and she needed to make sure he stayed that way.

"Your wife—I'm guessing she took care of running the household?"

Across the table, Mitch's lips tightened briefly. He nodded. "Evelyn—Eve—wanted to stay home with the kids. I was—am—running my own business, and my hours can be erratic, so it kind of just happened that she handled cleaning, cooking, organizing, kids' appointments, the works. And she made it look so easy. I used to tell people she was the family CEO. By the time we realized she wasn't going to get better, she was too weak to show me how to do things myself. My mother came to stay for a while, but she needed to go home to my stepfather." He grimaced. "I've just been trying to keep us afloat ever since. I'm pretty sure we're drowning at this point. You've seen the laundry room?"

The small bit of humor surprised a smile from Abby. "I started a load this morning."

"You're a brave woman." Mitch took a swig from his mug, watching her over the rim. "So what's your grand plan to get us on track to independence?"

"The first month, I'll clean and organize and figure out everyone's schedules. The second month, I'll start getting all of you involved in deciding who can do what once I'm gone, and I'll set up systems for you to keep track of everything. The third month, I'll hand things off to you a little bit more each week, so that by the end of it, you're running things yourself."

"You've given this quite a bit of thought, haven't you?"

All evening, right up until she heard the garage door open. "I have."

"What happens if your plan doesn't work?"

"We need to make it work, Mr. Abrams. *You* need to make it work because I'm not staying."

He stared down into his coffee, and his dark jawline

flexed. Then he met her gaze again. "Can I think about it and let you know tonight?"

"Of course."

He pushed back from the table and stood. "I'll go wake the girls for school. Are you making breakfast, or am I?"

"I made muffins yesterday, and I found some cans of peaches at the back of the cupboard. Will that do?"

He scrubbed a hand over his cropped hair. "Right. Groceries. I'll stop after—"

"If the vehicle in the garage runs and I can use it, I can get groceries today while the girls are at school."

"You were in the garage?"

"For the snow shovel. To clear the driveway. I didn't know how to use the snowblower, so..." Abby trailed off at his incredulity. "Did I do something wrong?"

"*You* cleared the driveway? I thought my neighbor —you did it by hand, by yourself?"

"Well, a shovel *is* pretty straightforward," she said dryly. "Even for a nanny. And the plow had come by, and I didn't want you to have to do it when you got home, especially since you were so late."

"I didn't mean it that way. And as far as last night..." Mitch had the grace to look somewhat ashamed. He cleared his throat. "I... uh..."

She waved away his words. "It's fine. Really. Fresh start, remember?"

"Yes, but still, thank you," he said. "And not just for the driveway. Thank you for feeding my kids and cleaning up around here and getting everyone into bed

—and especially for not walking out on me when I was such an ass."

"You're welcome."

He hesitated as if he might say more, then crossed to the counter and set his mug by the coffee machine before heading for the hall. He paused in the doorway. "You should have asked Rachel and Britt to help with shoveling," he said. "And you should have ordered a pizza for yourself, too."

The snort escaped before Abby could stop it. A furrow appeared between Mitch's brows.

"Something funny?"

"No. It's all good. We'll talk after you've made your decision."

Not until he'd left did she realize he hadn't answered her question about the vehicle. Oh, well. At least they had the soup she'd cobbled together yesterday if he didn't bring groceries home with him tonight. With a sigh, she stood and went to pour more coffee.

This was definitely going to be a two-cup day.

Three months. Three. Mitch climbed the stairs toward his daughters' bedrooms with heavy steps and a heavier gut. How in hell was he supposed to get himself, his house, his kids, and his business all back on track in just three months? Derek would cut him zero slack, and he couldn't blame the guy. At almost sixty-seven years old, his partner had his own set of issues, chief of which involved high blood pressure and instructions from the doctor to start slowing down and taking it easy. The guy had been the epitome of patience up until now, and he deserved a break. Besides which, Mitch would never forgive himself if Derek keeled over because of him.

But still... three months?

It would take a freaking miracle. Plus a small army. Maybe even two armies.

And this woman—this pale, fragile-looking stranger—thought she could manage it on her own? Mitch pushed open the door of Kiana's room and walked across to the bed. He should tell Abigail Jamieson where to put her offer, because there was no way she could pull it off. And he didn't need to be taking care of everything on his own; he needed someone to do it for him. Yes, he should definitely call the agency and demand they send...

Who, exactly? Mary Poppins?

He smiled down at his daughter's dark eyes peeking at him over the covers. Kiana would like that. Mary Poppins was her favorite movie of all time, and every night when she said her prayers, she asked to have the magical nanny come to their house and—he paused mid-thought as the hairs on the back of his neck prickled to life. Huh. Come to think of it, Mary Poppins didn't stick around, either. She taught some valuable lessons, danced with a few penguins and a chimney sweep, and then left the same way she'd come.

"Morning, Daddy." The rest of Kiana's head popped into view.

"Morning, pumpkin." Mitch leaned down to give her a gentle whisker rub along her cheek, and she squealed and disappeared again.

"Da-deeeeee!"

He chuckled and ruffled the ponytails that were still in place, albeit somewhat more crookedly than they'd been the day before. Then he poked at the t-shirt his daughter wore. "What's this? I thought we had a rule about wearing pajamas to bed."

"Abby said I could wear it. She said she didn't need to beat me over it."

"She what?" Mitch blinked.

"She means win," Brittany's voice said behind him, and he looked over his shoulder to find her leaning against the doorframe, yawning. "Abby said she didn't need to win the war. Or the battle. Or something. I like her. She's nice."

"Me too!" Kiana sat up in the bed, hands fluttering in her lap. "She helped me build a snowman and let me use her scarf and her hat for it. And then I made a bunch more snowmen, and she read me two stories."

"Did she, now? And did she also put you to bed on time? And make you brush your teeth?"

The crooked poofs bobbed up and down. "And she helped me say my thankfuls, too. I was thankful for you and Britt and Rachel, and for Abby. Is she going to live with us?"

"God," Rachel said, drawing out the word as she wedged herself between Britt and the doorframe, claiming the leaning post as her own and ignoring her sister's attempts to push her away. "I hope not."

Mitch regarded his daughter, decided it was way too early to get into it with her, and chose to respond to

Kiana's question instead. "I'm not sure," he said. "I haven't decided yet."

"Well, if you ask me—" Rachel began.

"I didn't," Mitch told her. "Because it's my decision, not yours."

His eldest crossed her arms. "You do know that we're the ones who have to put up with her, and not you, right? If you'd just let Jessica come over and help, we'd be fine. And it wouldn't cost you anything. Jessica says she's happy to lend a hand."

It was also *way* too early for Jessica Perkins to be part of the conversation, too. And since when had Mandy's mom become Jessica in the first place?

"It's Ms. Perkins to you," Mitch said. "And it's time to get ready for school."

"Jessica said—"

"Now, Rach."

Rachel gave him one of her best eye rolls—did she practice those things in the mirror for his benefit?—and her huffiest huff before flouncing away with a muttered, "What*ever*."

It was another stellar start to a day.

Just stellar.

CHAPTER 8

Abby's second post-school afternoon went pretty much as the first one had. Rachel refused a snack and stomped upstairs, muttering under her breath. Brittany and Kiana settled in at the kitchen island with the last of the muffins. Brittany worked on math homework while Kiana rocked sideways in her seat as she chattered happily to Abigail about her day at kindergarten. Nursing a cup of tea and the sore muscles that hadn't eased despite several hours of cleaning and tidying, Abby nodded and tried to ask appropriate questions when the child took a breath. Truth be told, however, only half her attention was on the girls. The other half waited with bated breath for the sound of the garage door heralding Mitch's return—even though it was hours before he was due home—and his decision about her proposal that morning.

A part of her wished he'd turn it down, because contrary to her hopes, staying wasn't getting any easier. In fact, every toy and book and discarded piece of clothing she'd picked up today, every surface she'd dusted and floor she'd mopped, every task she'd performed had been like a tiny blade nicking her soul, reopening her wounds. It was the little things that did the most damage. Finding a book she'd once read to

Olivia; lingering over the movie titles on the television shelf, so many of which had been their own family favorites; picking up the menagerie of stuffed animals rom Kiana's floor and discovering she had the same hippopotamus that Olivia had been given as a baby.

But another part—the part that kept her here, despite the pain of listening to another woman's daughters the way she would never again listen to her own—that part hoped Mitch would agree. Because the woman she'd seen in the photos on the living room mantel deserved to know her husband and girls could be a family, even if that family couldn't include Eve herself. And if the roles were reversed, if Abby had been the one to die instead of Olivia, she would have wanted someone to help her little girl, too.

"Abbyyyyyy, are you listening?" Kiana regarded her with mixed accusation and impatience.

"Sorry, sweet pea. My head was in the clouds. What did you say?"

"Your head wasn't in the clouds." Kiana frowned in puzzlement. "It was right here. I could see it."

Abby laughed. "It's an expression. It means my mind was elsewhere."

"I thought minds had to stay inside their heads." Kiana's eyes grew round. "Yours can leave? All by itself? Where does it go? How does it get out?" She leaned over and lifted Abby's hair away from one ear. "Does it come out your ears?"

"She meant she was daydreaming," Brittany told her sister, looking up from her homework. She shook her head at Abby. "You need to be specific with this one. *Very* specific."

"I'll remember that. Thank you."

The anticipated—dreaded?—sound of the garage door filtered into the kitchen. Abby's heart hit the floor, then bounced back up to lodge in her throat. He was early. And she was so not ready. Kiana, on the other hand, was pure unbridled enthusiasm.

"Daddy!" she shouted, scooting off her stool and running to the mudroom. "Daddy, Daddy, Daddy!"

Abby took a deep breath. She'd tried hard to stay busy today to keep from dwelling on what she'd do if her idea failed. The busy part had been easy with so much needing to be done in the house, but the other? Oh, she'd dwelled all right. Dwelled and stewed and worried... and come up with absolutely no idea. Because if Mitch turned her down—

The slam of a door came from the mudroom, followed by Mitch's muffled voice greeting his youngest. For an instant, Abby was thrown back into the past, when William had come home from the office and Olivia had run out to meet him, and Abby had stood in the kitchen, listening to her daughter's happy chatter and her husband's measured responses. Whatever issues she and William might have had between them, he had loved their daughter fiercely, and—

Footsteps headed for the kitchen.

Abby took a steadying breath and blinked back the tears blurring her vision. If she wanted Mitch to seriously consider her proposal, it might help to at least look like she was a semi-capable adult in control of herself. She grabbed the girls' empty plates and turned to the sink as he and Kiana came into the room.

"Daddy brought *food*!" Kiana announced, bouncing up and down on her stool, and Mitch chuckled.

"That may have been said with more enthusiasm than is healthy," he observed in a wry voice. "Things were that dire around here, were they?"

Her memories safely locked up again, Abby turned to find him setting two grocery bags on the island counter, Kiana dancing beside him. "Pickings were getting pretty slim," she agreed. "But there's still soup and biscuits for dinner, at least."

Still wearing his winter coat, Mitch dropped a kiss on the top of each daughter's head, then took a variety of packaged items from the bags and stacked them on the counter. Granola bars, crackers-and-cheese snack packs, boxed macaroni and cheese, cookies, frozen pot pies and pasta dishes, the works. Abby couldn't help but raise an eyebrow.

"No vegetables?" she inquired, trying to keep her tone neutral.

Mitch held up a bag of carrots in one hand and apples in the other. "And fruit," he said, but his look of triumph wavered. "Not what you had in mind, I'm guessing."

"It depends, I suppose."

"I suppose it does." He turned to his daughters. "Girls, how about you go upstairs and give Abby and me a few minutes to talk? Britt, you can finish that in a little while."

Wide-eyed and reluctant, the two girls shuffled

from the room, casting not-so-furtive glances over their shoulders as they went. Mitch followed them into the hallway, unzipping his coat on the way. He returned a few seconds later, shrugged out of the garment, and draped it over a stool. Without preamble, he asked, "Does your offer still hold?"

Refusing to second-guess herself any further, Abby nodded and cleared her throat. "It does."

"And three months is the best you can do?"

She nodded again.

Mitch scrubbed a hand over his graying hair. Then, hands on hips, he paced the floor on the other side of the island, first one way, then the other, then back again. Finally, he stopped and faced her. "Fine," he said. "But you have to know I'm not happy about the arrangement. When I hired you, I intended the position to be permanent."

With remarkable self-control, Abby refrained from pointing out that he'd tried to send her away, not hire her. She also didn't mention that unlike him, his eldest daughter would be elated. Instead, she murmured, "I understand that, yes."

He glowered at her. "I suppose we'd better discuss details, then. Hours and such."

"And ground rules," she agreed.

The glower deepened. "Ground rules?"

Abby nibbled on her lower lip. How to put this diplomatically? Could it *be* put diplomatically? "Your previous employees had some... issues, especially with Rachel, and they didn't feel supported by you. I'm going to need a certain amount of authority, and I need to know I can count on you to back me up."

"You're talking about discipline."

"Yes."

Mitch crossed his arms over his chest. "My daughters have been through a hard time, Ms. Jamieson. They lost their mother. They need time to—"

"Your daughters," she interrupted, "need to be part of a family, no matter how much the definition of that has changed. And they need you to be the head of that family." Mitch's expression turned thunderous, but she plowed on, following his switch back to formality. "It's the only way this will work, Mr. Abrams. And it's the only way *I* will work."

"Then I guess we don't have an agreement after all," he growled.

She sighed. "Do you know why I didn't have pizza last night?"

"Why—" He scowled. "What the hell does pizza have to do with anything?"

"Rachel placed the order."

Mitch opened his mouth to retort, then closed it again. His lips pressed together, and she knew the significance of her words had sunk in. "I see," he said finally. "And you think..."

"I *know*, Mr. Abrams. She made it clear when she informed me that I was the hired help, not her mother. Her words."

Her employer braced both hands against the counter and hunched his shoulders. "I'm sorry," he said. "She knows better. I'll speak to her."

But Abby shook her head. "I'd rather you didn't, except to tell her that I'm in charge in your absence, and that you support my decisions. And if you have an issue with something I've done or said, you discuss it with me, not her, and you do so in private."

The green eyes closed. "Fine. Anything else?"

"You said you run your own business. Construction."

Mitch opened one eye and regarded her. "Again, what does that have to do with anything?"

"I suspect it will take extra time to get it running the way you need to before you start taking over more here. So, for the first month, I'd like to propose that I not take time off except on Sundays. I'll run the house and look after the kids as much as you need me to."

The other eye opened, and he stared at her. "You'd do that for me—for us? But why?"

"Because you need the help. Because I can give it." *And because I'd want someone to do the same for my family if the roles were reversed.* She swallowed the bitter tang of sadness that was her constant companion and lifted one shoulder in a shrug. "There aren't many things I'm qualified to do, Mr. Abrams, but I can run a household. And I can teach you to do it, too."

Silence reigned for a long moment, and then Mitch cleared his throat. "Thank you," he said gruffly. "I—thank you. And please, let's make it Mitch."

Abby tried—and failed—to hide a smile. "You sure this time?"

He smiled back, a brief flash of white teeth against dark skin. "I'm sure." He straightened up from leaning on the counter. "I'll take your suitcases up to your room and find you some clean sheets—"

"They're in the dryer," she said. "I'll take them up later."

"Second door on the left," he said. "You share a bathroom with Rachel's room, but she'll use the main one with her sisters like she did when we had the other nannies here. I'll talk to them now and let them know what the plan is, and tomorrow I'll arrange for the snow tires to be put on Eve's—the SUV. You should have it by the next day." He turned to go but stopped again in the doorway. "For the record, I have no idea whether this plan of yours will really work, Abigail Jamieson, but for the first time in a long time, I actually feel hopeful about my family's future. Thank you for that."

This time, as she listened to his footsteps receding, Abby let her tears fall for the future her own little family had been denied.

Oh, Olivia...

CHAPTER 9

Mitch tapped on Rachel's door and poked his head inside. "Hey, kiddo. Family meeting in my room."

Rachel didn't look up from the homework spread across the bed where she sprawled. "I'm busy," she muttered.

"It wasn't a request."

Yup. There was the eye roll, right on cue.

"Fine," she huffed. "But if I fail my history test tomorrow, it's your fault, not mine."

"If you fail your history test tomorrow, it will be because of a far bigger problem than a fifteen-minute family meeting," he replied, nudging her shoulder with his as they walked down the hall together. "But nice try."

He was rewarded with another eye roll.

Kiana and Brittany waited for them in the chaos that had become Mitch's bedroom, lying on the unmade bed with their feet up against the wall. Mitch cleared his throat; the feet came down. He sat down on the edge of the bed nearest Kiana, and she crawled into his lap and leaned against his chest, her long legs dangling halfway down his. Brittany sprawled beside him on her stomach. Rachel stood with arms crossed, leaning back against the wall beside the door.

"Abigail is going to stay," he began.

"Yay!" Kiana clapped her hands and gave him a kiss on the cheek. "Thank you, Daddy!"

"Is that why all the stuff from the spare room is in here now?" Britt asked. "Cool."

"Seriously?" Rachel threw her arms wide. "Why? We don't need some stranger telling us what to do. We're fine on our own."

"Speak for yourself," Britt mumbled into the hands supporting her chin. "I like her."

"Everyone hold on," said Mitch. "There's more to it. Abigail is only going to stay with us for three months, just to help us get organized and on our feet. Then she'll be leaving."

"Aww, man!" Britt, with her usual flair for the dramatic, flopped onto her back and groaned. "But whyyy?"

"Because that's what we've agreed on."

"Doesn't she like us?" Kiana asked in a small voice.

"Of course she likes us, pumpkin. She just has other things to do."

"More important things than looking after us?"

Mitch sidestepped the knife in his heart, searching for the right words. "Nothing is more important than looking after you, Kiana, but that's supposed to be my job. Abigail is going to teach me how."

"In three months?" Rachel snorted, and Mitch turned a weary gaze on her.

"Gee. Thanks for the vote of confidence, Rach."

His eldest daughter looked down at her feet and scuffed at the floor with the bedraggled toe of a unicorn slipper, one of the last Christmas gifts she'd received from her mother. Mitch took a deep breath, reminding himself he wasn't the only one struggling here. He turned the conversation back to the issue at hand.

"Abigail and I have worked out a plan. For the first month, she'll do most of the stuff around here for me, so I can get caught up at work. That means I'm going to be out a lot, but I'll try to be home for bedtime, and we'll have Sundays together because that will be her day off. The second month, she's going to help us set up systems so we can make sure everything gets done, and the third month, we'll start doing things more for ourselves, with her help."

"And then she'll be gone?" Kiana asked sadly.

"And then she'll be gone," Mitch agreed.

"Can she still visit?"

"I'm sure we can ask her to."

"Or not," Rachel muttered.

Mitch ruffled Kiana's hair and set her on the floor, then poked Brittany in the ribs, making her squeak. "Right. I need a word with your sister," he said, standing up to open the door. "Why don't you two go down and see if Abigail needs any help?"

"You're in trou-ble!" Brittany sang to Rachel on her way out the door, ducking her sister's arm with the ease of long practice and sticking out her tongue for good measure.

"Britt."

"Sorry, Daddy!" she called over her shoulder as she raced Kiana for the stairs.

"Yeah, right," Rachel muttered. "Sorry-not-sorry is more like it."

Mitch closed the door and eyed his daughter, noting with surprise that she came up almost to his shoulder. When had she gotten so tall? He sighed and wordlessly looped an arm around her, pulling her in for a hug. For a moment, she resisted, and then she sagged into him, her arms stealing around his waist. "What's going on, kiddo?" he asked. "All this hostility—it's not like you."

Slender shoulders shrugged against his chest. "I don't know," she said. "I just—why her, Daddy? Why Abigail and not Jessica? We don't even know her, and I don't want another stranger telling me what to do. I'm thirteen—I don't need a nanny!"

"You're right," Mitch said, resting his chin on the top of her head. "You are too old for a nanny. But we need some help right now, Rach—*I* need some help, and it's too much to ask of a friend." Especially a self-proclaimed friend who made it clear every time she saw him that she was interested in more. A lot more. And, as attractive and available as Jessica Perkins might be, Mitch did *not* need another complication in his life right now. He could barely manage the ones he already had. Correction: He *couldn't* manage them.

"I'm more comfortable paying someone," he continued, "and that someone is going to be Abigail. Besides, it's only temporary, remember? Three months and she's gone, and we can run things ourselves around here. Doesn't that sound good?"

"Maybe."

Mitch smiled into the soft cloud of hair tickling his nose. "You're very much like your mother, you know that? Never give an inch unless you have to." He drew back to look down at his daughter. "Look, I know this isn't ideal. None of this is ideal. But we can't keep up the way we have, Rachel. It's not working for any of us. You don't have to like the situation, but you do have to accept it. And I need to know I can count on your cooperation. Please?"

Another shrug. Then a muttered, "I guess."

"Thank you." Mitch braced himself. Now came the hard part. "There are going to be some ground rules."

Rachel's eyes, the same pale green as his own, narrowed. "What kind of ground rules?"

"Abigail is in charge when I'm not here. She may want to do things differently than what you're used to, but what she says goes."

Incredulity warred with horror in Rachel's expression, and she pulled away from his embrace. "Are you kidding me? She doesn't even know us, and she gets to tell us what to do?"

"In a word, yes. And you have to listen."

"What if she beats us? Or locks us in our rooms? Are we just supposed to let her?"

Mitch regarded her. "Really, Rach?"

His daughter scowled. "Well, she might."

"Fine. If she beats you or locks you in your room, you have my permission to treat it as an emergency and call me on my cell phone. Otherwise, you listen to her and do as she says. And if you don't, she has my permission to punish you"—God, he hated that word—"as she sees fit."

"But—"

"That's final, Rachel."

"*Fine*," she snapped. "But if we all need therapy after this, it's *your* fault." And with that dramatic declaration, she whirled away, pulled open the door, and stormed down the hallway.

Mitch rested one hand on a hip and pinched the bridge of his nose with the other. Closing his eyes, he took a deep breath. Well. That had gone about as well as expected. And it seemed Abigail had been right about the girls—or at least Rachel—resenting the whole nanny idea. Another thing he'd missed in the mayhem that had become his life. He looked for the flicker of hope that had sparked in him when Abigail outlined her proposal. It had dimmed considerably in the wake of the confrontation with Rachel, but it had survived. Just.

He sighed. Man, he hoped Abigail could pull this off. He hoped *they* could pull this off, because he didn't know what they would do otherwise.

He dropped his hands, turned his back on the pile of boxes he'd removed from Abigail's room, and headed back downstairs.

During her first week in the household, Abby's days settled into a rhythm. Mitch left in the mornings before she went downstairs—no easy feat, considering she got up at 5:30 herself—leaving her to feed the girls breakfast and get them ready for school. Her biggest morning challenge turned out to be Kiana's hair.

Over the little girl's objections, she decided on Thursday that the omnipresent and ever more crooked ponytails atop the child's head needed to be redone. When she removed the elastics, however, the puffs exploded into a mass of coils that made her blink in surprise.

"Oh, my," she said. "That is a *lot* of hair."

Kiana giggled, using her fingers to tease the mass even larger. "I *told* you not to do this."

"You did," Abby agreed, wishing she'd listened to the objection. "But the big question is how do I *undo* it?"

"Good luck with that," Britt said. She stood in front of the bathroom sink, regarding her reflection as she patted her own short-cropped tight coils. "This is why I keep mine like this."

"Any suggestions?" Abby asked, eyeing Kiana's head.

"Not while it's dry. Daddy always puts the pony-tails in on Saturdays, when her hair is still wet from wash-day."

And you couldn't have mentioned that before I removed the elastics? Abby thought. "Wash day?" she asked.

"We only wash our hair once a week," said Rachel from the doorway, her arms crossed and her voice disdainful. "Natural black hair gets damaged if you wash it more often, and it needs special care. Don't you know *anything*?"

Abby gritted her teeth and mustered as pleasant a smile as she could manage. "Not ever having possessed it myself, I haven't needed to know before now. And if you have any suggestions for what I can do for your sister between now and Saturday, I would appreciate hearing them. Should I just leave it down?"

Kiana shook her head at the suggestion. "It gets in my eyes."

Abby pursed her lips. "Rachel?"

Rachel stared at her narrowly for so long that Abby thought she would refuse to help, but finally she heaved an exaggerated sigh—more out of pity for her sister than for her, Abby suspected—and dropped her arms to her sides. She pulled open the drawer nearest her and extracted an oversized, covered ponytail elastic. "Here." She tossed it to Abby. "You'll never get it into two ponytails when it's dry. She'll have to have just one."

"But I don't like having just one," Kiana objected. "My hat doesn't fit right."

"You can use my slouchy hat," Britt offered. "It will go over your hair and still keep your ears warm."

"The purple one?" Kiana asked. "I like purple."

"Excellent. That's settled," Abby said, with more than a little relief. "Thank you for your help, ladies. You can start breakfast while I do Kiana's hair. There's French toast keeping warm in the oven for you. Britt, can you pass me a brush before you go?"

"No brush!" Britt and Rachel shrieked in horrified unison, startling Abby into dropping the elastic.

"Never, ever use a brush on her hair!" Rachel added. "We don't even own one. You have to use a wide-toothed comb, and only when it's wet, and only if you need to."

"No brush. Noted." Abby leaned down to retrieve the elastic, wishing she had access to a computer and the internet to do some research. Failing that, however, she'd just have to do the best she could—and tolerate being condescended to. Joy. "All right, sweet pea," she said to Kiana. "Here goes."

By the time the unflaggingly cheerful Jessica Perkins (Abby had begun thinking of her rather uncharitably as Perky Perkins) stopped by to pick up the two older girls at 8:30, breakfast had been had, coats were on, and Kiana's single large ponytail had been successfully stuffed into the borrowed hat. Abby returned Perky's enthusiastic wave as she and Kiana passed the car on their way to walk the dozen or so blocks to the kindergarten class at the local primary school. After that, as she had on all the other days that week, she returned to the house to sift through another corner that had become buried under more than a year's worth of a family life in crisis.

Mitch had been as good as his word with regard to the SUV, and just after 10:00 on Friday morning, the doorbell heralded the vehicle's return. A thrill of excitement ran through Abby as she accepted the keys from the young man standing on the porch and signed the form he held out to her. Wheels. She had wheels for the first time since the sheriff had taken away William's Mercedes along with the house, leaving her stranded and homeless in one of L.A.'s most exclusive neighborhoods.

She stared at the vehicle sitting in the driveway, debating where to go first. She had a list as long as her arm, there were so many things she needed to do. A proper grocery order would be a good start. Mitch had given her a bank card with access to the household budget account the night before, and she really needed to get the kids eating vegetables other than carrots. She also needed a new driver's license to replace her American one. And decent winter boots to replace the ridiculous fuzzy things William had given her when they'd gone skiing last—no, Christmas *before* last.

Abby's shoulders curled forward protectively as she realized she faced her second Christmas alone. Except she wouldn't be alone, and she wouldn't be able to fold up under the tree and weep her way through this one. She'd be here, well into her second month with Mitch and the kids, who would expect at least a modicum of participation from her leading up to the season. Dear Lord, she hadn't thought that one through very well, had she? She drew a shaky breath. Time enough to worry about it closer to the date. For now, she'd—

A sudden desire to see her sister seized her. She hadn't spoken to Gwyn since the day she'd left to move in here. Her sister had no landline, and Abby hadn't thought to get her cell number from her so she could call to let Gwyn know she was safe. Yes, Gwyn's house would be an excellent first foray, with a stop for groceries on her return.

Her idea seemed even better when she pulled into the space in her sister's driveway where Gareth's vehicle usually sat beside Gwyn's minivan. As decent as her brother-in-law had been to her on the surface, there had been an undeniable coolness underlying his demeanor, and Abby couldn't help but breathe a sigh of relief at finding him gone. So when the front door opened to reveal him rather than Gwyn after all, sheer surprise made her blurt, "Oh. It's you."

A muscle flexed in the jaw of her ridiculously good-looking, movie star brother-in-law. "Nice to see you, too."

Heat scorched Abby's cheeks. "Sorry, I just—Gwyn's vehicle—"

"She and Julianne went to a friend's for lunch. They didn't need the minivan for just the two of them."

"Oh. I didn't think—I guess I should have called—except I have no phone, and—" *For heaven's sake, stop yammering, Abby.* She took a steadying breath. "I just wanted to let her know that I'm okay. I thought she might be worried. Will you tell her I was here?"

Gareth studied her for a moment, then held the door wide. "I've just made coffee."

As far as invitations went, it wasn't much of one, but Abby found herself caving to impulse and stepping across the threshold. If she wanted to mend bridges with Gwyn, she'd have to find a way to get along with Gareth, too. Even if he didn't seem inclined to make it easy, she thought, following his broad back down the hallway. In the kitchen, Gareth pointed toward the table and then went to pour coffee.

"Cream or sugar?" he asked.

"Black, thank you," she said, because she didn't want him doing anything more for her than the bare minimum.

He joined her at the table, setting down two brimming mugs and taking a seat across from her. "How's the new job?"

At least he was polite.

"It's good," Abby replied. She still wore the coat he hadn't offered to take for her, and she huddled into its warmth. "The kids are nice. Mitch—Mr. Abrams—is, too."

Gareth nodded. Silence fell again.

Abby wrapped her hands around the mug, welcoming the burn against her palms as a distraction from the real pain in her life. "You don't like me much, do you?" she asked, surprising herself as much as Gareth.

Her brother-in-law's level gaze met hers. Like her, he didn't mince words. And each of the ones he chose felt like a blow to her gut. "When Jack left her with the twins and she asked for your help, you refused. And then, years later, without a word of apology, you waltz back into her life and expect her to be there for you. I don't know you well enough to like or dislike you, Abigail, but I do know I don't like how you've treated my wife. And as sorry as I am for what's happened to you, Gwyn is my priority. Not you."

Hot tears flooded Abby's eyes. She stared down at the table between her and the mug of coffee in her grasp, but no amount of blinking helped. A tear trickled down her cheek. Another followed. Gareth swore under his breath and stood. A second later, a box of tissues appeared under her nose. She sniffled and plucked one out. Gareth sat again.

"Gwyn would have my head for making you cry," he said. "And rightfully so. This is between the two of you, and I should mind my own—"

"William wouldn't let me come," Abby blurted, cutting him off. There. She'd said it aloud. For the first time ever. And instead of the usual guilt that swamped her when she though ill of the dead, a weight lifted from her shoulders. She took an unsteady breath and looked up from shredding the tissue to meet Gareth's narrowed gray eyes. "William wouldn't let me come," she said again. "I wanted to, but he said he and Olivia needed me more."

"And you accepted that?"

Gareth's tone was neutral rather than accusatory, for which Abby felt supremely grateful, because it allowed her to continue rather than bolting out the door. "I didn't have a lot of choice," she said. "My husband was... old-fashioned in his thinking. All the accounts were in his name only, and I was entirely reliant on him. I had no means of getting here without him, and I was too ashamed to tell Gwyn."

"Bloody hell," Gareth said. "Was it always like that?"

Abby nodded.

"He wasn't old-fashioned. He was a controlling ass."

"I know that now. But when I was young—" She paused, remembering the charming businessman who had swept her off her feet and into his palatial Los Angeles home, where he treated her like something rare and fragile—until the honeymoon, quite literally, was over. She shrugged. "I was nineteen when we met. William was twenty-six years my senior. He was rich and handsome, and he gave me everything I could possibly want and then some. He said he wanted to look after me. I thought it was romantic."

"And when you realized otherwise, you didn't leave?"

"And go where? I had no money, no job, no friends that weren't his friends. And then I had Olivia."

Understanding flashed in her brother-in-law's eyes, along with a dark anger that made Abby think he would make an unpleasant enemy.

"You should have told Gwyn. She would have—"

"What, offered to take in me and Olivia? Gwyn had her own problems, remember? Besides, William made it clear he would never let me take Olivia from him, and I had no money to fight him. I didn't stand a chance. And it wasn't like he was abusive, really. I was well provided for. Big house, nice clothes, fancy parties, exotic holidays. Our relationship was... complicated, but he was good to me in his own way, and he was a wonderful father."

His mouth tightened. "What about now? You said William was well off."

"Most of the money came from his family, I think. I kept the books for his company and I know it was profitable, but that was it. I didn't have access to any of the accounts, he had no life insurance, the house was in his name and his sister's, and he didn't leave a will."

"Probate?" Gareth winced.

"And a nasty fight with his family, if I want it. I don't. His sister kept house for him for more than twenty years before he married me. She feels she's owed for that."

"But California probate law—"

"I don't want the money. I—" Abby squeezed the mug until it should have shattered. She was vaguely disappointed that it didn't. She gave Gareth a smile that felt more like a grimace. "What I want, I can't have. All the money in the world won't change that."

The silence between them lasted longer this time, but it didn't have its earlier edge. Instead, it was... sad. The kind of sad that came from resignation mixed with helplessness. The kind of sad that made Abby search for a way to break it. She looked at her watch. "Goodness, is it already that late? I still have to get groceries before the girls get home from school, and—"

"You haven't touched your coffee."

"I—no. Maybe another time." She pushed the mug into the center of the table, then looked across at Gareth again. "Please don't think I'm looking for sympathy here, because I'm not. I'll figure things out. Besides, I have a job. That's a good start, right?" She didn't tell him it would end by her own choice—her own need—in three short months. Instead, she smiled and stood, and Gareth followed suit.

"That, plus telling Gwyn what you've told me," he said.

Her stomach dropped at the idea. Gwyn would have so many questions, and there was so much to unpack in their relationship, and...

"I don't think—"

"Well, I do think," Gareth said, his voice discouraging argument. "She deserves to know, and each of you deserves to have your sister back."

"Maybe. One day." Abby swallowed the lump in her throat, desperate now to leave. She'd shared more with Gareth—of all people—than she had with anyone in her life. Ever. And now she wanted to retreat into a corner and decide how she felt about that. About telling anyone at all. She led the way down the hall to the front door and stooped to pull on her fuzzy boots. "Tell Gwyn I said hi, and Gareth—thank you for listening. I don't usually dump on people like that."

Gray eyes assessed her. "No. I don't imagine you do. And yes, I'll tell her. Do you have a number she can reach you at? She might want to call."

"Sorry, no. I didn't think to take down the number of Mitch's landline, and I don't have a cell phone."

"Hang on." Gareth opened the closet and reached into a basket on the top shelf. "Here. It's the one we give Katie when she's going to a friend's after school. It's nothing fancy and there's no data, but it calls and texts. Gwyn's number is programmed in already. So is mine."

"But Katie—"

"I'll pick up another tonight."

"You won't..."

"Tell Gwyn about our talk?" Gareth shook his head. "No. It's your story to share, not mine." He opened the door for her. "But, Abby?"

She stopped on the top step to look back.

"I know a good law firm in L.A. If you change your mind, call me. The money might not buy what you can't have, but it's yours, it would help, and you should have it. At least think about it?"

Without replying, she walked down the stairs to the SUV.

CHAPTER 11

The next day, on Abby's first Saturday in the Abrams household, a persistent tapping on her shoulder pulled her from the warm, comfortable cocoon of sleep. She reluctantly pried open her eyes to find morning light flooding the room—and Kiana standing by her bed. Her gaze flew to the digital clock on the nightstand. Ten past nine? But she *never* slept in. How—?

"I'm hungry," Kiana announced, pushing her hair back from her eyes. The ponytail holder seemed to have disappeared overnight, and her hair had again achieved the volume it had on Thursday. She looked adorable.

"And Daddy's gone, and Rachel won't make breakfast for me," she continued. "She said I should wake you up instead because it's your job."

Abby held back a sigh. Of course Rachel said that. Whatever Mitch might have told his eldest in their family meeting seemed to have made zero impact on her hostile attitude toward Abby. It was exhausting. Abby raised herself onto an elbow, propping her head in her hand. "I should think you're starving," she responded, poking a finger into the girl's belly. "I'm surprised you can even walk, you must be so weak from hunger."

Kiana giggled. "It's not *that* bad." She pointed to

Abby's bedside table and the photo propped there. "Who's that?"

Abby looked over into William's dark, smiling eyes and Olivia's suntanned, laughing face. It was her favorite photo of them, taken on a beach vacation. She couldn't remember where, anymore. William had whisked them away to so many destinations that they'd all blurred together, losing their glow. But Olivia had loved it, and Abby had loved seeing her daughter's happiness.

"Just someone I knew once," she answered Kiana.

"Are they why you're sad?"

Abby gulped, thrown again by the child's astuteness. Her grandmother was right about the five-going-on-eighty thing. But remembering Kiana's own loss, she forced a light cheerfulness into her voice as she tucked the framed photo into the nightstand drawer. "Sad? How can I be sad with you to keep me company?" she asked. "Inconceivable!"

"You know *Princess Bride*!" Kiana clapped her hands together. "That's my almost-most favorite movie. 'My name is Inigo Montoya. Prepare to die!'"

"Nice catch, kid."

"I didn't catch anything."

"I meant that your brain caught my reference to the movie." Kiana still looked perplexed, and Abby tried again. "You knew I was quoting from *Princess Bride*."

The mass of hair bobbed up and down, and Kiana grinned. Abby pushed aside the duvet and swung her feet to the floor. "So, if that's your almost-most favorite movie, what's your most-most favorite?"

"*Mary Poppins.*" Kiana cleared her throat, then launched into the chorus from the chimney sweep song, her pitch perfect.

"Wow, that's pretty good," Abby said. "I'm impressed. Do you know all the words?"

Kiana nodded. "And all the songs, too. I'm good at 'membering. Wanna hear *Supercalifragilisticexpiali-docious?*"

"I would love to hear it. Want pancakes? You can sing to me while I make them." It had taken her a while, but she'd managed to salvage the frying pan Mitch had discarded on the back terrace. Thank goodness for virtually indestructible cast iron. "Give me two minutes to get dressed, and then I'll meet you in the kitchen, okay?"

"Okay. I'll get the eggs out for you. And the blueberries." Kiana danced from the room, singing the chorus from *Supercalifragilisticexpialidocious* at the top of her lungs, so that even when the door slammed behind her and her voice grew muffled, the words still came through clearly.

"Kia!" Rachel's bellow filtered through the door. "I'm trying to sleep!"

Kiana's volume increased to a return bellow. "Supercalifragilisticexpialidocious!"

Abby sighed as the girl *um-diddle-diddled* her way downstairs to the accompaniment of Rachel's continued outrage. A whole day with all three of them at home.

This ought to be interesting.

While Abby would have liked to take the kids some-where for the day, Rachel—when she finally rolled out of bed at 11:00 and scorned the leftover pancakes in favor of cold cereal—refused all suggestions. Museums were deemed boring, the art gallery idea received an eye roll, and an indoor amusement park was 'for kids.'

"Besides," Rachel mumbled around a mouthful of cereal, "I have homework."

"All weekend?" Abby asked, trying to keep her voice mild.

"No. But I'd rather spend my free time with Dad, not you."

A valid point, though it could have been more politely phrased. Abby gave up the argument. "Fair enough. I'll take the others outside for a while and give you some peace." Heading out of the kitchen, she paused in the doorway. "Oh, and can you please put your dishes in the dishwasher when you're done, this time? I may be the hired help, but I'm not your personal maid."

A mutter followed her from the room, but in the best interests of everyone concerned, Abby didn't bother returning to ask Rachel to repeat the words she hadn't quite made out. She'd told Mitch the girl would come around in her own time, but with zero easing of hostility after four days, she was beginning to wonder. With a sigh, she went to inform the others that they'd have to settle for playing outside rather than going out anywhere. She threw in an offer of hot cocoa and a movie afterward, however—they settled on *Mulan*—and everyone was happy.

It had snowed again the night before, so Abby divided her time between shoveling and fort construction, making sure most of the snow from the driveway ended up on the lawn as building material. By the time they'd finished, the fort had taken on impressive dimensions, easily dwarfing the two girls. It boasted window openings, Kiana's army of snowmen at its center, snow benches, and a path to a second, smaller walled creation that housed an armory of snowballs and hopes of a snowball fight with their father the next day.

Abby had just gone to put away the shovel so they could head inside for the promised cocoa when Jessica Perkins's car pulled into the drive. Abby hung the shovel from its hook and stuck her hands into her jacket pockets as Perky herself emerged from the vehicle, along with her daughter.

"Good morning," Abby said. "I wasn't expecting you today."

"And I wasn't expecting you to be here on a Saturday. I brought Mandy over to work on her project with Rachel."

Abby would just bet she hadn't expected her to be here. She stamped her feet to rid her boots of the caked-on snow. "Mitch has a lot of catching up to do at work right now, so I offered to work extra days for a while."

"How kind of you." Perky tipped her head to one side. "I don't suppose that offer extends to evenings as well, does it? So that he can get out for some...adult time?"

You don't suppose right, Abby thought, but she settled for a politer, "Unfortunately not."

"Hm," was the response. Assessing were the eyes. Then Perky shrugged. "Oh, well. I've waited this long to get that man to relax for an evening. I suppose I can wait a little longer."

Abby was sure Mitch would be profoundly grateful to hear that. Her gaze traveled to Mandy, who stood to one side watching their exchange with wide eyes. "You can go inside, if you like, Mandy. Rachel is up in her room."

Mandy sidled between them and headed for the porch, casting glances over her shoulder. Abby could just imagine the upcoming conversation between Rachel and her friend as they analyzed the exchange between nanny and mother, most likely punctuated by giggles and gasps and multiple exclamations of *"No way!"*

The front door closed behind Mandy, and Abby looked back to Perky. "I'll make sure she calls you when they're done."

"Oh, she knows to do that. But seeing as how Mitch isn't here, and I was hoping to invite myself in for a coffee..."

"I promised Kia and Britt that I'd make hot cocoa and watch a movie with them."

"Another time, then."

"Perhaps."

Perky grinned and shook her head. "You needn't be so shocked by me, you know. Nanny or not, you're still a grown woman, and I'm sure you can understand my interest in your employer."

I can, but I'm darned if I'll admit it to you. Or myself.

"Your interest in Mitch is none of my business," Abby replied. "But his desire not to have you 'organizing his closets'—she emphasized the words ever so slightly—"is."

To her surprise, Perky took no offense at her words and instead burst out laughing. "You're too funny," she declared. "You make a great watchdog, Abigail Jamieson, but I'm a determined woman, and I'm used to getting what I want."

"Is that supposed to be a warning of some kind?"

"Let's call it a declaration of intent. I hope you'll honor it."

Perky was back in her car and halfway down the street before Abby managed to close her jaw. She stared after the disappearing taillights. Well. That had certainly been blunt. She honestly had no idea how to respond to Perky's overt intentions, but a part of her admired the woman's sheer confidence. How must it feel to know what you wanted and simply go after it like that? Abby stamped her feet again, shedding the last of the snow from her boots, and then headed into the house.

CHAPTER 12

Abby had just finished loading up a tray with cocoa and snacks, destined for the basement television room, when she heard the garage door open, followed by the rumble of Mitch's truck. She hesitated, then set the tray aside and took down another mug from the cupboard. By the time Mitch came in through the laundry room, she had a fourth cup of cocoa heating in the microwave. Mitch's head poked through the doorway, followed by the rest of him.

"I swear I've hired a human dynamo," he said, crossing his arms and leaning against the side of the pantry. "I came home early to clear the driveway before you could get outside, and you still beat me to it. Do you ever stop moving?"

"You didn't hire me to sit around doing nothing," Abby pointed out.

"No, but I didn't hire you to work yourself to the bone, either. Especially when you're putting in six days a week. You *are* allowed to take a break now and again, you know."

And have time on my hands for thinking? No thanks.

"I like being busy, and besides, I'm about to watch a

movie with Britt and Kiana. That's almost two hours of sitting."

He snorted. "Will you survive?"

Abby flinched from the squeeze of pain in her chest at the innocent question. She'd been asking herself the same thing since she and the girls had come into the house, steeling herself to be snuggled up on a couch with two warm little bodies, neither of which was her daughter. Trying, so very hard, not to let herself think about the awful hollowness at her center.

The fact that Mitch hadn't meant his question that way mattered not at all.

Mitch's brows twitched together. "You okay?"

"Of course. I'm fine." But the brittleness of her tone said otherwise even to her, and Mitch's eyes narrowed. Fortunately, the microwave beeped just then, and she turned away to remove the mug and give the cocoa a final, brisk stir, grateful for the chance to recover. Then she set the mug on the island countertop. "For you," she told Mitch. "I was making some for the girls when I heard the garage door."

For a moment, she thought he might not follow the change in subject, but at last he unfolded his arms and straightened away from the pantry.

"Thank you," he said. "Do you mind if I take it into my office with me? I have a project estimate I need to finish today so I can have tomorrow free for the girls."

"Of course."

With a last thoughtful look over his shoulder, Mitch carried the mug from the kitchen. Abby put the almond milk back into the fridge, then closed the door and rested her forehead against the cool stainless steel. It would probably simplify things if she told him about William and Olivia so he understood her occasional odd response to something he or one of the girls said, but it didn't seem right. His family had suffered a loss of their own, and she was here for their benefit, not hers. Besides, any show of sympathy right now was likely to result in her dissolving into a puddle—as it had with Gareth yesterday. It wasn't a scenario she cared to repeat, especially with her new employer.

The whole *talk about it* approach recommended by therapists might work for others, but she much preferred the *bury it as deeply as you can* method. She just needed to try harder.

She pushed away from the fridge, picked up the tray, and went to join her charges.

"We're hungry," Rachel announced a few hours later, marching into the kitchen with Mandy on her heels.

Abby looked up from peeling potatoes as the girls seated themselves on the stools at the island. She studied the determined set of Rachel's jaw and the challenging tilt of her head. Then she glanced at Mandy, whose round-eyed gaze darted from her friend to Abby and back again. Finally, she went back to the potatoes.

"Dinner is in an hour," she said. "But there are some veggies cut up in the fridge if you'd like to have those."

"We don't want vegetables. We want the muffins you made yesterday. With jam."

Abby peeled another potato. "It's too close to dinner for muffins."

"I don't think you understand, Abigail. I said, we want—"

"I'd like you to go upstairs to your room, Rachel." Abby turned on the tap to rinse the colander of potatoes. "Mandy, it's time to call your mother and ask her to pick you up, please."

"Excuse me?" Rachel's voice rose an octave—and several decibels—in indignation. "Who do you think you are, ordering me and my friend around? When I tell you to do something—"

"Rachel Marie Abrams!" Mitch's voice boomed through the kitchen, making all three of them jump—and Rachel squeak.

"Daddy! You're home!"

Mitch stalked into the kitchen, his scowl like an impending storm. He pointed at the doorway to the hall. "Upstairs," he growled at his daughter.

"But I—"

"*Now.*"

Rachel jumped again at the bark of a word. Tears filling her eyes, she slipped from her stool and scurried out of the room. Mitch turned his attention to Mandy.

"Abby asked you to call your mother. Get your things from Rachel's room and wait for her in the front hall."

Mandy's head jerked up and down as if pulled by a string. "Yessir," she croaked, trotting wide-eyed in Rachel's wake.

Silence descended over the kitchen. Abby watched

Mitch curl his hands into fists at his sides and take a deep breath, his shoulders rigid and jaw clenched. Then he turned to her, his gaze hard.

"Has it been like this all week?"

"Actually, no. And yes, I would have said something if it was," Abby replied. "I'm not the pushover you and your daughter both seem to think I am. She was showing off in front of Mandy. I was handling it."

"I never thought you were a pushover," Mitch disagreed, "but you shouldn't have to handle *that*. Not in my house. Apparently, I didn't make that clear enough to my daughter."

"It really is okay," she said. "Rachel is still figuring things out, that's all."

He snorted his disbelief. "Fine. Then I'll help her figure."

Abby filled the pot with enough water to cover the potatoes, set it on the stove, and switched on the burner. Then she turned to Mitch. "Look, I don't want to interfere between you and your daughter, Mitch, but I'm asking you to please not intervene on my behalf. I really can take care of myself where Rachel is concerned, and I would prefer to do so."

"You're serious." Mitch stared at her. "After what she just said?"

"Especially after that. You riding roughshod over her is just going to increase her resentment."

"You're suggesting I not speak to her?"

"I'm suggesting you let me handle it my own way."

Temper still simmered behind Mitch's gaze, and Abby could see the war he waged with himself, but at last he gave a single, terse nod. "Fine. But you need to keep me in the loop, so I know what I'm supposed to back you on."

"Of course. Are you eating with us tonight, or do you want a plate in your office?"

"I have an estimate to finish, so office. Please." He looked like he wanted to say more, but after a last shake of his head and tightening of his jaw, he headed back down the hall.

Mitch closed the door to his office and stood for a moment with his hand resting on the knob, staring at the shambles within but not really seeing it. His mind was too preoccupied with the kitchen scene. His daughter's outrageous behavior; Abigail's quiet, measured response, so unlike the overreactions of her predecessors—or his own, for that matter. He thought back to the slammed doors and raised voices over the last year and realized with a start that there hadn't been any of the usual drama in the house since Abigail's arrival.

Well—his mouth twisted—no drama except from Rachel.

Where the hell had that attitude come from? Had it been there all along? Was that what all the other nannies had been trying to tell him? A twinge of guilt rippled through him. He'd been so busy trying to keep himself afloat that he hadn't had time to listen—and, he admitted to himself, he hadn't wanted to hear or deal with it, either. He hadn't wanted to deal with a lot of things. Still didn't, if he was being honest, but Abigail hadn't left him a lot of choice with her three-month deadline.

What she *had* done, on the other hand, was bring an efficient confidence into the family that made it possible for him to breathe for the first time since Eve's diagnosis—something he hadn't been aware he'd stopped doing until now, when he realized his children were well enough cared for that he really might be able to get his act together.

Even the obnoxious oldest child.

Mitch's temper flared again at the memory of Rachel's haughty words. A part of him still wanted to storm up the stairs and ground her for a month, but another part of him—a surprising one—trusted Abigail to handle it as she'd asked. Trusted her judgment. He gave a soft snort. It was unfamiliar territory, this trust thing, because he certainly hadn't felt it where any of the other nannies were concerned. Maybe it was the age difference between her and the ones who'd seemed hardly old enough to look after themselves, never mind three children. He shook his head at himself. No, it was more than that. There was something else. A depth the others hadn't had. A compassion rooted in what felt like empathy rather than sympathy. Like there was more to Abigail's story than simply needing a job as a nanny.

He'd seen it in the haunted shadows in her eyes when she'd first arrived, and again when she'd informed him she would only stay for three months. He'd ignored the shadows because he had enough to worry about, he'd told himself, and because Abigail's business was her own. Which it was, except...

Except he couldn't help but wonder who was looking after Abby's problems while she looked after his.

CHAPTER 13

Balancing a tray in one hand, Abby tapped on Rachel's door with the other. There was no answer. She tapped again and then turned the knob and pushed inside. The bedside lamp was on, but there was no sign of the girl other than a mound under the duvet. Abby carried the tray across the room and cleared a spot for it on the nightstand.

"I thought you might need a bit more time to yourself," she told the lump of bed covers, "so I brought your dinner up for you."

The lump didn't respond.

Abby chewed on her bottom lip. She'd run through a dozen conversations with Rachel in her head before coming upstairs, all of which felt like she'd be treading on the thinnest ice possible if she attempted them in real life. Finally, she'd decided on the simplest approach. But simple still didn't mean easy.

"I'm not your enemy, Rachel, and I won't let you make me into one," she said. "Like it or not, your dad needs help getting things on track around here, and it's my job to give him that help. Part of that means looking after you girls, and yes, that includes discipline issues when they come up." The mound of covers shifted.

Abby waited, but no body parts emerged. Holding back a sigh, she kept her voice neutral. "That said, I've asked your dad to give you a one-time pass on what happened downstairs earlier. No lecture, no repercussions, nothing. As far as I'm concerned, it never happened. But it doesn't happen again, either."

This time, the top of Rachel's head appeared from under the covers and pale green eyes, inherited from her father and swollen from crying, peered at Abby. "Daddy agreed?" she sniffled. "That's it?"

"It is if you want it to be." Abby walked back to the door and stood in the opening, looking back at the girl in the bed and seeing the pain and loss behind the suspicion. She wanted to take Rachel in her arms and tell her that she understood more than the girl would ever know, but she didn't, both because she knew Rachel wouldn't welcome the sympathy and because she didn't trust herself not to come apart in the telling. So instead, she gripped the doorframe and said, "Whether you like it or not, I'm here until the end of January, Rachel. It's up to you to figure out how to deal with that."

Softly, she closed the door behind her and went to run a bath for Kia's wash-day—and to learn how to properly look after the very patient child's hair.

Abby stared at the mug of cocoa that appeared between her and her book, then at the dark hand holding it, and then at Mitch.

"It's the powdered kind and not nearly as good as yours, but you've been waiting on this family hand and foot since you came," he said, his expression inscrutable. "I figured it was my turn."

"I've only been doing my job."

"Maybe. But the hot chocolate is made now, so you might as well drink it."

She hesitated, then laid aside the book and took the mug. "Thank you."

"You're welcome." He indicated one of the armchairs opposite the loveseat where she'd wrapped herself up in a blanket after tucking Kiana into bed. "May I?"

She hid a little smile. "My job, your house."

"Good point." Mitch settled with his own mug into the chair, lifting his feet onto the coffee table between them. "Thank you for overseeing baths and bedtime tonight. I was afraid if I stopped working on the estimate, I wouldn't be able to get back into it. Any trouble with Kia's hair?"

"Now that I know what I'm doing, no. Thank you for the instructions."

"You're welcome. I'm sorry I didn't think to give you a heads-up about it when you started here."

Abby shrugged. "We had a lot of other stuff to deal with. I managed." Not well, but she'd managed. "So did you get the estimate done?"

He nodded. "I sent it off a few minutes ago. Now I cross my fingers."

Abby sipped at her hot chocolate. It was sickly

sweet, but given Mitch's reputation with his daughters for cooking—and his burnt pancake history—she didn't suppose from-scratch cocoa was in his repertoire.

"Construction is a tough business," she said. "How long have you owned your own company?"

"Three years. I bought into my boss's business. We're still partners—for now."

"For now?"

"Derek is quite a bit older than I am, and his health isn't good. His husband has been nagging him about retiring."

"Will you take over his share?"

"Ideally? Yes. Practically? It might be difficult." He nodded at the mug in her hands. "How is it?"

"It's good," she said. "Thank you again."

He regarded her lazily. "You're just being kind, but you're welcome." He waved off her objection with a grin. "I recognize the tone. Eve used it whenever I made her something, too. I'm pretty sure she was just glad she didn't have to do it herself."

Abby tugged the blanket closer around her shoulders. "You must miss her."

Mitch gave a soft snort. "I do when I have the time. There hasn't been a lot of that."

He said it as a statement of fact, rather than a ploy for sympathy, but Abby's heart twisted a little at the sadness underlying the words. She'd had nothing *but* time in the year since William and Olivia had died, and she'd never stopped to consider that others might not have the opportunity to grieve. Odd how she and Mitch had lived two sides of the same coin.

"So what's your story, Abigail Jamieson?" Mitch rested his head against the chair back, watching her. "How come someone like you is working as a nanny?"

Abby tried not to react to the question, but a watchfulness in Mitch's gaze told her he'd noticed her stiffen. She buried her nose in the mug, clinging to it as if to a life preserver while she pretended to sip from it. "No story," she said when she emerged. "I like children. And I'm good at running a house."

Mitch didn't say anything for a minute, then he raised an eyebrow. "No dreams or aspirations of doing something else? You never went to university?"

She shook her head. "Not really. I—" *I married young and had a child and then I lost everything, and...* "I did a semester in psychology once. Maybe one day I'll go back to finish."

"Why didn't you continue?"

Because my husband refused to pay for my classes, and I couldn't save enough out of the house budget he gave me because I was already saving for—

"It wasn't financially feasible."

"And now?"

Now there were too many feelings and memories welling up inside for her to continue this conversation. Abby leaned over and set her mug on the coffee table, careful to keep her gaze averted so Mitch didn't see the sheen of tears she blinked back. "It's getting late," she said. "I should get some sleep."

"You haven't finished your hot chocolate," he pointed out. "Besides, tomorrow's your day off. I'll keep the kids quiet so you can sleep in."

"It's been a long week. I'm tired." She stood and, hands trembling, folded the blanket, then laid it across the back of the loveseat. "Thank you again for the drink."

"You're welcome, but—"

"Goodnight." She fled before the expected tears overflowed, but by the time she reached her room, they had retreated, replaced for the first time ever by the prickles of an unfamiliar anger. Not at Mitch for asking the questions he had, but at William, for never having asked about such things himself. For not caring about her dreams and aspirations. For holding her back and down and making certain she stayed where he wanted. What he wanted.

The other wives among their couple friends had led much the same life as Abby, but if they'd felt the same restlessness and resentment, they'd never spoken about it. The few times Abby had asked, the subject had been changed, and she had slowly learned to suppress her discontent. Olivia became her sole focus, and that was as it should be, William told her—that, and caring for him. It had been easier to agree than to continue fighting a battle she stood no chance of winning, and over time she had convinced herself that she was—well, if not happy, then at least satisfied.

Until William had discovered her secret savings account and screamed at her that he would take Olivia away forever, and then slammed out of the house with their daughter and—

And they had never returned.

Victims of a drunk driver, the police had told her. An accident William had no chance of avoiding.

But Abby had known better. She'd known that if she had just done as her husband had asked, if she could have been happy with the life he'd given her, then he and Olivia would both still be alive. She would still have her daughter. Instead, the rest of her life yawned before her like an immense, immeasurable void into which everything had disappeared. Pleasure, happiness, love, dreams. Until now, when twice in the space of two days, two different men had made her remember that, once, she had wanted more. Dreamed of more. Been more.

Now, when the restlessness that had killed her husband and daughter was back.

Abby went into the adjoining bathroom, switched on the light, and stared at her reflection. Blue-gray eyes in a pale, near alabaster, face stared back at her. She still wore her hair pulled back in the tight knot William had favored on her. He said it made her look more maternal, and he liked being the one to release it at night, to turn her from mother into wife. She hadn't let it down except to wash it since he and Olivia had died.

The blue-gray eyes scowled at her. She put up both hands and plucked out the pins holding every stray hair in place, letting them fall like metallic rain into the sink. The hair elastic went next and, released from its prison, her hair tumbled in wild, spirally disarray around her face and shoulders. Abby's insides quivered nervously in response, and her chest went tight.

It felt dangerous, like the start of a rebellion.

And? her reflection's eyes asked.

Abby had no answer, so she switched off the light again and headed for bed.

But she left her hair down.

Chapter 14

Mitch found Abby sitting in a sunbeam in the kitchen the next morning, knees drawn up and feet on the chair, mug of coffee at hand and face turned to the warmth. She looked so relaxed and peaceful that he hated to disturb her, but the rest of the gang would come thundering down the stairs at any moment anyway, and so he headed to the coffee machine.

"You look like your first day off is starting well," he said. He was glad of that. He wasn't sure what he'd set off in her last night, but he'd begun to suspect his new nanny carried quite a bit of invisible baggage with her.

"Mm," she responded. She gave a small smile but didn't turn her head or open her eyes. "I won't lie about how nice it is not to have to make breakfast and rush everyone out the door."

Mitch added a spoon of sugar and a splotch of almond milk to his coffee, then picked up the mug and strolled over to stand beside her. The back yard was a blanket of brilliant white diamond-dust, sparkling in the sunshine. "Nice day," he said. "Any plans?"

"I'm considering sitting in this sunbeam for the entire day."

He chuckled. "Sadly, it will disappear around the

side of the house in about a half hour. No windows there."

"Figures." Abby sighed. "Would you mind very much if I hung around here? I won't get in the way. I'm just not inclined to go anywhere at -23."

"That cold?"

Eyes still closed, she pointed vaguely in the direction of the thermometer he'd mounted in a shady spot beside the sliding doors. "Unless it's miraculously changed in the last five minutes."

"Well, I guess that settles it. The science museum it is for us."

"On a Sunday when every other parent in the city is thinking the same thing? You're a brave man."

"It's either that or stay inside with a sulky teen and two others who are pinging off the walls. But whether we're here or not, you're more than welcome to stay in. This is your home for as long as you're here."

"Thank you." The shadow from a cloud passed across Abby's face, and she cracked open one eye to glare at it. Mitch grinned again. She reminded him of a cat, all curled up and content until something disturbed it. A fuzzy, pale blond cat.

His gaze settled on the tumble of curls around her shoulders. *That's* what was different. He'd thought it was just because she was so relaxed, but no. It was her hair. And it was...gorgeous. He cleared his throat. "You didn't put it up today," he said. "Your hair, I mean."

Abby put a hand to her head and gave a self-conscious half shrug. "I decided I needed a change."

"Abby!" Kiana thundered into the kitchen on slippered feet and skidded to a halt by the table. "Ohhh... your hair is so pretty! You look like a golden fairy. Doesn't she, Daddy?"

Mitch sipped his coffee, watching over the rim of his mug as the color climbed into Abigail's cheeks. He didn't think he'd ever seen anyone as pale as she was, as if her skin had never seen the sun. Kiana pulled on the bottom of his sweatshirt, demanding an answer, and he tweaked a ponytail in response. "Indeed she does," he agreed.

The red in Abby's face glowed brighter.

Deciding to take pity on her—and not entirely comfortable with the direction the conversation was taking—Mitch set down his mug and swung Kiana up in his arms. "So," he said. "What do you think? Museum today?"

"Science?"

"You read my mind."

"Yay!" Little arms clasped around his neck. "Can Abby come with us?"

"It's Abby's day off today, sweetie. I think she'd appreciate some quiet time, don't you?"

Kiana tipped her head to one side and pursed her lips, considering his words. "I s'pose," she allowed at last. "But I wish she could. She's fun."

"She's confused," a new voice drawled, and Mitch noted a fine tensing around Abby's eyes before he turned to a pajama-clad Rachel.

"Who's confused about what?" he asked, not sure he wanted to hear the answer. He set Kiana on the floor and picked up his coffee again. Sure enough, Rachel responded first with an eye roll, then a huff.

"Kiana, of course. She's confused about Abigail only working for us because you're never home anymore, and the *nanny* runs the place like it's her own."

Mitch stared at his eldest, not quite believing his ears. Rachel had become so prickly and difficult these days, he hardly knew her anymore. He certainly didn't see any of the sweet, funny, generous little girl he remembered. He steeled himself for a confrontation he didn't want to have, particularly in front of Abigail. A touch on his arm distracted him, and he looked down at Abby. Her blue eyes gave a roll that outdid his daughter's six ways from Sunday, and he caught back a surprised snort of laugher. He was even more surprised when she gave a small shake of her head and a discreet, sideways hand movement that said, *"Don't."*

Mitch's lips tightened. It went against his grain to allow such disrespect in his house, and this was the second time in the space of twenty-four hours. He practically itched to send Rachel back up to her room until she'd improved her attitude. Abby's fingers waved side to side again. He glowered, then turned his attention to his daughter, whose tense body told him she, too, was braced for a fight. Perhaps even looking for one.

"You're right," he said, sparking surprise in her eyes. "I haven't been around much. We had a lot of work piled up, and Derek needed my help. We're lucky Abby has been so willing to pitch in." He watched Rachel's gaze narrow, then slide back and forth between him and Abby, as if suspecting a trap. Huh. Maybe Abby was onto something with this less punitive approach. At the very least, putting Rachel off balance like this was more fun than grounding her. He strolled over to give her a one-armed hug. "How about I promise to do better this week? Even if I have stuff I need to finish on a job, I'll come home for dinner every night and stay until bedtime. Does that work?"

For a moment—well, a split second, at least—the little girl inside Rachel shone through, and she forgot herself long enough to give him a happy nod before the scowl returned to her face. "I suppose," she muttered.

"Yes, yes, yes!" Kiana hopped around in her usual on-the-spot circle, hands flapping like the wings of a grounded bird.

Mitch put a hand on her head to slow the bounce. "Breakfast out," he announced. "We'll give Abby the house to herself, and no one has to eat burned pancakes. Deal?"

Perhaps predictably, the rate of bounce increased again.

Remaining seated in her chair while Mitch got the kids ready and out the door was equal parts bliss and torture for Abby. While she loved that she had no responsibility for the day, a part of her longed for the distraction of the happy chaos happening in the front entry—and dreaded a day with nothing to focus on but her own thoughts. She hadn't been alone in a house since she'd arrived on Gwyn and Gareth's doorstep in August. It would be so much easier to tag along with Mitch and the kids, but that would be doing them a disservice. They needed time on their own, without an outsider, if they were going to function as a family by the end of her three months here.

She sighed. Maybe it would be better if she *did* go out... but where? The thought of wandering around a mall or a museum by herself held no more appeal than sitting in the house, plus it required going out into a bone-chilling cold for which her California-acclimatized body was seriously unprepared. Visiting Gwyn and Gareth was equally unappealing, given the freshness of her conversation with Gareth and the certain grilling she expected from Gwyn about how she was holding up on the new job. Which left what... a movie? A book? Total panic at the idea of hours of empty time on her hands?

A chorus of goodbyes reached out to her as the troops filed from the front hall through the laundry/mud room and out into the garage. She really did need to sort things out so that everything was in one place—especially for the winter. Doors slammed. A vehicle started. The garage door rumbled shut. Silence descended.

Abby stared at her coffee, now cold in the mug on the table. As Mitch had predicted, half her sunbeam had already disappeared, leaving behind a chill.

"Well, damn," she said to the kitchen. And then she stood, crossed the kitchen to dump her cold coffee down the drain, and set about keeping her thoughts at bay the only way she knew how.

CHAPTER 15

By the time Mitch and the kids arrived home just before dinner, Abby had made the beds, moved all the winter gear from the front hall closet into the mudroom (where she sorted it into labeled baskets beneath the bench), dusted and vacuumed the entire house, completed a pile of mending, written out the week's menu and accompanying grocery list, cleaned the fridge, made spaghetti sauce, and was in the middle of peeling apples for an apple crumble.

"Really?" Mitch asked from the kitchen doorway, surveying her efforts. "Your first day off, and you spend it cooking?"

"I like cooking," she replied, avoiding his gaze and keeping the mending and cleaning part to herself.

"Daddy, Daddy! I have my very own basket in the mudroom with my name on it and everything!" Kiana's voice floated in to join them. "And a coat hook, too!"

Mitch raised an eyebrow. "Cooking *and* organizing?"

"There's a lot to do if I'm going to have everything ready for you to take over."

"So much that you can't take a day to yourself?"

She sighed. "I told you I'm not very good at sitting."

"I'm beginning to believe you."

Brittany bounded into the kitchen, Kiana close behind, and peered into the simmering pot on the stove. "Ooh, spaghetti! With meatballs?"

"Is there any other way?" Abby asked, ruffling the girl's short, bouncy curls. "And there's apple crumble for dessert, if someone wants to help me peel the apples."

Two voices clamored to volunteer, and Abby dug out two peelers and got Britt and Kiana settled on stools, all the while conscious of Mitch's continued presence in the doorway. Then, when she picked up her own knife again, he plucked it from her fingers and pointed it at the third stool.

"Sit," he said. "It's time I learned how to make an apple crumble. How many apples do we need?"

"The rest of the pile, but I—"

"You have done enough for one day." Mitch raised his voice to call, "Rachel! We need your help in here."

Supervising a kitchen full of people was a new experience for Abby. William had expected her to take full responsibility for meals—three a day—and year after year, he had decreed Olivia too young to help. Abby had often felt more like the hired help than a wife and mother, but then her husband would arrive home with an unexpected and extravagant gift, and guilt would once again hold her silent. Watching Mitch and his girls pitch in to complete the meal she'd started was a revelation... and then some. All those years of preparing food, and she'd had no idea kitchen work could be so much fun. Even Rachel cracked a smile a few times and let a giggle slip through once, when

Mitch's vigorous stirring of the crumble topping raised a cloud of flour dust that turned his beard strip and eyelashes white.

It took a little longer than it would have if she'd worked alone, but at last the crumble was in the oven, the pasta was drained, and the table was set. Mitch served up spaghetti and meatballs, the girls carried their plates to the table, and then he brought his own and Abby's over—and, for the first time since her arrival, sat down to join them.

Eating a meal with him at the table was different from eating alone with the girls. Rachel didn't spend the entire time glowering at her plate, there were no awkward silences, and Abby—refreshingly—didn't feel like an interloper. In fact, halfway through her plate of pasta, she realized that she felt very much like a part of the family. Which raised a whole lot of other issues for her—primarily, paralyzing guilt at the thought of enjoying herself with someone else's children when her own was gone.

The idea sucked the air from her lungs, and she pushed a meatball around her plate as the table talk and laughter flowed around her. Desperately, she tried to recall the sound of Olivia's laugh, a sound she had once loved more than life itself, but her memories stayed stubbornly silent. A knife slipped beneath her ribs. She'd forgotten. She'd forgotten her own—

"Abby?"

She blinked and looked across the table at Mitch, his brow creased. Her gaze searched his for a hint of the same shadows she carried inside her. He had lost his wife. The mother of his children. Did he ever look at them with the same guilt that Abby felt? The grief counselor had assured the bereaved parents' group that it was normal. Survivor's guilt, she'd called it. The ache of remaining alive and daring to find happiness, no matter how small, without your loved one.

"Everything okay?" Mitch asked.

All three girls watched her.

"It's fine," Abby said, hearing catch in her voice. "I think I just overdid it today. Do you mind if I excuse myself?"

"Don't you want dessert?" Kiana asked.

"You can save mine for me." Abby forced a smile. "I'll have it for lunch tomorrow." She stood and pushed back her chair, but when she made to pick up her plate, Mitch's voice stopped her.

"I've got that," he said. "You go and rest."

And, once again, Abby found herself fleeing.

CHAPTER 16

Abby's second week in the Abrams household was a replica of the first: getting the girls off to school in the mornings, followed by more cleaning and organizing while they were gone. With the main living spaces under control, she turned to the hidden ones: closets, basement storage, and even (with some trepidation) the garage workshop, so that she could park the SUV inside *and* still open all its doors. Halloween decorations were separated from the Christmas ones and given their own containers, camping gear was pulled out from under the workbench, sports equipment found a home in a bin, and so on. The afternoons found her picking up Kiana at three o'clock, supervising homework and snacks, and preparing dinner.

Mitch was as good as his word, arriving home in time to eat with them each evening, to the great delight of his children. Through sheer determination, Abby got through the dinners without having to leave the table, reminding herself again and again that it was part of her job, and it didn't mean she was pushing aside memories of her own daughter if she smiled at one of Mitch's.

Even if she still couldn't remember Olivia's laugh.

Each night after dinner, Mitch recruited the girls to help him clean the kitchen and supervised bedtime, leaving Abby free to curl up on the loveseat in the living room with her book again—and to reflect that, at this rate, the family wouldn't need her for the full three months after all. That begged the question of what in heck she'd do next and led, in turn, to more stressing than reading—but not as much stress as Mitch's habit of bringing her tea did.

He started on Monday, holding out a mug to her with a smile. "Chamomile," he said. "You didn't look very enthused about the hot chocolate the other night. Eve used to say this helped her sleep."

Abby curled her fingers around the book she'd been staring at but not reading. "Thank you, but—"

"I think," he said, "you're supposed to stop after *thank you.*"

"Well, yes, but—"

Mitch raised an eyebrow, still holding out the mug.

Abby snapped her mouth closed and took the steaming mug from him. "Thank you."

"That's better. And you're welcome. I have to go back out for a couple of hours, but I'll be back before midnight. You okay with watching the kids?"

"Of course."

She settled back to listen to the sounds of his departure, a little nugget of warmth at her core that had nothing to do with the heat of the mug she cradled.

Well, not directly, anyway.

On Tuesday night, it was peppermint.

"You really don't need to do this, you know."

"*Thank you, Mitch,*" he coached.

She blushed. "I didn't mean to sound ungrateful. I just—"

"You're just not very good at letting other people do things for you."

With a tiny shock, she realized he was right. With a much greater shock, she realized it was because she hadn't had a lot of experience at it. For all his lavish gift-giving and jetting her around the world, William hadn't been a thoughtful man—or a generous one, for that matter. At least, not in the everyday sense. And she'd never seen it until now. To cover her discomfiture, Abby set her book down on the coffee table and accepted the mug from Mitch. "Thank you," she mumbled.

"You're welcome. And I really hope that wasn't as painful as it sounded."

His words surprised a smile from her. "No, it wasn't painful. And I meant it. Thank you."

Mitch smiled in return. "Much better. And you're welcome." He hitched up the pant legs on his jeans and dropped with a sigh into the armchair opposite.

Abby noted that he had a glass containing ice and an amber liquid. "Long day?" she asked.

"Long few days." He sipped from the glass, then frowned. "I'm sorry, I should have asked you if you'd prefer something stronger than tea."

"Thank you, but no. I'm a bit of a lightweight when it comes to alcohol. It's best if I avoid it when I need to get up early."

His green gaze turned assessing. "All work and no play? I've heard that's not good for you."

"Said the pot, calling the kettle black."

"Touché." He tipped the glass toward her in a small salute. "So. Your second week with us. How are you finding things? Not too much trouble getting the girls off to school in the mornings? Kiana can be a bit..."

"Delicate?" Abby suggested, and he chuckled.

"That's as good a word as any," he agreed, with a wry twist of his mouth. "I probably should have warned you that she doesn't like to be rushed. Any problems?"

Abby shook her head and took a sip of the peppermint tea, which happened to be one of her favorites. "Not really. My—" Her throat closed against what she had been about to say, and she swallowed. "I've had experience with another girl like her. I give her lots of lead time. It helps."

"I have to say, I'm a little surprised at how easily you've settled in here." Mitch swirled the liquid in his glass as he regarded her. "In one week, you've done more to organize this house and my family than I've seen anyone accomplish in more than a year, including my mother. The girls are happy, and—"

"Well, maybe not all of them," Abby said, partly to correct him, but mostly to divert him from where she thought he might be going with this. Because she wasn't going to change her mind. *Couldn't* change her mind.

He smiled. "True. But the majority rules, and Kiana and Brittany are more relaxed than I've seen them in a long time. Are you sure you won't—"

"I can't. We agreed on three months, Mitch. I can't stay longer, and I would appreciate it if you wouldn't ask again. Please."

In the long silence that ensued, she darted a quick look in his direction and found him watching her, the index finger of his free hand tracing the fullness of his bottom lip. She wrenched her gaze away again.

"I'd venture to guess that you have quite a story behind that request," he said at last, "but all right. I won't ask again." He levered himself up from the chair and, glass still in hand, strolled toward the hallway, pausing in the doorway. "If you ever want to talk, however, I've been told I'm a decent listener. Goodnight, Abigail Jamieson."

Abby didn't even try to respond.

CHAPTER 17

On Wednesday evening, despite the turn the previous night had taken, she found herself unable to focus on reading as she waited for Mitch and the tea she had begun to expect after the girls had gone to bed. When half an hour slipped by after he'd come back downstairs from saying goodnight to them, and there was still no sign of him, she leaned forward to peer down the hall at his office door. It was solidly closed. Had he forgotten? Decided she was more drama than he cared to deal with anymore?

Abby sat back again, staring at her open book without seeing it. She'd spent the better part of the day working on her defenses—again—so that she wouldn't have another semi-meltdown, and now she wanted the opportunity to test her newly forged determination to carry on a normal conversation. She and Mitch were the only adults in the household—heck, he was the only adult in her life at the moment—and, as the girls' father, he deserved to be able to talk to his nanny without feeling as if he was treading on eggshells.

Setting her mouth in determination, Abby put the book on the coffee table, stood, and draped the blanket over the back of the loveseat. Then she tiptoed past Mitch's office to the kitchen, where she made tea for both of them and tried hard to convince herself she could handle this. Because if she couldn't, how on earth was she going to manage the next ten weeks?

She straightened her spine, left her own cup on the counter, and marched down the hall to Mitch's office with his. There, she tapped on the door and waited.

Mitch's voice, sounding distracted, called, "Come in."

Abby turned the knob and stepped inside, and he looked up from the avalanche of papers across his desk. A look of dismay crossed his face when he saw the cup in her hands.

"I forgot your tea. I'm so sorry—I lost track of the time."

Abby waved away his apology. "I don't expect you to bring me tea every night," she lied. "Besides, I figured you must be busy."

He leaned back in his chair and linked his hands behind his head. "So you *were* expecting me."

"That's not what I—I just thought I—" She bit down on her jumble of words, gathered herself, and crossed the floor to his desk, sidestepping a stack of books and a giant roll of blueprints. She set the mug down on his desk with a thump that didn't quite send the liquid spilling from it. "I made you some instead."

"Wait." Mitch stood and reached out and caught her wrist when she turned to leave. An unexpected electric tingle shot up her arm, and she caught her breath. Mitch went still for an instant and then released her with a muttered, "Sorry. I shouldn't have done that."

Abby sidled a few steps away as the tingle spread across her chest and made her breath hitch. The silence between them grew awkward. She contemplated outright flight as an alternative if he didn't speak soon, because *she* sure as heck couldn't think of anything to say.

Mitch rubbed the back of one hand over his neatly trimmed beard. "I wasn't trying to guilt you. I was just teasing. Making you a cup of tea in the evening is the least I can do when you're putting in fourteen hours a day, six days a week around here. I enjoy doing it, otherwise I wouldn't. Okay?"

She nodded.

"And I'm sorry I grabbed you like that," he added, his gaze serious. "I wasn't thinking. It won't happen again."

Abby squashed a ripple of disappointment—because she wasn't supposed to react to his touch at all, let alone want him to touch her again—and tried not to want to disappear into the floor. Could she be any more gauche? "It was nothing," she squeaked. Squeaked? *Dear Lord, Abigail, you need to do better than that.* "I know it was just a reflex."

Nope. Husky voice wasn't any better than squeaky. Time to leave.

"Well. Goodnight, then." Giving in to the urge to flee, she turned and promptly tripped over the stack of blueprints, sprawling face first on the floor. Mitch was at her side before she'd even registered the impact—or the whoosh of air from her lungs.

"God, Abby, are you okay?" Strong hands scooped

her off the hardwood and set her on her feet, then remained on her shoulders to steady her.

Abby opened her mouth, but no response emerged —not even a sound. Then she realized she couldn't draw a breath, and panic set in. Her fingers clutched at Mitch's shirtfront. His hands left her shoulders and curled around hers.

"It's all right," he said. "You've just knocked the wind out of yourself. Give it a minute, and your diaphragm will relax again. Just keep trying to breathe."

Diaphragm. Her brain zeroed in on the paralyzed body part, suddenly aware of the intense, taut pain centered there. For long seconds, the *just keep trying to breathe* part of Mitch's instructions remained impossible, but little by little, the muscle relaxed again, and air returned to her lungs. At last she was able to suck in the deep, albeit shaky, breath her body craved... and then her brain found other things to zero in on.

Such as how Mitch's breath feathered against her face. And how dark and warm his hands were against her own skin. And how she was leaning into his taut, muscled strength and the pale green of his eyes seemed to be deepening and—

Cheeks burning, she pulled away and stepped back, stumbling over the blueprints again but managing to stay upright this time. A new jumble of words piled up on her tongue, spilling out in random order. "I'm so sorry. I haven't knocked the wind out of myself since I was a kid. Thank you. The last time I did that was when I jumped off the garage roof. I'm not usually that clumsy. I—"

"You jumped off a garage roof?" Mitch interrupted. He'd slid his fingers into the front pockets of his jeans and watched her with equal parts amusement and something Abby couldn't—no, didn't *want*—to identify. "Why on earth would you jump off a garage roof?"

He was changing the topic, Abby thought with relief. Well, not exactly the topic, but at least the direction of their conversation. Not that they'd been talking about anything in particular, and certainly not about whatever that had been between them just now, but— she slapped brakes on her runaway brain.

"We were trying to parachute," she said. "With bedsheets. I was the youngest, so I got to go first."

Mitch laughed. "Sounds about right," he said. "My older brother made me try the toboggan jump he made when I was six. I ended up with a broken collar bone. My mother was not pleased."

Abby managed a smile in return, but all she could think about was how much she wanted to try leaning into his strength again, how warm his hands had been, and how wrong her thoughts were. "Well," she said. "I should let you get back to work. Goodnight."

Mitch's goodnight followed her out the door as she made good her escape, this time without incident. She didn't bother returning to the kitchen for the cooling tea in which she'd lost all interest.

CHAPTER 18

Sleep eluded Abby for a good part of the night, and morning found her tired, groggy, and unfocused. Which was how she found herself staring down at Kiana in full meltdown mode after she took away the girl's unfinished breakfast in an effort to hurry her along. It didn't matter that Abby had offered her a muffin and banana to eat on the walk to school instead. It mattered only that she had moved too quickly for the five-year-old, and now Kiana sat on the floor with her arms wrapped around her knees and her face tucked out of sight, rocking back and forth and humming to herself.

"Now you've done it," Rachel observed, leaving her plate on the table and walking past Abby on the way to the hall. "She'll never make it out the door today. Awesome job, *nanny*."

Abby glared daggers after the teen's retreating back, but she didn't respond. Rachel was right, she'd messed up, and poor Kiana was paying the price. But in her defense, what the *heck* had that been last night with Mitch? She'd spent most of her sleepless night trying to convince herself she'd been mistaken about that spark between them, about the look in his eye, but she wasn't that naive. Mitch Abrams had looked at her as something more than his employee last night, and he'd liked what he'd seen, and she had responded, and oh *hell*, but she didn't need this.

Taking a deep breath, Abby crouched at Kiana's side. "Kiana, sweetie..."

The humming intensified. Abby stared down at the crooked black puffs held in place by fuzzy purple ponytail holders decorated with unicorns. When Mitch had asked how things were going with Kiana, she'd responded that she'd had experience with another girl like his daughter—and she was beginning to wonder just how much truth was in that statement. Was it possible...?

"Here." Brittany shoved Kiana's beloved stuffed bunny into Abby's face. "This helps sometimes."

Abby took the plush toy. "Thank you, sweetie. Anything else I should know that helps?"

"Not really. Except don't try talking to her or touching her. She'll snap out of it on her own. But Rachel's right. There's no way she's going to school today."

"That's all right," Abby said, with another regretful look at the problem she'd created just because she hadn't had the patience to wait for an extra few minutes. "We'll bake cookies instead."

"Chocolate chip and oatmeal?" Brittany's dark eyes lit up.

"Why not? But for now, we need to get you ready to go. Ms. Perkins will be here any minute." Abby set the rabbit on the floor, tucking it against Kiana's leg. Then she stood, because if her suspicions were right, hovering over the little girl would just make matters worse. "Got your lunch?" she asked, turning her attention to Britt. "And your homework?"

"All packed." Britt hefted her bulging knapsack as evidence, then stooped and planted a kiss atop Kiana's head. "Bye, Kia. Be good. And remember, chocolate chip and oatmeal."

Kiana continued humming and rocking.

Rachel and Brittany were all of two minutes behind schedule, but when Abby opened the front door for them to leave, she found Perky Perkins on the other side with her hand raised to knock. Perky flashed her a bright smile and then a look of concern.

"You look like you're having a rough morning, my friend. Everything okay?"

"It's fine, thank you. I just didn't sleep well last night."

"Probably because you're exhausted, the way Mitch has you working six days a week like that. I'll have a word with him. If he really needs the extra time for the business, I can come help out on Saturdays so you get a break."

Abby couldn't imagine anything less helpful, at least from Mitch's perspective. Still, it was a nice offer, and so she summoned a ghost of a smile through the headache nagging at her temples. "Thank you, but I'm honestly doing fine," she said. "Today is just a bit of an anomaly."

The not-very-charitable part of her wondered what Perky would think of the reasons behind that anomaly. She filed the thought away with the others that had plagued her since the encounter in Mitch's office, because she didn't want to be thinking any of them. *Shouldn't* be thinking them.

"Are you sure? Because I really don't mind."

I'll just bet you don't.

Abby sighed at herself. "I'll call if I need help," she promised.

"Please do. And in the meantime, remember it's just for a few more weeks, right?"

"How—"

"Rachel mentioned it. It wasn't a secret, was it?"

"I'm just not sure Mitch would like her discussing family concerns that way." Abby flashed a narrow look at Rachel, but the girl brushed past her and headed down the sidewalk to the waiting vehicle. If she'd heard, she wasn't letting on.

Perky snorted. "Oh, pooh," she said. "We're friends. He wouldn't mind. Well, I have to get these three off to school. I hope your day gets better!" With her trademark cheery wave, Perky jogged down the stairs and along the walkway to her car.

Abby closed the door. Darned if she could figure out that woman. Perky's interest in Mitch was clear, but she wasn't behaving at all the way the women in Abby's L.A. social circle had done in similar situations. There was no cattiness, no insincerity, no underhandedness— none of the hallmark behavior with which Abby was familiar. Instead, Perky had been upfront about her intentions, confident in her quest to achieve them, and seemingly quite genuine about her offers to help Abby —all at the same time. It was weird.

Abby returned to the kitchen, where Kiana remained on the floor, but now had her arms wrapped around her stuffed bunny. In silence, Abby scooped fresh oatmeal into a bowl, heated it in the microwave, and added a drizzle of maple syrup and some almond milk. She placed the bowl on the island.

"Your breakfast is on the counter," she said. "I'm going to go vacuum the upstairs. You let me know when you're done, and I'll walk you to school."

The little girl's voice stopped her at the doorway. "I still get to go?"

"Of course. We'll just be a little bit late, is all."

"Will Madame Sylvie be mad?"

"I'll talk to her," Abby reassured her. "No one will be mad."

"What about the cookies?"

"We'll bake them before we go."

It was the tail-end of lunchtime by the time they made it to the school, and Kiana's kindergarten class was out on the playground under the watchful eye of their teacher. Abby sent a bundled-up Kiana off to play with her friends, then went to join Madame Sylvie by the monkey bars. The other woman greeted her warmly, and then asked, "Is everything okay?"

"Just a rough start to the morning," Abby said, pulling a face. "I tried to rush her at breakfast and it didn't go well."

"Ah. Yes, she does take a little gentle coaxing, doesn't she?" Madame Sylvie moved away to support one of Kiana's classmates, small for his age, as he swung himself across the bars. "*Très bon*, Michel!" she praised him, and a dazzling smile of triumph rewarded her. She stepped back to Abby's side again, looking sideways at her. "You look like you have something on your mind."

"How is Kiana in class?" Abby asked, watching her young charge building a snowman with her friends. A full head taller than any of them, she'd been put in charge of lifting the head into place. "Have you noticed anything that raises concern?"

Madame Sylvie's expression turned cautious. "I'm not sure I can discuss this with you," she replied. "You're not a parent or a legal guardian..."

Abby had expected as much. She tried a different tack. "Her father hasn't mentioned hearing from the school. Is there something I should be asking him?"

"There might be," the teacher allowed, "if he'd ever come in to speak with me."

"You've asked?"

"Several times. He's canceled two appointments with me already. I'm trying to give him as much space as possible, knowing what the family has gone through."

Abby nodded, unsurprised. She'd half expected that, too. She considered how to continue. "I have some experience with ASD," she said carefully around the memories she didn't want to stir up. She could still hear the words spoken by Olivia's pediatrician a scant year before the accident: *autism spectrum disorder*. She steeled herself to go on. "Some of Kiana's behaviors are red flags for me. The hand-flapping and bouncing, the way she won't always meet my eyes when I'm talking to her, the difficulty in changing direction, her fixation on certain things. But I feel I haven't known her long enough to suggest to her father that there's an issue. If you've noticed the same things, however, it will give me something more to take to him."

Madame Sylvie stared out over the playground for a long moment without answering. Then she sighed. "Snowmen," she said.

"Pardon?"

The teacher nodded toward the fence on the far side, and for the first time, Abby noticed the veritable army of snowmen clustered there—at least twenty of them, of varying sizes and shapes, some with sticks for arms, others with stubs made of more snow.

"Kiana?" she asked.

Madame Sylvie nodded. "She draws them on everything, too. And every craft we do gets turned into one. She's quite creative about it."

Abby tried not to smile, thinking about the tray of chocolate chip cookies they'd made before leaving the house, meticulously placed so that three cookies baked together—but not altogether evenly—into snowmen shapes.

"At the beginning of the school year, it was penguins," Madame Sylvie said, "after we read a book about them." She turned to Abby as the school bell rang, signaling the return to class. "Kiana is an extremely bright girl, Ms. Jamieson, but yes, I think you should speak to her father. And I think he should keep his next appointment with me."

CHAPTER 19

It was with more than a little trepidation that Abby listened to Mitch making tea in the kitchen that night. Both her conversation with Madame Sylvie and the previous evening's encounter remained fresh in her mind, and as she plucked at the blanket, awaiting his appearance, she preferred not to think about which was the primary cause of her jitters. Mitch's silence when he did arrive didn't help.

He handed her one of the cups he carried, then indicated his usual armchair with his freed-up hand.

"Of course," Abby said. "I need to talk to you about something anyway."

Mitch's mouth drew tight, and a muscle flexed in his jaw. When he sat, he didn't lean back like he usually did, but instead sat forward with elbows on knees and head bent, staring into the cup he held.

Abby took a deep breath. "It's about—"

Mitch held up a hand but still didn't look at her. "Please," he said. "Let me go first. I know I made you uncomfortable when I grabbed hold of you last night, Abby, and I cannot begin to tell you how sorry I am. I don't know why—and you're right, it's none of my business, so I won't ask—but being here in the house with us is hard for you, and the last thing I want is to make it harder. So please, give me another chance?"

"Another..." Abby blinked at him. "You think I'm quitting?"

"Aren't you?"

"No! Of course not. This isn't about—it's not—I need to talk to you about Kiana."

"Kiana?" Mitch's head came up at last, and he frowned. "What does Kiana have to do with it?"

Briefly, Abby outlined her conversation with Kiana's teacher that morning, including her own observations and concerns, and ending with, "I know it's difficult to think there might be an issue, but have you ever considered having her evaluated? It might be nothing, but—" She broke off as Mitch, looking inexplicably stricken, set his cup on the coffee table and stood.

"I'll be back," he said, and a second later, she heard him opening and closing what sounded like file drawers in his office. He returned when Abby had drunk half her tea. "Sorry, it took a while to find it." He dropped a file folder onto the table.

Abby looked askance as he resumed his seat.

"It's Kiana's medical file," he said, resting his elbows on his knees again. This time, however, he didn't hold his cup but instead rubbed his hands over his face, looking wearier and more haggard than Abby had seen him so far.

No, not haggard. Tortured. She reached for the file.

"Kiana has trisomy X," Mitch said as she began flipping through the reports and letters inside. "Also known as triple X syndrome. It's a genetic—"

"A genetic abnormality," Abby broke in. "Affecting one in a thousand women, most of whom go undiagnosed because they have no symptoms—or because their doctors don't know to test for it."

"You're familiar with it?" Surprise laced Mitch's voice.

"I've... come across it before." She'd researched it half to death when Olivia's pediatrician had recommended the DNA test. It was his standard next step when autism was confirmed in a female patient, he'd told them, even though the syndrome still wasn't well known in most of the medical community. In Olivia's case, the test had come back negative, much to Abby's great relief. Autism on its own would have been challenging enough, but if it had resulted from triple X, there could have been a whole host of other issues as well. Abby paused at a cardiology report, relieved to read that no heart abnormalities had been found in Kiana. Ditto for the kidney exam results. She looked across the top of the folder at Mitch. "When did you find out?"

"Not long before Eve was diagnosed. She was able to look after some of the follow-up work"—Mitch nodded at the file—"but once she started treatment, she was too sick to do more. And I..." The tortured look returned. "I never even opened the file after she died because I forgot about it." He rubbed his hands over his face again, steepling his fingers against his mouth.

"Freaking hell," he muttered. "What kind of father forgets about his daughter's health?"

"One that's been stretched a little too thin for a little too long," Abby replied, but the torment remained on Mitch's face. Without thinking, she leaned across to put her hand on his knee. "Hey, ease up on yourself. You've singlehandedly kept your family and business afloat for a year, remember?"

He raised an eyebrow. "Seriously? You can say that after the disaster you walked into last week?"

Abby smiled. "The house was still standing when I got here," she countered, "and the girls had been fed—"

"Is that what we're calling granola bars for breakfast?"

"And your business is still running—"

"More thanks to Derek than to me."

Exasperated, she lifted her hand and gave his knee a poke. "Enough. Like it or not, you've done better than you give yourself credit for, and I'm going to get you on track so that it's easier. Even with this." She waved the file folder at him. "You just need a plan, is all."

Mitch stared down at the knee she'd prodded, then he stood up from the chair and picked up his untouched tea. "I'll keep telling myself that," he said, his gaze meeting hers with a quiet despair that went straight to her core. "But you need to know that you're way more optimistic about this three-month thing than I am, Abby. Way more."

Abby listened to his steps retreat down the hallway, first to the kitchen and then past the living room again to his office, where the door clicked shut. She wrestled with the desire to follow him and offer more reassurance, but her better sense won out—underlined by the memories of the evening before and the tingle in her palm from its contact with his knee. Settling back on the loveseat, she opened the file again and began reading about Kiana.

CHAPTER 20

"Abby, there's someone at the door for you!"

Abigail pulled her head out of the washing machine and raised her eyes toward the ceiling. Her third Saturday on the job, all the girls at home, yet another confrontation with Rachel, a washing machine that refused to drain...and all before nine in the morning. And now what was most likely a door-to-door marketer. Maybe she'd get lucky and it would be kids selling chocolate bars to raise money for a school project, and she could buy their whole inventory, and—

"Abby!" Brittany yelled again.

With a sigh, Abby wiped wet hands against the seat of her jeans. "Coming," she called back, heading into the hall. She stopped short of the entryway. "Gwyn! What—how—?"

Her sister grimaced, looking guilty. "Tracking app," she said. "On the phone Gareth gave you. You haven't been returning my calls, and I got worried."

"You tracked me?"

"Sister's prerogative?" Gwyn hedged. Then she scowled. "Seriously, Ab. I was worried. Why didn't you call me?"

It was Abby's turn to hedge. "I was busy."

Gwyn raised an eyebrow. Heat suffused Abby's cheeks.

"And I wasn't ready to talk."

"You talked to Gareth."

"He told you?"

"Yes, but he didn't give me details. He just said you and I had some clearing of the air to do." Gwyn waited, still bundled in her winter coat and boots, hands stuffed into her pockets. Then she sighed. "If you're not ready, I can respect that. Today, I really did just want to know you're safe."

"I'm fine."

Her sister's gaze took in her wet shirt front and jeans. "I'm catching you at a bad time."

"Yes. No. Kind of. The washing machine decided not to drain. I thought maybe something was jammed, but I've taken the whole load out, and I can't find anything."

"Sounds like your water pump. Ours went last year. You'll need someone to come in."

Abby groaned. "You've got to be kidding me. I stripped all the beds this morning, and I have six loads to do, including school clothes. And I haven't been in a laundromat in—" She broke off and frowned. "Do they even have laundromats in Ottawa anymore?"

Gwyn laughed. "They do, but why don't you and the girls come to our place instead? You can have lunch with us and use our machines. Our four would love the company."

Abby hesitated.

"And I promise not to grill you," Gwyn added. She

began stripping off her coat and scarf. "Point me toward the laundry room and I'll put things in bags while you get your troops organized. Make sure everyone has their snow gear, and I'll see if I can talk Gareth into taking them tobogganing while Julianne naps. There's not a huge amount of snow yet, but our crew insists there's enough. And our van seats eight, so they can all squeeze in to get to the hill, and Amy's coming by this afternoon, so she can help out." She paused in her efforts to divest herself of her boots. "Why are you looking at me like that?"

"I'd forgotten how bossy you can be."

"Would you really rather drag three kids to the laundromat with you for the day?"

Abby rolled her eyes and pointed down the hallway toward the kitchen. "Hallway on the right, just past the stairs. Bags are on the top shelf of the cupboard over the sink. I'll get the girls."

Predictably, Brittany and Kiana were thrilled with the idea of going out for the day, especially when the possibility of tobogganing was raised. Equally predictably, Rachel was not.

"You're kidding, right?" From her usual sprawled-on-belly position on the bed, she regarded Abby as she might something distasteful on the bottom of her boot. "You expect me to spend the day with a bunch of little kids I don't even know, just so you can visit your sister? I don't think so."

"It's not so I can visit Gwyn, it's so I can do *your* laundry. I told you, the machine is broken, and Gwyn was kind enough to offer the use of hers. It's either that or the laundromat, and I guarantee her place is nicer."

"Right. How convenient." Rachel returned her attention to the laptop open before her. "I have an English essay to write. I'm staying here."

Abby drew her lips between her teeth and bit down so hard that they burned. While things had improved between her and Rachel immediately following the blow-up last weekend, they had slowly devolved again over the week, until it felt like they were back to square one, and Abby was getting more than a little tired of the constant friction. Tired, too, of the attitude. Already today, Rachel had refused to strip her bed so Abby could wash the sheets. She hadn't outright informed Abby that it was part of her job this time, but she had certainly insinuated as much. Abby counted to a slow ten, weighing and discarding options such as throwing an all-out hissy fit or just turning the entire mess over to Mitch after all. Then inspiration struck. Calmly, she crossed the floor to the bed, closed the laptop, and picked it up.

"Hey! That's mine!" Rachel screeched.

"Your English essay," Abby said, "is coming to Gwyn's. And so are you. Bring your headphones and your charging cord, and we'll find you a quiet corner to work in. I'll see you in the front hall in five minutes."

"And if I'm not there?" Rachel demanded of her back as she headed out of the room again. "You can't make me, you know! You're not the boss of me, Abigail!"

Abby pulled the door shut, closed her eyes, and

leaned against the wall, listening to the string of inappropriate curses filtering into the hallway and wanting very much to slide down onto the floor and curl up in a ball. How in the world was she going to survive another two months of this?

"Jessica would never treat me like this!" Rachel's muffled voice yelled, and Abby's eyes snapped open. She twisted her head to look over her shoulder at the teen's door, letting that last bit percolate in her brain. Was *that* the problem? Could Perky Perkins really be so small that she'd stoop to—

Abby thought back over how the woman had cheerfully insisted on continuing to pick up Brittany and Rachel for school every morning. Could her helpfulness have hidden some kind of ulterior motive? Sure, she'd made her interest in Mitch clear, but would she stoop to deliberately poisoning Rachel's mind like that?

Well, hell.

"Abby, we're ready!" Kiana called from the front hallway. Abby detached herself from the wall, gave Rachel's door a last, thoughtful look, and headed for the stairs.

"Four minutes and counting, Rachel," she called over her shoulder. The thud of something hitting the door was the only response.

Gwyn looked up from zipping Kiana's jacket as Abby joined them. "Trouble in paradise?"

"Whatever gave you that idea?" Abby muttered, setting the laptop she carried on the entry table beside her keys.

"Let me guess, thirteen going on eighteen?"

"I'm five going on eighty," Kiana volunteered. "Grandma said so."

"I can believe it." Gwyn tapped the little girl's nose with a fingertip, then pushed to her feet and surveyed the pile of gear by the door. "Right. Snowsuits, mittens, hats, scarves, spare socks, laundry, favorite plushie, and"—she nodded at the table—"laptop. I think you have everything you'll need, and I have spares at home if we forgot anything. I'll head out now and get the wet load into the machine to start, and you follow when you have everyone on board." She zipped up her own coat and tugged on her gloves. "Mac and cheese for lunch, and tobogganing after. Sound good?"

Kiana hopped up and down in her familiar spin, hands flapping. "I love tobogganing! And I love macaroni and cheese!"

"Glad to hear it." Gwyn turned her smile on Abby. "See you soon?"

Abby raised her gaze to the ceiling and grimaced. "Soon-ish is more like it, I'm guessing."

To her surprise, her sister reached out and gave her a quick hug. "Deep breath, sweetie. You're doing great."

CHAPTER 21

Abby shuffled Kiana, Brittany, and their winter gear out the door and into the vehicle she'd forgotten to put into the garage the day before, making yet another mental note to ask Mitch if there was a spare remote for the opener. Then she loaded two giant bags of laundry into the back and swept away the previous night's snowfall from the SUV's windows while they waited for Rachel to grace them with her presence. At last the front door slammed, and Rachel stomped down the path to the driveway, school backpack hugged tight against her chest. She passed Abby without so much as a glance and got into the back seat with her sisters. Abby finished brushing off the windshield, returned to the house to lock the front door, and, shoulders squared against the hostility rolling her way, slid into the driver's seat.

Rachel's stony silence lasted the entire way to Gwyn's house, out of the SUV, and up the stairs. But when Abby's movie-star brother-in-law opened the door to her knock, the girl's jaw nearly hit the porch floor, and Abby found her elbow clutched in a surprisingly strong grip. Knowing she was taking way too much pleasure in the situation, she looked around at the girl and asked with deceptive innocence, "Rachel? Is something wrong?"

Round eyes blinked at her, and Rachel's gaze moved swiftly between her and Gareth and back again. Her mouth remained open. Gareth cleared his throat and held out a hand in greeting.

"You must be Rachel," he said, flashing his best smile and making Abby want to hug him. "I'm Gareth. Please, come in."

The teenager released her grip on Abby's elbow, brushed her fingers against Gareth's and snapped her teeth shut. "Pleased to meet you," she croaked.

Without missing a beat, he looked down at Brittany and Kiana. "And you," he said, "must be Charlie and Fred."

Kiana giggled and returned his offered fist bump. "Yes," she said. "I'm Fred."

"Now you've done it." Brittany rolled her eyes. "She's gonna wanna be Fred all day now."

"Oh. Oops." Gareth stepped back and swept an arm wide in invitation. "Well, Kiana-Fred and Brittany, come on in and meet the others."

A tug on her jacket sleeve stopped Abby from following the younger girls into the house. She met Rachel's awed brown gaze.

"You know that's Gareth Connor, right?" the girl hissed. "*The* Gareth Connor?"

Abby held back a smile. "I'm aware, yes."

"And you're *related* to him? Why didn't you tell me?"

Abby regarded her in silence for a long moment,

until Rachel's gaze slid away from hers. Then she stepped inside, leaving the teen to trail behind her.

"Well?"

Abby looked up from folding the last load of laundry to find her sister watching her over the rim of a coffee cup. Baby Julianne lay on her back on the floor at Gwyn's feet, happily chatting with her toes as she tried to chew on them. A familiar pang of envy shafted through Abby. She pushed it away and responded, "Well, what?"

Gwyn rolled her eyes. "Well, the kids and Gareth will be back any minute, and you still haven't told me a thing about this job of yours. Spill, sister."

Abby waved a pair of socks in the air, one in each hand, rolling her eyes. "This *is* my job. This and dishes and meals and driving... I hardly think I have to tell you what goes into looking after three kids and a house."

"No, but you *could* tell me something about the family. And why you're working on a weekend."

"Not the whole weekend. Just Saturdays, and I offered. Mitch—Mr. Abrams has his own construction firm, and things fell apart when his wife got sick and..." she trailed off and shrugged. "He needs a little extra help getting back on his feet."

"Understandably."

Abby shot a look across the table. Had there been a double meaning in that response? Something directed at her own situation as well as Mitch's? Gwyn's noncommittal gaze met hers, giving nothing away.

"Go on," Gwyn said.

"Yes. Well. Like I said, I offered to work Saturdays, so he'd have extra time for the business." Abby rolled the socks together and added them to the neatly folded stack of clothing on the table. She'd have to get the girls to help sort it when they got home, because she had no idea yet what belonged to whom, especially when it came to Brittany and Rachel, who wore the same size in underwear and most shirts.

"The girls are lovely."

"They are, aren't they? Well, Rachel is a bit of a handful, but the others are a breeze."

"Even Kiana?"

"You noticed." It would have been difficult not to. Kiana's little quirks—the hand-flapping and spinning— became decidedly more prominent when she was excited, and the promise of a tobogganing adventure had proved very exciting.

"Autism?" Gwyn asked.

"She's on the spectrum, yes, but it's part of a bigger thing called trisomy X, or triple X syndrome. She carries a third X chromosome."

"I've never heard of it."

"I learned about it when they tested Oliv—" Abby corrected for the shake in her voice and tried again, "Our doctor tested Olivia for it when they diagnosed her autism."

"You never told me she was on the spectrum."

"When was I supposed to? In my annual Christmas card?" Abby set aside an odd sock and plucked a Kiana-sized pair of jeans from the basket. "Season's greetings, and oh, by the way, Olivia is autistic?" She folded the jeans. "Besides, most people didn't know. William didn't do well with the idea." An understatement if there ever was one—and one of the main reasons Abby had never considered leaving Olivia behind, no matter how much William loved his daughter.

"You had a lot to deal with."

Abby regarded her sister for a moment, wondering if the *it served you right* she detected behind the words was actual or imagined. She opted for imagined and gave a shrug. "I managed."

"And did she have the X thing?"

"Fortunately not."

Gwyn frowned. "Is it that serious? Kiana seems healthy."

"There can be some physical things, such as heart and kidney anomalies, but Eve had Kia checked for those, and she's fine. She does have a lot of the other symptoms, though. Low muscle tone, autism, a hand tremor when she gets tired, and a potential host of learning disabilities that showed up on her evaluation a couple of years ago. Those will be more of a problem as she goes through school, along with a strong chance of anxiety and depression."

Her sister's eyes had widened. "Good Lord, that's a lot for your Mr. Abrams to have to deal with on his own. Can he handle it, do you think?"

"It is, and yes, I think he can." *If I can get him organized enough in the next couple of months. No pressure.*

"So. Nice guy, then?"

"Mitch? He's very nice."

"Dating anyone?"

Gwyn's uber-casual tone—and the sudden change in topic—made Abby's hands stop in mid t-shirt fold. "Excuse me?"

"I'm just curious." Blue eyes blinked innocently.

Abby wasn't buying it. "You know we grew up in the same house, right?" She finished folding the t-shirt. "I know you, Gwyn."

"Fine." Gwyn sighed. "Look, I know it's none of my business, but you really rushed into this job, Abby, and I can see how much you care for those kids already, and you're still so vulnerable, and—" Her gaze dropped away from Abby's glare. "I'm overstepping, aren't I?"

"Only by a mile or two."

Gwyn set her coffee cup on the table but didn't release it. "Gareth told me I should keep my mouth shut, but I can't help but worry about you. You've been through *so* much, and I'm just afraid you'll..."

"That I'll what? Throw myself at the nearest man in an effort to fill a void?" Abby felt equal parts angry and betrayed—and all parts sick to her stomach.

"No! That's not what I meant. Lord, Abby, you've said how desperate he is, and I just don't want him taking advantage of you, is all."

"Advantage, how? By sweeping me off my feet and proposing marriage so he has a new mother for his children? I've been there less than three weeks, Gwyn. That's hardly enough time for him to get to know me well enough to—" Abby broke off, the air leaving her lungs as sudden understanding dawned. Well, hell. Long seconds passed as she stared at her sister, at the careful way Gwyn avoided looking at her and the way her knuckles had whitened in her hold on the cup. She drew a shaky breath. Then, just to be sure, she asked quietly, "This is about William, isn't it?"

Gwyn pressed her lips together.

Well, double hell.

Trembling, Abby snatched up one of the bags in which she'd transported the laundry and began stuffing clean clothes into it. Folded or unfolded, it didn't matter. Not through the tears prickling behind her eyes. She blinked furiously, refusing to let Gwyn see her hurt. Her sister had made her disapproval of Abby's whirlwind marriage to William crystal clear at the time —that's what had driven the initial wedge between them. Now, thirteen years later, she seemed determined to finish the job. Well, that was just fine by—

"Wait," Gwyn said, catching hold of her arm. Abby shook it off. Gwyn caught hold again, her grip stronger this time. "Abby, wait. Let's talk about thi—"

"I hear the kids outside," Abby interrupted, pulling away a second time. "I need to get them home for dinner."

"I thought maybe you could stay. I made—"

"No." Abby didn't even attempt politeness. She tied the three bags shut, hefted two of them off the table, and lugged them down the hall to the front entry. She set them on the floor as the door opened to a tumble of snowy, happy children, eyes bright with lingering excitement, all chattering at once.

"... so much fun!"

"... go again?"

"Next week!"

"Gareth said—"

Following in the crowd's footsteps, Gareth's oldest daughter, Amy, put two fingers in her mouth and whistled sharply. Silence descended, and all eyes turned to her. "Much better," she said. She looked at Abigail and the bags. "You're ready to leave?"

Throat tight and not quite trusting her voice, Abby nodded.

"All right. Those staying here, take three steps toward the closet," Amy directed. "Those leaving, back out onto the porch. Rachel and Brittany, each of you take one of the bags for Abby."

Another flurry of activity ensued as bodies tangled together for goodbye hugs and everyone tried to get out of each other's way, but finally the staying and going groups sorted themselves out and Abby was able to get her own coat and boots on. Then it was her turn to receive icy wet hugs from her nieces and nephew.

"I like your new family, Auntie Abby." Maggie planted cold lips against her cheek. "Can you come again soon? Tomorrow?"

Abby's heart shredded at the innocent words. She gave the six-year-old an extra squeeze. "They're not actually my new family, sweetie," she managed past the pain. "I'm only looking after them for a little while to help out their dad. But maybe we can come again one day." She disentangled herself from the soggy snow-suited arms and stood to face her sister, who held Julianne in one arm and the last bag of laundry in the other. Abby held out a hand for the latter, but Gwyn's grip tightened when she tried to take it.

"I'm sorry," she said. "I had no right."

"No, you didn't," Abby agreed. "Just like you had no right thirteen years ago."

Gwyn continued to hold firm to the bag. "You were my kid sister, you'd known him a month, and I was worried about you. But maybe I could have dealt with it better."

You think? Abby wanted to ask but didn't. Instead, she continued to grip the laundry bag until, finally, Gwyn released her hold. Abby turned to leave, passing Gareth in the doorway as he came in. She paused on the porch to look over her shoulder at Gwyn. "Thank you for the use of your laundry facilities," she said. "And lunch. And if it makes you feel any better, I have no intention of becoming involved with anyone again on any timeline, fast or slow. As it turns out, you weren't all wrong about William. Gareth can tell you the details."

CHAPTER 22

Rachel sat in the front passenger seat on the way home, shooting Abby sidelong glances the entire way. After the confrontation with Gwyn, Abby was disinclined to engage in conversation, however, and so she drove in silence. It wasn't until they turned onto the Abrams's street that Rachel cleared her throat.

"It was fun today," she said. "I'm glad I went."

"And I'm glad you enjoyed yourself. You didn't get have much time for homework, though."

"It's okay. The essay isn't due until the day before Christmas vacation."

Rachel didn't seem to remember her earlier fit, and Abby pressed her lips together to avoid reminding her.

"It's pretty cool that Gareth is your brother-in-law," Rachel continued, staring straight ahead. "I didn't know you had someone famous related to you. I thought..." She trailed off.

"You thought I was just paid help," Abby supplied, signaling for the turn into the driveway. "Seems to me there's a lesson in there about judging people."

The teen shrugged a shoulder. "I guess."

Abby pulled the SUV to a stop, put it in park, and switched off the ignition. She turned to face Rachel. "Want to start over again?"

Rachel still wouldn't meet her gaze, but she nodded.

"Me, too," said Abby, reaching over to give the girl's hand a squeeze. "Now I don't know about you, but I'm hungry. Let's get all this into the house and have some dinner, shall we?"

With Brittany and Kiana in charge of carrying the wet winter things inside and hanging them in the mudroom, Rachel helped Abby with the laundry bags.

"Why do you do it?" she asked on their second trip.

Abby handed a bag to her as, in her coat pocket, her phone chimed. She fished it out, glanced at the text message, saw Gwyn's name, and stuffed it away again. Then she took the last bag out of the vehicle and slammed the hatch shut. "Do what?"

"Work as a nanny for us when Gareth is rich. Couldn't he look after you?"

"Probably. But I don't want him to. I want to be able to support myself."

"Can't you do anything else?" Rachel hugged the bag close. "Didn't you go to university or anything?"

"I didn't have the chance."

"Do you like looking after us?"

"Most of the time."

The pale green gaze, so like her father's, dropped. "I guess I haven't exactly made it easy for you sometimes, have I?"

"Not exactly, no." Abby watched her for a moment, then sighed. "I meant what I said about starting over, all right? Clean slate. You good with that?"

She got a nod in response, but Rachel still wouldn't

look at her. Ah well, might as well get it all out of the way while they were at least speaking.

"Starting Monday," she said, "I'll be driving you and Britt to school myself. Please text Mandy to let her know."

"What?" Rachel's head came up at last, and she stared wide-eyed at Abby. "But why?"

"Because that's how I want to do things from now on. That bag of laundry can go upstairs, by the way, and I'd appreciate it if you'd sort it and make sure your sisters put it away." And with that, Abby walked up the sidewalk to the front porch and went inside as her phone chimed another alert. She ignored it.

CHAPTER 23

Mitch leaned against the kitchen doorframe, watching Abigail clear away the remains of dinner. Her back was to him, and her movements smooth and efficient. God, but he envied her comfort level in this room. And in the house in general, come to that. He'd hugely underestimated the amount of organization and know-how that went into running a home when Eve was alive. She'd made it look effortless, and so he'd never paid that much attention to it until he'd had to take it over himself. He grimaced. He had, in fact, taken his wife very much for granted, as she had so often accused him of doing. She'd be relieved to see things back under control at last. And she was probably laughing herself silly at the agreement he and Abby had come to.

Just over two months left to get his act together. The business, the house, the kids and all their goings-on, and likely a slew of appointments for Kiana, now that Abby had reminded him to look after his youngest's special needs. Were there enough hours in a day to make it possible? Maybe they'd get lucky and Abby would change her mind before the time was up. Maybe she'd stay longer. Maybe—

Mitch realized his gaze lingered on the soft round curves of Abby's rear as she stretched up on tiptoes to put a bowl on the top shelf of a cupboard, and he straightened away from his leaning post with a cough of embarrassment.

Looking over her shoulder, Abby dropped down onto her heels, bowl still in hand. "All done with stories?" she asked.

Mitch nodded, trying to regain his equilibrium. Once again, he was noticing things about his employee that he had no business noticing. Things he'd never noticed about any of the other women that had paraded through the house over the last year. They'd all seemed like girls, fresh out of college and far closer in age to Rachel than to him. Abby, however, was different, with fine lines at the corners of her eyes that crinkled when she smiled at one of his kids, and an air of weary sadness that made him wonder again what her story was.

"Everything okay?" Abby's voice recalled him to the here and now.

He tucked his hands into his jeans pockets. "I'm fine," he said. "And, yes, stories are done. Kiana fell asleep halfway through, and Britt and Rach are both reading in their rooms. They're all pretty wiped from tobogganing today. Thank you again for getting them out like that."

"Don't thank me—thank your washer. And my brother-in-law." Abby stretched back up and tried again to slide the bowl onto the shelf. Against his better judgment, Mitch stepped forward to help—and told himself he absolutely didn't notice her warmth and nearness as he stretched his arm up over her.

Or the faint scent of strawberries that accompanied said warmth and nearness.

He put the bowl in place and stepped back, then focused on her mention of the washer. He cleared his throat. "I'll call the repair place on Monday. Any preference for day or time?"

"Yesterday?" she suggested wryly. She shook the blond curls she'd taken to leaving down. "Not really, as long as it's not when I'm taking the girls to school or picking them up."

Mitch frowned. "Girls, plural? Has Jessica canceled on you?"

"Not at all."

Well, that was informative. He raised an eyebrow. "So... why?"

"I just think it's best that way. It will give me a chance to chat with Rachel a bit more. She's always tied up with homework after school."

Mitch would have bet his last dollar that there was more to it than Abby's explanation, but she'd gone back to wiping counters and didn't seem inclined to continue. And frankly, he'd be happier not owing Jessica Perkins any more favors than he already did, because he was pretty sure she had every intention of trying to collect someday. Still, he felt he should at least put in a token objection.

He folded his arms over his chest and leaned back against the island counter. "You sure you want to take on something extra like that? You're already putting in longer hours than I have a right to ask, and now with the Kiana stuff—"

"You didn't ask. I offered. And I'd much rather be busy than trying to invent things to do." She wrung out the dishcloth and hung it over the faucet, then pulled the plug from the sink. The water disappeared in a gurgle and slurp down the drain. Wiping her hands on a dishtowel, she looked askance at him. "Was there something else you wanted?"

Nothing I should even be thinking about, never mind asking for.

The thought slipped unbidden into Mitch's mind, and for the first time in a long time, he had reason to be profoundly grateful that his skin hid color changes, because otherwise, he'd be glowing neon red right about now. "Ah," he stammered, desperately searching for something to say. "Rachel," he croaked. "How are things with Rachel going?"

Abigail gave him a half smile. "Better since this afternoon. I think we may have reached a turning point."

"Oh?"

"She didn't tell you?"

"Only about the tobogganing."

"My brother-in-law is Gareth Connor."

For a second, Mitch couldn't place the name. Then he stared at her. Then he gaped. "*The* Gareth Connor? The *actor* Gareth Connor?"

A corner of her mouth twitched. "The same," she agreed.

He had no idea how he held back the *well, shit* that hovered on the tip of his tongue as his esteem for one of Hollywood's finest took a serious tumble. His gaze traveled the pristine kitchen. The guy must be worth millions, and he let his sister-in-law wash dishes and clean up after someone's kids instead of helping her out?

"I see," he said, for want of something more scintillating. "That will definitely move you up in her estimation."

Abby regarded him. "I wouldn't take it," she said.

"Take what?"

"Gareth's money. He offered to set me up in a place of my own when I came to Ottawa and to help me get on my feet. I refused. It's time I learned to... I want to stand on my own feet."

Once again, Mitch suspected the words she left unspoken would have filled an entire book. And once again, he decided it wasn't his business to pry, especially when she'd asked him not to.

"Fair enough," he said, and then he returned to safer territory. "So, things are better with Rachel. How about with Kiana? We haven't had much time to talk this week..." He trailed off, unable to complete the lie he'd rehearsed about having dropped the evening tea routine that he'd barely begun because of workload— and loath to admit he'd dropped it because he hadn't been able to stop thinking about that encounter in his office.

"It's all right," Abby said. "I know you've been busy."

Was she deliberately keeping her voice neutral, or was that just his guilt talking? Either way, he needed to do better. Needed to remember he was an adult sharing his home with another adult—who happened to be his employee, no less—and not some crass college kid who hadn't been out on a date for too long.

Not that he was thinking in terms of dating Abby.

Or anyone.

Because no. Just...

Freaking hell.

He jerked his attention back to Abby, who had rested a hand on the counter on either side of herself and continued talking.

"... good," she said. "I've been reading up on trisomy X, and I've made a list of questions up that might help when you take her to the pediatrician appointment."

"Pedia—" Mitch fought to keep his gaze away from the intriguing swells beneath Abby's sweater. *For God's sake, Abrams, get with the agenda.* "Right. You left a note on my desk."

"With an appointment time that you put on your calendar?" she encouraged.

"With an appointment I'm *going* to put on my calendar the second I go back to my office," Mitch agreed. Damn, but he liked the way her eyes crinkled at the corners when she tried not to smile. "Anything else I should know about?"

"I don't think—oh, wait. There is something. Brittany's teacher sent home a note yesterday saying she's having trouble seeing the board and suggesting she have her eyes checked. If you can give me the other girls' medical information, I can make optometrist appointments for all of them. Dentist, too, if you want. That will get everyone caught up before I—before you take over."

Mitch grimaced and rubbed one palm along a jawline in need of a shave. "Eve handled all the appointments, and I have no idea who any of the practitioners are. But I think she kept files somewhere in my office. I'll look for them this week."

Another silence descended, this one stretching out until Abby shifted her feet and shot furtive glances at the doorway to the hall while Mitch thought about the faint scent of strawberries. And on that note...

He straightened up from the counter. "I'm, uh, going to finish up in the office," he said. "Enjoy your day off tomorrow."

CHAPTER 24

The following Thursday, Abby headed upstairs to the linen closet with a loaded laundry basket balanced on one hip. Not until she passed her bedroom door did she register the fact that it wasn't quite closed. She retraced her steps and pushed it open.

A startled Rachel stood up from the side of the bed, framed photo in hand and eyes wide. "I—uh—the door was open, and I—uh—wanted to make sure Kiana hadn't gotten into any—" She broke off as Abby, tight-lipped with anger and betrayal, walked across the room and held out her hand for the picture.

"My door might have been open," Abby said, "but my bedside table certainly wasn't." She slipped the photo back into the drawer and slid it shut. "Care to explain?"

"I'm sorry," Rachel mumbled. "I was curious."

"That's no reason to go through my private things, Rachel. Think about how you would feel if you found me snooping through *your* room."

The girl's gaze dropped from hers. "I'd be really mad."

"And I am, but I'm sad, too, that you would break my trust like that." Abby sat on the bed and patted the spot beside her in invitation. After a second's hesitation,

Rachel perched beside her. Abby took a deep breath. "Sweetie, I'm running out of ideas here. Every time things seem to be getting on track between us, something happens to throw them off again, and I don't know why. Am I really that bad a person to have around?"

Rachel shook her head.

"Then why?" Abby asked. "Why do we keep having issues, Rachel? Why would you come into my private space and—"

"I thought you were trying to get Daddy to marry you."

Jaw hanging open, Abby stared at the teen. A mix of anger, embarrassment, and defensiveness stared back. Abby shook her head. "Where on earth did you get that idea? I'm only staying three months, remember? We're actually down to just over two, and—"

"Mandy's mom said we shouldn't be surprised if the two of you got hitched. She said that's why women like you take jobs as nannies."

Women like...

"I see." Abby said, curling her fingers into the duvet beneath her. Well, that answered her previous question about Perky having an underhanded motive behind that cheery façade, didn't it? "So, you were...?"

"Investigating you."

"Ms. Perkins' idea?"

"Me and Mandy. We looked you up online, but we couldn't find anything there like we could with the others."

"The oth—the other nannies? You've done this

before?" Despite Abby's efforts to keep her voice neutral, a sharpness had entered it and Rachel's shoulders hunched miserably as she nodded. "Ms. Perkins thought all of them wanted to marry your father, too?"

That earned her a snort and an eye roll. "Of course not! They were too young. But Mandy and I decided that as long as we have a nanny..." Rachel trailed off and then launched into a babble. "She just wants to help us, and she's really nice and fun and everything, and she likes Daddy and us, and maybe if he gave her a chance, they could fall in love and then we could—"

"Whoa." Abby held up both hands to ward off the sudden flow of words and her deepening suspicion. "Clarify that last bit for me. Who wants to help?"

Another eye roll. "Jessica, of course. Mandy's mom? She's been offering and offering, but Daddy keeps saying no, and Mandy and I think it would be cool to be sisters."

Oh. Dear. Lord.

Abby stared at the girl beside her. She didn't even know where to start with this mess, apart from throttling Perky—which might not actually help matters, although it would give Abby great satisfaction. She took a deep, steadying breath, then reached out and turned Rachel's chin so the girl had to look at her. "Right," she said, "so here's the thing. First, I'm not looking to get married. Not to your dad or anyone else. Second, I'm pretty sure your dad isn't looking to get married again, either. Third, even if he was, or is, or will one day, *who* he marries is up to him, not you and your friend."

Or your friend's meddling mother.

"And fourth, you need to let me do the job I came here to do because your dad really, really needs the help. You guys need to learn how to be a family again, Rachel, and you need to do it with just the four of you because there's no guarantee that another marriage will ever happen. Life just isn't that simple or predictable."

Rachel sat quietly beside her, scuffing a toe against the hardwood floor. "I miss her," she whispered at last.

"I know, sweetie," Abby said. Impulsively, she put an arm around the girl's shoulders. She expected resistance, but to her surprise, Rachel leaned into her, burying her face against Abby's collarbone. Abby's second arm joined the first, and she rested her cheek atop the soft, dark cloud of curls piled on the girl's head. "I know," she said again.

They sat together for a long, quiet minute, and then Rachel pulled away to look at Abby. "Have you ever known someone that died?"

"Both of my parents are gone," Abby said, offering the least painful of her stories, "but I was older than you when they died."

"What happened?"

"A drunk driver." Proving that lightning really did strike twice, because that was how Olivia and William had died, too.

"I'm sorry."

Abby brushed a tiny spiral of hair back from Rachel's forehead. "It was a long time ago," she said. "But thank you. And I'm sorry that your mom died."

"Do you ever stop missing someone?"

Abby's gaze strayed to the closed drawer as she

thought about the hollow agony she'd lived with since that awful day, its edges sharp and raw, scraping at every breath she took, every beat of her heart. Except... except sitting here with Rachel, being in this house filled with so much life and so much need... was it just her imagination, or were the edges of her pain just a tiny bit duller? She realized Rachel waited for an answer and set aside the possibility for closer examination later.

"I think," she said slowly, remembering the words of the leader of the bereaved parents group she'd briefly joined in the weeks following the accident, "I think we always miss them, but time takes away some of our pain, so that it's not as hard to remember them."

"I don't want to forget her."

"And you won't. You can't, because you get to see her every time you look in the mirror or at one of your sisters. She's as much a part of you as your dad is, sweetheart. Death doesn't take that away."

"I guess."

"And you can talk about her, too, you know. With your sisters, with your dad... even with me. I'd like to hear about her."

"You wouldn't mind?"

"I'd be honored to listen."

Another few seconds slid past, and then Rachel stood. "Thank you," she said. "And, Abby? I'm really sorry I've given you such a hard time. I promise I'll do better."

"I know you will."

Abby waited until the door closed behind the teen,

and then she opened the drawer and took out the photo. Gently, barely touching, her fingers caressed the lines of her daughter's face. Her words to Rachel had been true. The girls really would have a part of their mother with them always, but for Abby... for Abby, it was different, because she would never again see Olivia in someone's smile or hear her voice in someone's laugh. Every trace of her daughter had disappeared except for images printed on paper and memories stored in her mind—both of which would inevitably fade with time.

She would never forget her daughter, but neither would her memories be as vivid as she desperately wished them to remain. Because the bereaved parents' leader had been right about life and time going on, and—

A screech from Brittany downstairs sliced through her thoughts. "Kia, stop it! Abby, Kia won't stop bugging me, and I have homework to do!"

With a sigh, Abby tucked the picture into the drawer, glanced at the cell phone—with its many unanswered texts from her sister—on the bedside table's surface, and then went to attend to the life that seemed so determined to prove the parents' group leader right.

CHAPTER 25

"Did you know Abby was married before?" Rachel asked. "At least, I think she was."

Mitch paused in the doorway, his hand on the light switch as he looked back at his daughter sitting up in bed. "What makes you say that?"

"I saw a picture in her room."

"And what were you doing in her room?"

"I was checking to make sure Kiana hadn't gone in." Rachel hugged her knees under the covers. "And I was snooping. But Abby and I already talked about it, and I apologized."

Mitch crossed his arms and leaned one shoulder against the doorframe. "I see. That's a pretty serious transgression, kiddo."

"I know, and I'm really sorry, Daddy. I won't do it again, I promise. And I'm going to try harder for her. We talked about that, too."

"I'm very glad to hear it."

"But did you know? About her being married before?"

"Abby's private life is none of my business—or yours." Mitch tamped down a flash of curiosity that disagreed.

"There was a girl in the picture, too. I think she's around Britt's age."

"Did you ask her about it?"

Rachel shook her head.

"And did she offer to tell you?"

Another shake.

"Then it's none of our business," he repeated.

"But the picture makes her sad, and—" Rachel broke off with a sigh when he raised an eyebrow. "Yes, Daddy."

"Good girl. Now, sleep. You have school tomorrow." He reached out and switched off the light.

"Daddy?"

"Yes, kiddo?"

"Are you ever going to get married again?"

Mitch turned the light back on. "What? Where did that come from?"

"Abby and I were talking. She said there was no guarantee you'd ever get married again. That's why you need to learn how to do things yourself around here, and we have to help."

"I see." Back to crossed arms and leaning. "Well, to be fair, me learning how to look after you guys and the house is something I need to do whether I get married again or not. Your mom was amazing at doing everything around here, and it was easy for me to let her, but it wasn't fair to any of us. I'm sorry I didn't do my share of things."

"But will you get married again?"

"I don't know, kiddo. It's not the sort of thing I can

predict. Maybe, one day, if I meet someone, I suppose I might think about it."

"So you haven't thought about it yet?"

Why, why, *why* did these deep discussions always have to happen at bedtime? Mitch gave up on the idea of a quick goodnight and returned to his daughter's bedside. "Scoot over." Rachel shifted out of his way and he sat down beside her. "I take it you've been thinking about it?"

"A little. Mandy and me were talking, and—"

"Mandy and I."

Rachel rolled her eyes. "Mandy and *I* were talking, and we thought it would be cool if you and her mom got married so that we could be sisters."

Mitch didn't even attempt to hide his choke. "Me and Mrs. Perkins? Um... no. She's a very nice lady, and I'm glad you and Mandy are such good friends, but—no."

"That's okay. I don't think it would work anyway. I know you don't like her that way, and I've decided that having two sisters is enough for me. But what about Abby?"

"What about Abby?"

"You could marry her."

Shock rendered him speechless. Then made him sputter. "I—Abby—we—" He stopped, pulled himself together, and tried again. "Abby is also very nice, but she's my employee, and—"

"You look at her differently than you look at Jess—Mrs. Perkins."

"I—what?"

"You do. You watch her when she's not looking."

Mitch frowned. "You make me sound like a stalker."

"You know that's not what I mean. You watch her like you like her. A lot. And I think she likes you, too."

"I hardly know her."

"She lives with us. You sometimes make her tea at night. And she already knows what you take in your coffee and what kind of pizza you like."

Mitch wondered how his daughter knew about the evening tea, but he decided to stick with one topic at a time. "Just because she's observant doesn't mean she likes me."

"Not even if she's watching you when *you're* not looking?"

Mitch stared at his daughter. When had she developed that archness peculiar to women making a point? And when had she become so damned observant? And was Abby really watching him the way he—

Hell. He *was* watching her, wasn't he?

"You know what I think?" he asked, standing up. "I think Abby is here to do a job for us, and she and I both have enough on our hands without you imagining things between us that aren't there. And now it really is bedtime." Mitch stooped to kiss the top of his daughter's head, her cloud of hair tickling his nose. "Straight to sleep, and a little less focus on my love life in future, okay? Please?"

"Maybe." Rachel grinned as she flopped onto her back and pulled the covers up. Her muffled voice followed him to the door. "But no promises!"

~

"I hear you and my oldest daughter have been discussing marriage," Mitch said, holding out a mug of tea to Abby.

Abby looked up in surprise, both at Mitch's conversation opener and the tea. Did this mean the return of their evening ritual? She'd be lying to herself if she said the idea didn't please her. She wrenched her mind back to the opener. "She told you?"

"She did. She was quite chatty, in fact. I gather I've been the topic of much speculation."

"Much," she agreed, accepting the mug and hiding a smile. "But for what it's worth, I think you and Perky would make a lovely couple."

"Perky?"

Her blush extended from head to toes. "I, uh..." Dear Lord, she'd known it was just a matter of time before she slipped up with that.

"You mean Jessica," Mitch said. Not a question. "Jessica Perkins."

Abby's blush grew hotter.

"You call her Perky Perkins?"

"Not to her face," Abby defended, but she should have saved her breath, because there was no way Mitch could hear her over the roar of laughter he let out. And continued letting out. She scowled at him. "It's not *that* funny."

"Oh, but it is. I just wish I'd thought of it myself," he said, still chuckling. "I had no idea you had that in you."

"It should have stayed in me," she mumbled.

"I disagree, because it's perfect. You have no idea how determinedly cheerful—and cheerfully determined—that woman has been."

Oh, Abby was pretty sure she had an excellent idea after that Saturday driveway exchange. But she kept the observation to herself because she didn't think it appropriate to tell her employer he'd been the subject of such a discussion. Instead, she focused on the realization he was still standing and carried no cup. "No tea tonight?"

"I'm heading out to finish some work at a job. But I picked this up for you today." He dropped a rolled-up brochure onto her lap. "It's the course catalog for Carleton University. I thought you might like to take a look at their psychology program. Their winter term starts in January. You won't be quite done here, but I'll be taking over a lot by then, so you'll have the time for at least a class or two. Something to think about." He headed for the hallway. "I'll see you in the morning. Sleep well."

He was gone before she could blink—or muster the wits for a thank you. The garage door opened, the truck started, the door closed again. Then, and only then, did she put aside the memory of William taking from her the last catalog she'd held and dropping it into the recycling bin before storming out of their kitchen. Then, and only then, did she pick up the catalog Mitch had given her as if it were a rare and precious gift.

Because, in truth, that's what it was.

CHAPTER 26

"Abby? Abby, wake up. There's a dog at the door, and Kiana wants to let him in."

Abby struggled up from the cottony softness of her duvet and sleep. She blinked at Brittany's face, illuminated by the glow of the digital clock on the bedside table. Then she blinked at the fact it was still dark enough for the clock to illuminate anything. Then at the clock itself.

"It's three in the morning," she mumbled. "What are you doing out of bed?"

"There's a dog," Brittany repeated patiently. "At the door. Kiana heard it crying, and she woke me, and now she's sitting on the porch with it because I told her it couldn't come into the house."

"She's on the porch in her pajamas?" Abby gaped at the girl, then fought to untangle herself from the covers. "It's freezing out there!"

"I know. That's why I woke you. She says she won't come in without the dog, but it's really big and dirty, and I told her it had to stay outside."

A big, dirty, unknown dog alone on the porch with a five-year-old while the rest of the world slept. Abby almost fell over in her haste to get to the door because, yeah, there was no way this scenario could go wrong. She raced down the stairs, flicked on the porch light, and tore open the door. "Kiana? Kiana, sweetie, you need to come into the—" She stopped and swallowed. Hard. Brittany hadn't been kidding about big.

A massive black head lifted from Kiana's lap and turned to regard Abby. Snow coated the animal's back, and he—she?—shivered sporadically. As did Kiana, whose teeth clacked together. Abby moved toward the girl but stopped again when a low growl rumbled across the porch. Her throat squeezed tight. *Please, please, please don't hurt her,* she silently urged the watchful animal. *Please.*

She made herself take a calming breath. "Kiana? I need you to come over here with me, sweetheart. Slowly, so you don't startle him, okay? We don't want him to get scared and bite you."

"Don't w-w-worry," the little girl said, patting the dog's head as she shivered. "He won't hurt me. He's m-m-my friend."

"We don't know that for sure." Abby tried hard to keep the panic from her voice, hyper aware of the dog's suspicious brown gaze fixed on her. "He could be sick or hurt, and he might bite you by accident."

A hairy black lip lifted away from strong white teeth, as if to underscore the imminent threat, and Abby's knees sagged a little. She clutched the doorframe. Not taking her eyes from the duo on the porch, she said over her shoulder, "Britt, go wake your dad and tell him we need him, okay? Tell him it's import—"

"Daddy's not home. That's why I woke you. Should I call the police?"

Shit. Abby bit her lip, swallowing the curse just in time. Thoughts jumbled through her brain. The police might be a good idea. Who else was she going to call at three in the morning to remove a potentially rabid animal from the front porch? Three in the morning. Where in God's name was Mitch at three in the morning? He couldn't possibly still be working at this hour, could he? Which begged the question of what else he could be doing, and none of those questions helped—at all—with the current problem of a potentially rabid animal on the front porch.

Abby pushed a strand of hair out of her eyes. One more attempt to talk Kiana inside, she told herself. If that didn't work, she'd have no choice but to call for help. She schooled herself to calmness again.

"Kiana—"

She broke off as Kiana's arms stole around the big dog's neck, wrapping it in a hug and earning herself a small, wet kiss on the cheek in return. Two sets of brown eyes turned to Abby, managing to look sad and hopeful all at the same time.

"P-please can he c-c-come in?" Kiana asked. "He'll die outside by himself."

For the first time, Abby wavered. Her priority was getting Kiana into the house and warm again, and to her, the animal looked strong enough to withstand the cold for a few more hours, but what if she was wrong? What if he'd already been out in the cold for days, and their porch was his last resort? What if, heaven forbid, Kiana was right, and they woke in the morning to an enormous black carcass in front of the door?

"P-please?" Kiana asked.

She and the dog shivered again, and a low, pleading whine reached across the porch. Abby caved.

"Fine," she said, "but only for tonight, and he stays in the laundry room."

"Yay!" Kiana got stiffly to her feet and tugged on the dog's matted fur. "Come on, dog. I'm *freezing.*"

For a giant hairy monster, Kiana's new friend proved remarkably cooperative about being confined in the laundry/mud room. After turning around a half dozen times on the blanket Abby put down for him, he collapsed with a long half sigh, half moan, and curled into a tight ball. Abby was pretty sure he was asleep before she closed the door, much the way she herself wished she could be, but first she had to see to the half-frozen and wide-awake Kiana. It took two blankets, a mug of hot cocoa, and twenty minutes of lap time before the five-year-old stopped shivering and starting yawning, and another twenty minutes to get her and her sister back into their beds.

By the time Abby dragged herself back to her own room, it was past 4:00 a.m. and there was still no sign of Mitch. So, of course, that meant another hour or so of lying in bed waiting for the sound of the garage door and wondering if she should call him to make sure he was all right.

Except if he'd been out all night, then he was very

likely with someone. And a phone call from the nanny checking up on him would be uncomfortable all round. Not to mention that it was none of her business, because whatever that shared moment had been the night before, she had no right to wonder about his private life—and no right to be sharing moments, either. Or any interest in doing so, she reminded herself.

A last glance at the clock marked the time at 5:10 when she finally turned over and drifted off to sleep, only to be jolted awake again by an unholy commotion. For the second time, she bolted from her bed and ran down the stairs, her feet landing on the main floor before she was even awake enough to identify the racket as a dog snarling—and a man bellowing. Wincing, she hurried to the laundry room and opened the door to find Mitch clinging to one end of a baseball bat and their overnight guest to the other, locked in a tug of war and hurling insults at one another through the partially open door to the garage.

Mitch spotted her through the crack. "There's a dog!" he yelled. "In my house!"

"I know. I should have texted to warn you!" She, too, had to shout over the dog's growls. Dear Lord, but that thing had a big voice. She eyed the sharp teeth clamped onto the baseball bat and decided it would be foolish to become involved in the fray. She motioned to Mitch and shouted some more. "Let him have it and come in through the front door!"

Mitch tugged a couple more times on the bat, then relinquished it to the dog and slammed the door shut. Hastily, Abby did likewise, leaving the giant, hairy beast snarling in the laundry room as she scurried to open the front door. A scowling Mitch was already on the porch, hands on hips.

"What. The. Hell?" he asked.

Shivering, Abby folded her arms across her chest, altogether too aware of the thin fabric of her pajama t-shirt—especially when Mitch's gaze followed the movement and his expression darkened further.

"He turned up on the porch in the middle of the night, and Kiana heard him," she said. "She went out to sit with him, and—"

"By herself? Where were you?"

"I didn't hear her get up. Brittany—"

"My five-year-old daughter went outside by herself in the middle of the night," he repeated, "and you didn't *hear* her?"

"Your five-year-old daughter went outside by herself in the middle of the night," she snapped back, "and *you* weren't even home."

Mitch glowered at her so fiercely, he looked like he might burst a blood vessel. Abigail glared back, shivering again and wishing he'd just come inside already so she could close the door, but he showed no sign of moving. Then he closed his eyes and drew a deep breath, held it, and then blew it out again in a gust.

"You're right," he said. "That wasn't reasonable of me. But a *dog*?"

"She wouldn't come inside without him."

"The thing is huge. How did you get him into the laundry room without him killing one of you?"

"Can we please continue this with the door closed?"

Mitch's gaze dropped to her chest again, and her cheeks heated. Why couldn't she have grabbed a sweater before coming downstairs? She stood aside, giving him plenty of room to pass, and he stepped into the house and closed the door. The entryway promptly shrank three sizes, and Abby sidled away another few steps while he stripped off his coat and boots. His clothes underneath were caked with white. His hair was, too, now that she saw him in the light.

"I was finishing up some drywall work on a house," he said, his hand following her gaze upward to touch his hair. "My drywall guy is out sick, and we have the painters coming in today. I was too tired to trust my driving when I finished, so I slept on the floor." He grimaced. "It was supposed to be just a nap. Were the girls worried?"

"I think they were too distracted by the dog. Who, by the way, is like a lamb with Kiana. She's the one who put him into the laundry room for me."

"But she knows we're not keeping him." The scowl returned to Mitch's face.

"She wants him to go back to his family. I'll take him to a vet today to see if he has a microchip."

"And the shelter after that if he doesn't?"

"That would be your decision, not mine."

"I'll talk to Kiana before I leave again. I'm just home to shower and change, and then I need to go let the painters in." Mitch headed for the stairs.

"You haven't forgotten your meeting with Madame Sylvie before school starts, have you?"

Mitch stopped with one foot on the bottom step, and from the back, Abby saw his head and shoulders droop. His hand tightened on the railing. He turned, heaved a sigh, and said quietly, "Pardon my language, but *shit*."

Having muttered that very sentiment under her breath several times as she'd dealt with kids and a hairy black monster a few hours before, Abby could sympathize with Mitch's word choice—and with the haggard weariness that settled over his expression. The poor man looked ready to drop. She bit her lip.

"Can I let them in for you?"

"What?"

"The painters. Can I let them in for you? I can't take over the meeting with Madame Sylvie, but I can—"

"You'd do that for me?"

"Of course. I'd be happy to."

He regarded her in silence, then said gruffly, "If it wasn't so highly inappropriate, Abigail Jamieson, I swear I would hug you right now."

Abby's toes curled into the floor at both the statement and her reaction to it—a twisty warmth that wriggled through her and whispered, *"Yes, please!"* In a rather desperate attempt at levity, she forced a smile and replied, "And then we'd both need a shower."

The wrongness of the words hit her the second they left her mouth.

Mitch stared at her.

She stared back.

To her everlasting despair, however, the floor beneath her remained uncooperatively solid and refused to swallow her.

"I'll, um, make coffee," she whispered at last.

And then she fled.

CHAPTER 27

The morning plan, already a work in progress, went to hell in the proverbial handbasket when the girls rolled out of bed and came downstairs for breakfast. Before Abby could call out a warning to Kiana to leave the laundry room door closed, the little girl had opened it and released the monster within. Chaos ensued.

Their overnight guest barreled into the kitchen, around the table, and back down the hall to the living room, accompanied by shrieks of alarm from all three girls.

"What *is* it?" Rachel squealed, ducking behind Abby. "It looks like a mammoth!"

"Dog!" Kiana yelled. "Watch out for the lamp!"

Crash, tinkle, tinkle.

"Abby!" Britt yelled louder. "He ate the blanket you gave him!"

"Dog! Get off the couch!"

Momentary paralysis held Abby prisoner. It was too early for her brain to deal with this.

Thud, skitter, skitter.

Way too early.

"No, Dog! Not Daddy's office!"

"ABBY!"

Abby jolted out of her stupor. She jammed the

coffee pot back into the machine and bolted for the kitchen doorway, tripping over Brittany, who was headed in the opposite direction.

"Blueprints!" the girl gasped, her brown eyes wide with horror. "He has Daddy's blueprints!"

Abby set her aside and ran to the office door. Inside, the stacks of books on the floor had been scattered far and wide, and Kiana and the dog were engaged in a tug of war with a roll of—yes, Abby saw with a horror that mirrored Britt's—blueprints.

"Bad dog," Kiana scolded, and the dog grumbled back.

But it wasn't an angry grumble. In fact, Abby could have sworn the thing was laughing and having the time of his life. She put a hand on Kiana's shoulder. "Let go, sweetie. He thinks you're playing."

Kiana did as she asked, and the dog immediately dropped his end of the roll, too. Then he sat in the middle of the overturned stack of books and other papers, brown eyes bright behind a fringe of matted hair and pink tongue lolling, as if to say, *"That was fun. Let's do it again!"*

Abruptly, the tongue disappeared, replaced by large, white teeth as the dog snarled a warning. Abby felt a presence at her shoulder and raised her gaze to Mitch's thunderous expression.

"What," he said in a growl to rival the dog's, "is that *thing* doing in my office? What is he even doing out of the laundry room?"

"I wasn't quick enough—" Abby began.

"Daddy, Daddy, Daddy!" Kiana squealed, throwing herself at his legs. "This is Dog! Isn't he beautiful?"

"Not now, Kiana," Mitch snapped at his daughter. "I'm talking to—" He broke off mid-sentence, closed his eyes, and pressed his lips together in what Abby recognized as a bid to recover his patience. But even as he reached for Kiana to apologize, the meltdown had already begun.

Small hands flapped at the little girl's sides and she rocked sideways from one foot to the other, her gaze unfocused. Abby grabbed at Mitch's outstretched hand, but she was too late. As gentle as his touch was, the contact was enough to set off the downward spiral. Humming loudly, Kiana dropped to the floor, tucked her head down, and wrapped her arms around her knees. Mitch's hand hovered for a second, then returned to his side. His expression made Abby's heart hurt.

"Freaking hell," he muttered. "Kiana, I'm so sorry, sweetheart. I didn't mean to snap at you like that."

The humming increased in volume. Mitch tipped his head back to stare at the ceiling, radiating guilt, self-blame, and helpless frustration.

"Now you've done it," Brittany observed.

"Britt, your breakfast is getting cold," Abby intervened. "Rachel, you too."

When the two older girls were gone, dragging their heels in obvious reluctance, she turned back to Mitch. "I really am sorry," she said. "They're excited, and I should have expected them to go straight to the laundry room. Let's just give Kiana some time to recover, and I'll help you pick things up so you can see if there's any damage."

A hand wrapped around her forearm, rooting her to the spot with surprise as much as its firm grip. Surprise and... Abby swallowed. She really needed not to feel that little warmth unfurling in her chest every time Mitch so much as brushed against her.

Really.

Heat crawled up her neck, but Mitch's whisper distracted her from it.

"Look." He nodded his head toward the floor, and Abby followed his gaze.

The giant, filthy, matted mutt had lain down beside Kiana and wedged his nose under her arms and into the space between her abdomen and upraised legs. As Abby watched in astonishment, Kiana's rocking and humming stopped, and her arms stole around the dog's neck, hugging him close. The dog's cropped tail twitched, and he gave a contented sigh. Dark, intelligent eyes looked up at Abby. *"I've got this,"* they said.

"I'll be damned," Mitch muttered, drawing her attention back to him—and to the hold he still had on her arm.

The warmth in her chest resumed its unfurling, and she gently extricated herself. "You have a meeting to get to with Madame Sylvie," she reminded him, "and I need to drop off Britt and Rachel so I can let the painters into the house."

"What about that?" He indicated the dog.

"I'll bring him with me and stop at a vet's office to see whether he's microchipped."

"Can't the shelter check for you? It will save you extra driving if he's not."

Abby looked at the child still hugging the dog on the floor. *Well, yes, but...* She backed away from the treacherous thoughts beginning to form. The ones that whispered that if the dog *wasn't* chipped, then maybe...

Because no. The last thing Mitch needed right now was another family member to look after. She steeled herself to do the right thing.

"Good idea," she said.

"Can I go with you and Dog?" Kiana asked, peeping around a hairy ear. "Then he won't be as scared."

Mitch and Abby exchanged a glance. "It might be easiest that way," she murmured.

He responded in the same, low-pitched voice intended for his daughter not to hear, "Even when you have to leave him at the shelter?"

"Good point. But what if saying no triggers another meltdown?"

"Also a good point." Mitch grimaced. "Suggestions?"

Abby sighed and shook her head. "None."

Mitch sighed, too. "All right. You go get the others ready, and I'll see what I can do here."

"Good luck," she whispered, and then, with a trace of guilt—but only a trace—she made good her escape.

Back in the kitchen, Abby focused on making lunches while straining to hear the words beneath the deep rumble of Mitch's voice coming from the office. Rachel and Brittany, unusually quiet at the island as they ate, appeared to be doing the same. And when Mitch and Kiana came into the kitchen together a few minutes later, the dog trailing them, all gazes fixed on them.

"So?" Abby asked. "What's the plan?"

"Kiana and I have agreed that the shelter is the best place for the dog," Mitch said, his tone pleasant but determined. "Because that's where his family will look for him."

"But—" Brittany broke off at a look from her father.

"She would, however," he continued, "like to come with you to say goodbye to him, if that's all right with you?"

Abby bit her lip. She had serious misgivings about the idea but couldn't bring herself to voice them in the face of the pleading looks directed at her by both dog and child. "Of course," she said. "Let's put him in the back yard to do his business while we get ready, and then we need to get moving so I can let the painters in on time."

CHAPTER 28

Twenty minutes later, parked in front of Britt and Rachel's middle school, Abby twisted around in the driver's seat of the SUV to stare first at Rachel beside her, then at Brittany in the back seat beside Kiana. "What do you mean, you're not getting out?"

"We're coming with you," Brittany said brightly. "We want to be there for Kiana."

"That's very sweet of you, but I'm more than capable of looking after Kiana," Abby replied. "I promise. Now, I'm already late for the painters, so—"

"Still not going," Rachel said. Arms crossed, she stared out the windshield.

Abby stared some more, nonplussed by the mutiny unfolding. She couldn't very well drag the two of them out of the vehicle, and Mitch was depending on her, and—

"It's getting even later," Rachel observed. "You should probably start driving."

Another few seconds passed while Abby debated threatening to ground the pair of them if they didn't move their butts, but truth be told, her heart wasn't in it. They all knew Kiana was in for a hard time when they dropped the dog off at the shelter, and her sisters' determination to support the youngest member of the family was... sweet, she decided. And heartwarming.

She put the vehicle into gear and pulled out of the parking lot and onto the street again. From the corner of her eye, she saw Rachel reach backwards over the seat for a high-five from both her sisters.

It was also a darned conspiracy.

She cleared her throat and tried for a stern note in her voice. "This isn't over, you know. We'll discuss it at home later."

"Yes, Abigail," the three of them chorused.

Yup. A conspiracy. For which she didn't blame them a bit, if she were honest. Abby glanced into the rear-view mirror at the dog, shook her head, and drove toward the address Mitch had given her for the painters.

Folded into a chair made for the average four-year-old— or perhaps a gnome—Mitch tried hard not to squirm as he waited for Madame Sylvie to close the classroom door and join him. Her heels clicked when she crossed the floor, and a string of pearls swung out from her neck as she stooped to seat herself in a chair identical to his. Only she managed it much more gracefully.

"*Bon*," she said. *Good.* "I understand that your nanny—"

"Abigail," Mitch interjected. "Abigail Jamieson."

Madame Sylvie raised an eyebrow and regarded him for a moment, as if wondering why his nanny's name might be important, and then repeated, "Abigail.

Of course. I understand *Abigail* has discussed some of her concerns with you regarding Kiana."

"She has," Mitch agreed, not sure himself why Abigail's name was so important in this context. "And it reminded me that I never gave this"—he held up a file folder—"to the school. In all of the upheaval of Eve's— my wife's—illness and then her death, I'm ashamed to say that it completely slipped my mind."

Pink polish-tipped fingers reached for the folder, and Kiana's kindergarten teacher took a moment to read through the cover letter at the front from the pediatrician. Piercing brown eyes from the folder to look at Mitch. "I am cognizant of your circumstances, Mr. Abrams, but there is important information here that is critical to your daughter's school career."

Mitch took a deep breath, trying not to feel as if he faced a trip to the principal's office. What was it about being back in a classroom setting that made him feel so small? It happened at every parent-teacher interview. Eve had laughed, teasing him that it was a guilty conscience left over from all his youthful escapades. The memory made him smile, which made Madame Sylvie's forehead stretch even more. He wiped the amusement from his face. "I know. And I'm sorry. I should have given this to you when I registered Kiana, but to be honest, I forgot it even existed. There was a lot going on. There *is* a lot going on."

"Hm." Madame Sylvie went back to the file, skimming through the other papers, most of which pertained to the psychological evaluation that Eve had insisted on getting when Kiana was only three and a half—just after her own diagnosis. The teacher looked up again. "We don't generally develop an IEP at the kindergarten stage, but based on what I'm reading here, I think you should request one be put in place before she enters Grade one. The earlier the intervention, the more successful the student."

"An IEP?"

"Individualized education plan. If Kiana does have the learning disabilities suggested here"—she tapped a finger on the open folder—"she'll need to have an IEP that allows for any accommodations she might need."

"Accommodations?" He was beginning to feel a bit like a parrot.

"Additional help with her reading, extra time on tests, assistance with planning, perhaps taking verbal tests instead of written ones—that sort of thing. Your daughter is very bright and remarkably confident for her age, Mr. Abrams, but if I'm seeing her struggle now, it will only get worse as she progresses in school."

Mitch looked past the teacher at a brightly decorated alphabet plastered along the top of the wall. His gaze settled on the "f" for "fan" and he swallowed a snort. "F" for "failure" was more like it, he thought bitterly. That seemed to be the ongoing theme in his life right now. He was losing count of the number of people he'd let down over the last year—more, if he counted the year and a half that Eve had been sick before that, because he'd let her down, too. Her, the girls, his business partner, half their employees and clients...

"Mr. Abrams?"

Madame Sylvie's voice jolted him back to the tiny, uncomfortable chair and the equally uncomfortable new information he'd been given. *How much more?* he wondered. How much more could he handle before his family and business both collapsed under the weight of the world he couldn't keep at bay? Elbows resting on knees almost at chest level, he spread his hands in a gesture he hoped didn't look as helpless as it felt.

"Tell me what I need to do," he said.

CHAPTER 29

After a quick stop at Mitch's construction project to let in the painters already waiting there—and to call Rachel and Britt's school to excuse their absence—Abby and her entourage continued on to the animal shelter. There, Abby found herself profoundly grateful to have all the girls along, because without a proper collar and leash, it took all of them working together to steer their hairy guest out of the vehicle and into building. And, once inside, she was certain only Kiana's presence kept the animal from running rampant through the place.

Perspiring and out of breath, she presented herself at the reception desk and waited for the woman behind it to finish a phone call. The woman craned her neck to look past Abby. Both her eyebrows rose.

"That," she said, "is a big dog."

Abby, who'd had to lift the thing out of the SUV, grimaced and brushed at the smears of dirt across her jacket front. "Tell me about it."

"Is this a surrender?"

"A what?"

"Are you giving up a family pet?"

"Oh! No. No, he just turned up on our doorstep last night."

"All right, let's put him into our holding area, and

then I'll get some details from you." The woman handed a leash across to Abby and then came out from behind the counter to lead the way to what looked like a bank of oddly sized lockers in a short hallway to the left. She unlocked the largest at floor level and opened the door. All three girls leaned down to peer inside.

"It's so small," said Rachel.

Abby looped the leash around the dog's neck and coaxed him to follow. She did a double-take when she saw the narrow space he was expected to occupy. "Don't you have something larger?" she asked. "He won't even be able to turn around in there."

"It's temporary," the woman assured her. "He'll only be in there until they scan for a chip and give him a quick health check, then he'll be moved into the back. If he's chipped, we'll try to contact his family."

"And if he isn't?"

"They'll have three days to come looking for him."

"What happens if they don't?" Brittany asked.

"He'll be evaluated by our team and get all his shots, we'll make sure he's neutered and give him a good grooming, and he'll be put up for adoption."

"Will he have to live in a cage until someone takes him?" Rachel asked.

"Once he's cleared for adoption, he'll get his own little room—we call them pods. Someone will take him out for a walk three times a day and give him playtime, and he'll get lots of cuddles and love. We'll take very good care of him because the more socialized he is, the better his chances are of getting adopted."

"How long can he stay if he's not?"

"As long as he needs to. It'll be tougher for him because he's so big, so it might be a while."

"What's the longest time a dog had to stay here?" Brittany again, bending over for another look at the holding cage.

The woman hesitated for a second, and her apologetic gaze met Abby's. "We have one who's been here for sixteen months," she admitted.

"That's almost a year and a half." Rachel's voice took on an accusatory tone, and three pairs of eyes fastened on Abby. No, make that four pairs.

Abby's fingers tightened around the leash, and she stared down into the dog's intelligent, trusting gaze, remembering how adamant Mitch had been that they leave the creature at the shelter. And how Olivia had long begged for a pet that had never materialized.

"Do we *have* to leave him here?" Brittany asked. "Can't we just file a report or something so he can stay with us?"

"Your dad—" Abby began.

"You absolutely can." The woman joined the others in looking at Abby. "If that's what you'd like to do?"

Kiana wrapped her arms around Abby's waist. "Can we?" she pleaded. "Please?"

"I don't—"

"*Please*, Abby?" Rachel and Brittany chorused.

The dog grinned up at her, tail stump wiggling.

Abby groaned.

It was definitely a conspiracy.

CHAPTER 30

Mitch stared at the heavyset man tipping back in the chair so that its front legs were well off the ground. "Say that again?" he asked hoarsely.

"You heard me the first time, Mitch. I'm done. Paul has had enough, and I can't blame him. I'm packing it in."

"But we talked—I told you—you said—" Mitch gave up on trying to string words together and put both hands up to cover a head that felt like it might explode. Every bone in his body ached from his night on the floor at the job, and he was still reeling from his meeting with Madame Sylvie, and how in hell was he supposed to respond to this? He tried again. "Freaking hell, Derek, we talked about this. You agreed to give me a month to get up to speed again, *failing* which you'd pull the plug. It's only been three weeks, and I've worked my ass off around here. You've seen me working my ass off!"

His business partner, Derek Simmons, rubbed one temple and looked away, his jaw tight. "I know. And you have. But—"

"But what? We had a deal, damn it! I have three kids depending on me to make this company work, and

I can, but you know damned well no bank is going to float me enough to buy you out right now." Hands on hips, Mitch paced the floor of Derek's cramped office. "What the *hell* am I supposed to do?"

"Paul has cancer."

The bombshell stopped Mitch in his tracks. He stared again at Derek, seeing for the first time the weariness in the older man's lined face—and the quiet, underlying terror he remembered so well from when he'd learned Eve's diagnosis.

"Shit," he said. He walked back to the desk and sat in the chair opposite his partner. "I'm sorry, man. So sorry. How bad?"

"Prostate. Stage 4A, which means it's regional and not just localized. He'll need treatment. I want to be there for him."

"Of course." In Mitch's mind, there was no question. "Of course you do," he repeated.

"He didn't want me to tell anyone."

Mitch had been there with Eve, too. He nodded. "Not a word," he agreed.

For a moment, they both sat silent. Then Derek released a shuddering sigh. "I'm not ready to lose him, Mitch."

We're never ready, Mitch thought. "What's the prognosis?" he asked.

"Decent, actually. The five-year survival rate is almost a hundred percent."

"Wow. That's excellent news."

"Yes. But a wake-up call all the same. I'm pushing seventy, Mitch, and my heart isn't getting any better. As much as I love and admire you, I love and admire my husband more, and I'd much rather spend whatever time I have left with him. Especially now."

"Of course," Mitch said again, because there was really nothing else he could say. "What now?"

"Paul starts treatment a week from today. We should be finished the Henderson job by then, and I won't be coming in after that."

"And financially?"

"I want to enjoy the years I have left, my friend. I can give you a month to raise the funds to buy me out, but after that, I'm going to want us to consider that offer we got last year."

"It's still open?"

"I checked last week."

Elbows resting on knees, Mitch leaned forward in the chair and stared down at his linked hands. A part of him wanted to throw those same hands in the air and walk away from the business right now. Away from the stress, the headaches, the impossible workload and—and what? Go back to the tools full time? As much as he enjoyed getting his hands dirty now and again, did he really want to go back to that amount of sheer physical labor all day, every day, in every imaginable kind of weather?

With three kids to feed, would he have a choice?

Not as long as you're sitting here feeling sorry for yourself, Abrams.

With a sigh, Mitch braced his hands on the chair arms and pushed to his feet. "I'll start making some calls," he said. "And I'll be ready to take over full management from you next week."

Somehow.

"I really am sorry about Paul," he added. "Let me know if I can do anything."

CHAPTER 31

Three hours, a drained bank account, and several stops after leaving the shelter, Abby and the dog arrived home again. No microchip had been found on the animal, so she had filed a "found report" with the humane society, following which the girls had insisted on accompanying her to a vet's for a quick checkup—and crowding into the exam room with her and the dog. The vet had pronounced the animal to be in relatively good shape with no sign of fleas or infections, but based on the dog's worn foot pads, the condition of his coat, and his prominent backbone and ribs, she suspected he had been on the streets for a while. She gave them a list of instructions, a nutritional supplement, and a handful of samples including treats and shampoo, and told Abby to bring him back for his shots in a few weeks if no one had claimed him.

From there, they'd made a trip to a pet store, where Rachel volunteered to remain in the SUV to make sure the dog didn't eat the seats the way he'd devoured last night's blanket. They'd bought food and a rawhide chew bone, along with a leash and a collar, because no matter when—or if—he was claimed, Abby had no intention of going another day without some semblance of control over the critter, especially after the morning's blueprint incident. After that, they'd stopped for hamburgers—Kiana's wrapped in lettuce with no bun—and french fries before Abby had finally been allowed to deliver everyone to school for the afternoon.

And now it was just her and an overgrown, filthy, hairy beast—identified by the vet as a Bouvier des Flandres—that took one look at the bathtub Abby had filled and immediately retreated into the far corner of the bathroom.

"Come on, boy," Abby coaxed, holding out a treat. "It's not so bad, I promise. And you'll feel much better when we're done."

The dog sat down on his haunches and regarded her, his expression clearly skeptical.

It took twenty minutes of pushing, pulling, coaxing, and swearing before Abby managed to get the animal near enough the tub to lift him into the water one end at a time—and then all of her strength and agility to keep him there. With one hand clutching the dog's new collar, she squirted the shampoo the vet had given them over his back and, with grim determination, lathered, scrubbed, rinsed, and repeated. Then, just as the last of the rinse water swirled down the drain and she reached back for the stack of towels she'd placed on the counter, she heard the sound of the front door opening, and Mitch's voice.

"Abby? I need that key I gave you this morning," he called.

The dog—no longer filthy but now very, very wet—lunged from the tub and over Abby, knocking her onto her butt in the tsunami that followed as he bellowed at the bathroom door. She rolled to her hands and knees on a floor awash in water and towels and grabbed again for the animal's collar, but she might have been an insect, for all the attention he paid to her. She switched tactics, scooping up towels and trying to spread the least wet ones across the broad, black back. If she could just get him a little bit drier before—

"Damn it," Mitch bellowed back on the other side of the door. "What in *hell* is that dog still doing here? I told you—"

"Wait!" she cried as the door handle turned, but she was too late. The door swung inward, the dog thrust head and shoulders through the opening, Mitch hollered, and then she was staring after the animal's disappearing hindquarters... and at Mitch's steel-toed winter boots.

Silence fell. And stayed.

"Perhaps," Mitch said at last, "I didn't make myself clear this morning."

Abby waved a wet, weary hand at him. "You were very clear," she said. "And I was ambushed by your daughters. They—"

"Wait," he interrupted. "You're going to blame this"—he indicated the disaster of a bathroom—"on my children? I'm sorry, did I miss the part where you abdicated your role as an adult?"

Shock dropped her mouth open. She snapped it shut again. "I didn't think—"

"You're right. You didn't. And now I have to go through the whole damned mess with Kiana a second time, because we are *not* keeping the bloody dog!"

"She doesn't—"

"Save it," he cut her off again. He looked as if he might say more—a lot more—but then he scowled and scrubbed a hand over his face. "The painters finished early and I need to lock up the house. Where is the key I gave you this morning?"

"My coat pocket," she said. "Left side."

"I'll be home for dinner. We'll talk then."

Still kneeling amid the soaked towels and puddles, Abby listened to the thud of heavy boots down the stairs, followed by the dog's deep bark, a not-so-muttered curse, and the slam of the front door—the latter loud enough to make her jump. A few seconds later, a damp black head peered around the door post at her, and she scowled at it.

"You, my friend," she said, gathering up wet towels, "had better be worth all this trouble."

The dog delicately tiptoed into the room and bestowed a wet kiss on her cheek, then stood quietly while she rubbed him down with the one remaining dry towel.

CHAPTER 32

Despite Abby's warning that their plan would likely fail, the girls went into a huddle in Kiana's room after school, working on their strategy for convincing Mitch to foster their guest—and ultimately adopt him. Every so often, one of them would thunder down the stairs with a question about costs and necessities, and Abby would drop what she was doing to help with research.

By the time dinner was ready and their father expected, they had compiled a list of wants and needs, come up with a budget that included paying Abby back from their allowances for the vet checkup and supplies already bought, and written and signed a contract promising to feed, walk, and clean up after the animal. Abby wondered if she should text a warning to Mitch about what he would be facing when he came home, but given the mood he'd been in when he slammed out of the house, she decided against it. There didn't seem much point in getting him all worked up again before he even walked in the door, and maybe the element of surprise would work in the girls' favor instead of against it. Besides, after that dressing-down he'd given her, a part of her rather liked the idea of him being ambushed.

She heard the rumble of the garage door opening, and her heart skipped a beat. She just hoped he'd at least hear his daughters out after the work they'd put in on their proposal. Leaving the salad greens in the spinner, she dried her hands on a tea towel and went to the foot of the stairs. "Girls! Your dad's home!"

"We heard!" came the muffled reply. "We'll be there in a minute!"

Abby hurried back to the kitchen, wanting to be occupied with something before Mitch came into the house. She needn't have worried, however, because for the first time since he'd begun joining them for dinner, his footsteps turned away from the kitchen and headed in the opposite direction. A second later, she heard him going upstairs to change. The nerves that had already been overwound throughout her body tightened another notch. With a sigh, she dumped the salad mix into a serving bowl, tossed it with the dressing already there, and set it on the table with the rest of the meal.

Dinner was a silent, somewhat tense affair, with a degree of formality between Mitch and Abby that had Britt and Rachel shooting each of them—and each other—sidelong glances. Abby did her best to keep the conversation flowing, but even Kiana, normally a chatterbox oblivious to any undercurrents, had only monosyllabic answers to questions.

At last, Rachel pushed her plate away and announced, "Daddy, we have something to discuss with you."

Mitch regarded her, then shot a narrow look at Abby.

"It was our idea, not Abby's."

The rise of an eyebrow expressed Mitch's doubt

about the statement, but he turned his attention back to his daughter. "If this is about the—"

"We have a plan." Rachel interrupted. She nodded at Britt, who half stood and pulled a creased sheaf of papers out from under her. Rachel rolled her eyes but took them and smoothed them as best she could as she cleared her throat. "We, Rachel, Brittany, and Kiana—"

"That's me," Kiana said proudly. "Because I helped."

"I see." Mitch's lips twitched. He sat back in his chair and crossed his arms. "Go on," he told Rachel.

"'We, Rachel, Brittany, and Kiana Abrams, hereby petition the head of household for permission to foster and maybe keep one large black Bouv... Bouv...'" Rachel looked to Abby.

"Bouvier des Flandres," Abby supplied, avoiding Mitch's narrowed gaze.

"Yeah. That." Rachel looked back to her father. "That's the kind of dog he is."

"I see," said Mitch again.

Rachel went back to reading. "'In return, we promise to use our allowances to repay Abigail Jamieson for expenses already incurred, and to assume financial responsibility for basic upkeep of said Bouv... dog. We also assume responsibility for his care, and we promise to feed, water, brush, walk, train, and play with him.'" She looked over at Mitch again, sliding another sheet of paper across to him. "We're watching videos on how to train and look after a dog so we know what to do, and we figured out how much it would cost.

That's a list of weekly and monthly expend... expend..."

"Expenditures?" Mitch asked.

Rachel nodded and slid a second paper his way. "Yes. And this is a list of incidents."

There was no denying Mitch's struggle not to smile now. "I think you mean incidentals."

"Money words are hard," said Brittany with a sigh. "Abby helped us."

"I'm sure she was a big help." Mitch's gaze touched Abby's and slipped away again, but not before she saw the light dancing in green depths. "Anything else?"

"We'd like to take him to obedience classes if we keep him, but that costs more money than we have."

"And you'd like me to pay for that?"

Rachel nodded. "We can pay for most of his dog food, though."

Mitch studied the papers he'd been given. "And all three of you are willing to give up your allowances for this."

Three heads nodded.

"What about any damage he causes? Such as the blanket he ate and the lamp he broke."

"We'll clean up after him."

"The yard, too? Big dogs leave a lot of business lying around."

"We'll take turns every day after school."

"You three have put a lot of thought into this." Mitch set aside the papers and sat back again. "I'm going to need some time to think about it, too."

Three enthusiastic nods accompanied by grins.

"I do have one major concern. As much as you might want him to be a family dog, what happens if he wants to be with one of you more than the others? Have you thought about that?"

"Of course," said Brittany. "We already know he'd be Kiana's dog."

"That's why we're doing this," Rachel added, tugging a puff ponytail on her little sister's head beside her. "For her. Once he settles down and learns some things, he can even be her support animal when she gets upset."

Abby didn't dare so much as look in Mitch's direction after that announcement.

CHAPTER 33

"Better?" Mitch asked as he handed Abby's tea to her later that evening. "You left the dinner table in a bit of a hurry."

"You weren't faring very well, either," Abby retorted, remembering the gruffness with which Mitch had ended the dog discussion and put the girls to work clearing the table.

"That last part caught me off guard, I'll admit." He lowered himself into the armchair and regarded her narrowly. "I take it you didn't know about it?"

Abby shook her head. "I had no idea."

"They're right, you know. We saw how he reacted to Kiana's meltdown this morning. He has potential."

Had that only been this morning? It felt like a week ago, with all that had happened in the interim. "We did," she agreed. "But without formal training, he won't be allowed to accompany her to school or anything."

"Formal, expensive training, I'm guessing?"

"I don't know, but even if he doesn't get the training, he can still go a lot of places with her. And I can make some calls tomorrow, if you'd like."

Mitch grimaced. "If I say yes to that, it feels like I'm saying yes to the whole damned dog idea."

Abby pressed her lips together to stop a smile.

"Where is he sleeping tonight?" she asked, already knowing the answer because she'd heard the click of toenails climbing the stairs behind Kiana, but she hadn't heard their return.

The question earned her a glower followed by a heavy sigh. "Touché," Mitch said. "But in my defense, I figured he'd cause less havoc if he was in with her rather than cooped up in the laundry room with nothing to do but chew on a blanket."

"Sure."

Mitch sighed again. "I'm in trouble with this, aren't I?"

"I suspect you are."

"Damn it," he muttered. "I really don't need another mouth to feed or take care of. Not right now."

Guilt slithered through Abby's belly. Was it just her belated conscience kicking in, or did he seem more haggard than usual tonight?

"Is everything okay?" she asked tentatively. It wasn't her place to pry—or any of her business—but Mitch looked much like she thought a drowning man might when he realized help wasn't coming, and guilt twinged again.

"Honestly?" Mitch closed his eyes for a moment, then opened them to regard her in despair. He was definitely a man on the verge of drowning. "No. I found out this morning that my business partner's husband is sick, and he's pulling out of the company to spend more time with him. As of next week, I'll be running everything on my own. And I have a month to come up with a way to buy him out before he sells his share in the company to someone else. And I'm not sure how much longer I can keep pretending I can do and have it all, and I suspect I'm going to have to make some serious changes, and frankly, it sucks, and—" He stopped and shook his head. "Wow. I can't believe I'm dumping on you like this, Abby. I'm so sorry."

Abby had no idea how to even begin responding—to his news, his dilemma, or his apology. How this man had managed to keep afloat for as long as he had was beyond her. And not just afloat, but functioning well enough to keep those girls cared for and loved and—

Abruptly, she stood, reached across, and plucked the mug from his hand, saying, "I'll be back in a minute."

She returned with a glass and the bottle of Scotch Mitch kept in the cupboard over the fridge, but instead of taking them from her, Mitch raised an eyebrow.

"Where's yours?"

She flushed. "I didn't want to be presumptuous..."

Mitch gave her an eye roll worthy of his eldest daughter. He pointed at the loveseat, ordered, "Sit," and disappeared back toward the kitchen. He was faster than she'd been—probably because he hadn't had to drag a chair over to access the Scotch cabinet—and soon they both held glasses with a healthy three fingers of Scotch in each. Abby vowed to limit herself to just one of the fingers, because that looked like a *lot* of alcohol for someone who hadn't had a drink for more than six months. Especially someone who'd been too tense to do more with her dinner than push it around her plate.

"Here," he said, raising his, "is to having survived this day."

Abby could surely drink to that. She tipped her glass to touch his, and then sipped the liquid fire within. It burned its way down her throat and into her belly and, much as she'd hoped it wouldn't, left her coughing and spluttering, eyes watering.

Mitch, not very helpfully, chuckled. "You weren't kidding about being a lightweight, were you?"

"Not even a little," she wheezed. She waited for the burn to pass, then cleared her throat. "So. Your business. What can I do to help?"

Giving a snort, Mitch sat back in his chair again. "Unless you have a magic carpet bag of some kind, not much."

Abby smiled at the *Mary Poppins* reference. "Sorry, no. And no chimney sweeps, either. But I know how to keep a set of books and run an office. I helped my—a friend with his company for a while." She was pretty sure William had given her the job just to shut her up about needing more in her life, but she didn't think Mitch needed that part of the story.

Brief interest gleamed in Mitch's eyes, but he shook his head. "I can't ask you to do more than you're already doing around here. But thank you."

She leaned forward, elbows on knees and glass cradled in her hands. "I'm serious, Mitch. I'm caught up on everything else in the house with the exception of the boxes in your room—which I assume are personal— and your office. I would love to have something to keep me busy while the girls are at school."

"Our newly acquired hairy monster won't be enough?"

"He can keep me company."

Mitch absently stroked a finger over his bottom lip. "You're really serious about this."

"Wait," she said in almost the same instant. "You're really serious about keeping the dog?"

"Was there ever any doubt?" He grimaced.

"I'm sorry," she said. "I should have just left him at the shelter the way you asked."

"It was a big ask," he said, waving away her apology. "Especially when you had the girls in the same vehicle with you. I know how united their front can be. Besides, they've been after me to have a pet for years. It was bound to happen eventually. I should have caved on the hamster idea when I had the chance."

Abby laughed, the sound surprising her. She didn't remember the last time she'd laughed. Smiled, yes, but laughed out loud? It would have been at something Olivia had done or said, no doubt, but she couldn't remember what or when.

"You do that a lot, you know."

"Do what?"

"Disappear somewhere up here." Mitch tapped his temple. "Somewhere sad."

She swallowed. "I'm sorry. I don't mean to—"

"You don't need to apologize, Abby. But you're welcome to talk, if you'd like."

For a moment, she was tempted. Perhaps if she hadn't already broken down in tears with Gareth, she might have taken Mitch up on his offer. But having her brother-in-law's sympathy had been one thing; it would be quite another to have Mitch's. She took another drink from her glass, managing not to choke this time.

"I'm fine," she said. "But thank you."

He regarded her in silence, then shrugged. "Have it your way. So. Just how good are these bookkeeping skills of yours?"

"Adequate, I suppose? I can do accounts payable and receivable, and our—my—" She stopped to gather herself and sipped again. She really had to stop stumbling over the "my husband" thing, or else just tell Mitch that she had once been married. If only she could be sure that information would satisfy his curiosity and not lead to a lot of other questions, followed by tears and that whole comfort thing she couldn't handle. Not when her fingertips still hadn't forgotten the warm strength of his shoulders when he'd lifted her from his office floor the week before. She gripped her glass a little tighter. "The accountant never had any complaints at tax time," she finished.

"If you take this on, I'll pay you extra."

"You're already paying me—"

"Not for office work on top of everything else."

"But—" She broke off as his jaw flexed stubbornly. "Fine," she said with a sigh. "I'll start on Monday while the girls are at school. Speaking of which, I didn't ask you how the meeting went with Madame Sylvie."

"Apart from having to sit in one of those ridiculously small chairs? I think they give you those on purpose. To put you at a disadvantage."

Abby took a swig of whisky, trying and failing to

picture Mitch in one of the undersized chairs—or at any kind of disadvantage. Also trying and failing to feel her toes anymore. Or her top lip. She was even more of a lightweight than she'd remembered.

"I took copies of the medical records in, like you suggested," he continued. "She was ticked about not having seen them before, but I've promised to do better. She's suggested that we have an individualized education plan in place for Kiana before she starts Grade one. I have to file a written request with the principal, and she'll submit it to a committee for consideration. We'll likely need an updated psychological assessment for her, but the school doesn't pay for that before Grade three, so I need to see if my extended health plan will cover it."

"Wow. That's..."

"A lot of work?" He rubbed a hand over his eyes. "Yeah. I know."

Abby drained her glass. The last of the liquid fire slid down into her belly, joining the pleasant warmth already there, and then prompted her to say, "You're doing it again, you know."

"Doing what?"

Abby blinked at her unexpected bravado. Then she shrugged and answered, "Feeling sorry for yourself."

"I beg your pardon?" Mitch scowled at her.

"It's because you're overwhelmed," she said, nodding at the wisdom of her own words, even as a part of her whispered an alarm. *Too much whisky*, it told her. *Too much, too fast.*

Too late, the buzz responded, edging her forward so

she could pat Mitch's knee, then encouraging her hand to linger there.

"Whenever you look at the big picture, you panic," she informed Mitch and shook her head. "Big picture bad."

Mitch's scowl faded, replaced by a raised eyebrow and a glimmer of amusement. "Big picture bad?"

"Very bad. It's like trying to move a mountain."

"A picture is like moving a mountain?"

"Yes. No. *Looking* at a picture is like moving a—" She stopped and frowned. That wasn't right, was it? She squeezed Mitch's knee. "My point is—" Wait, that wasn't his knee, it was his thigh. And holy wow, how in heck had she moved from sitting on the loveseat to sitting on the coffee table in front of him? She drew back from the sudden scorch against her palm.

"I think we might want to continue this conversation tomorrow," Mitch said.

How interesting, Abby's buzz said. *His voice is all rough and gruff again, the way it gets when he's—*

Nope. Not interesting, her whisper disagreed. *Nothing to see here, Abigail. Move along!*

But—

"And that means we should end it now," Mitch added, standing up from his chair. He plucked her empty glass from her and held it with the other in one hand, then reached down to help her to her feet.

Dear Lord, woman, you're swaying!

Mitch's free hand clamped onto her shoulder. "You okay?"

She opened her mouth to reply, but then her gaze

settled on *his* mouth. His lips were so full. Way fuller than William's had been. Her buzz wondered how it would feel to—

"Bedtime."

She blinked. Even her buzz was surprised by that. "Wow. That's a little fast, don't you think?"

Mitch rolled his eyes. "*Not* what I meant." His hand still clamped on her shoulder, he towed her out of the living room and to the foot of the stairs, where he released his hold and pointed upward. "Next time you tell me what a lightweight you are?"

"Mm?"

"I'll believe you. Good night, Abigail Jamieson."

She never would have done it without the whisky in her system. Heck, she wouldn't have thought it possible *with* the whisky, and she was a thousand percent certain she would regret it, but as Mitch turned to leave, she caught hold of his t-shirt front, stretched up on tiptoe, and pressed her lips to his. Then she turned tail and ran.

CHAPTER 34

Abby woke to silence on Saturday morning. That alone wasn't unusual, but accompanied by bright sunshine rather than the pale light of dawn? That was definite cause for worry. She scrambled out from the tangled duvet and reached for the cell phone face down on the nightstand. She blinked at the time it displayed. It was 9:30? Really? She'd slept in *again*? That was twice in less than a month. Mitch would think—

Mitch.

Abby put her hands up to molten cheeks.

She'd kissed Mitch.

Stood on tiptoe, reached up, and pressed her mouth to his, and—

Warm. His lips had been warm, and soft and firm at the same time, and he'd smelled of citrus and mint, and—

Abby flopped onto her back, pulling the duvet over her head.

It had been the whisky. It had to have been the whisky. She hadn't had a drop of alcohol in more than six months, not since single-handedly emptying William's well-stocked, climate-controlled wine cellar, and she'd been too wound up to eat more than a bite or two at dinner, and...

And she'd kissed her boss.

And now she had to go downstairs and face him. And his children. And her conscience, because, dear Lord, what kind of woman threw herself at another man—at her boss—less than a year after her husband and daughter died?

The duvet became suffocating. Abby pushed it away and gasped for air. The house stayed silent. She frowned. Then she sighed and swung her feet out of bed. As awful as facing Mitch would be, she couldn't very well remain in her room all day. She had kids to feed, and laundry to do, and a dog to walk, and—why in heaven's name was it so quiet around here? Had *everyone* slept in?

She tugged on a cardigan over the t-shirt she wore as a pajama top, then padded across the cool hardwood to the door and pulled it open. She listened. Nothing. No kids' chatter, no deep Mitch's voice, no—

"*Oof!*"

Abby frowned. "Dog?" she called.

"*Oof!*"

She pulled the cardigan closer and headed down the stairs. The main floor was as deserted as the second level, with the exception of the snuffling sound coming from the base of the laundry room door. Abby turned the knob and pushed. A very enthusiastic something on the other side pushed back.

"You have to move, you silly creature," she told him.

"*Oof! Oof!*"

"Seriously." She shoved harder. "Back!"

The door gave way with a suddenness that sent her

stumbling into the room to land on the floor beside the dog, who whuffled happily in her ear and licked the back of her neck, then lay down beside her, brown eyes joyous behind their fringe. Abby stared into them. Intelligence stared back. Slowly she pushed to her knees, then to her feet.

"Sit," she said.

The dog's front end bounded up; its rear stayed glued to the floor.

"Well, I'll be," she murmured. "Down."

The dog dropped back down.

"Um... stand?"

He did.

And his blanket was intact, too. Maybe the girls had been right about him just needing a chance to settle in. Or maybe he'd just taken out his fury on it at Mitch's armed attempt to come into the room that night.

"Huh," she told him. "Keep this up, and you might even win over the guy you need to impress."

Speaking of whom, where was he? And where in the world were the girls? All their coats were missing, as were their boots. At least, she hoped the items were missing and not ingested. She looked at the dog. "You wouldn't, would you?"

The animal grinned up at her, and for the second time in the space of a few hours, she laughed out loud. It felt easier this time, and not quite so foreign. With Dog trailing her, she headed for the kitchen, remembering how, once upon a time, she had laughed often and easily. It would have made Olivia sad to know she'd stopped.

Dog trotted to the sliding glass doors and regarded her expectantly over one shoulder. Someone, Abby thought as she walked over to join him, had spent a great deal of time and effort in training this animal—which did not bode well for the burgeoning hope among certain household members that they might be able to keep him.

"Guess we'll just have to wait and see, won't we, buddy?" She pulled open the door and shivered in the draft as the dog bounded out into the snow.

She found the note Mitch had left taped to the coffee machine, smiling as she pulled it free because she couldn't think of a better place to leave something that needed to be seen by an adult in the morning. She unfolded the paper marked with her name and read: *Took the day off to get the tree with the girls. Back after lunch. Girls have a favor to ask of you.*

Abby skipped past the 'favor' part and frowned at the strong pen strokes in the word 'tree'. What tree? Why would anyone need a tree in the middle of win—

Her stomach dropped to the floor like a stone, taking her heart with it. Oh, hell. Of course. Christmas. Her second without her family—not that she remembered much about the first beyond a blur of neighbors knocking at her door with casseroles and baked goods that she'd thrown out because she hadn't been able to eat. Hadn't been able to swallow. Had felt much like she did again right now.

Abby sank to the floor along with her vital organs and buried her face against drawn-up knees. She'd been so busy keeping busy, so focused on putting one foot in front of the other day after day, that she'd forgotten Christmas was closing in on her again. Forgotten she would be a part of a family over the holiday. A family that would expect her to participate in... whatever nannies were supposed to participate in.

Such as baking cookies, wrapping presents, listening to carols...

Decorating a tree.

Her lungs folded in on themselves and refused to inflate again. Panic stirred at the base of her throat. Then she heard the soothing murmur of Mitch's voice in her ear, *"Give it a minute, and your diaphragm will relax again. Just keep trying..."*

Having a thought knock the wind out of her wasn't quite the same as landing face first on the floor, but she latched onto the memory anyway and schooled herself to calmness. Slowly, the spasm at her core relaxed. She drew a shallow, careful breath, then a deeper one. The pain didn't return.

She had no doubt it would again, but for now—for as long as she could keep the memories at arms' length —she was safe. And—

"*Oof!*"

And the dog needed to come in again.

Note still clutched in one hand, Abby heaved herself to her feet and padded back to open the door. The black dog bounded inside and skidded on the floor, sending a chair crashing into the table. "Easy," Abby cautioned. "You'll have a better chance of staying if you don't knock the house apart."

She glanced again at the note. *Back after lunch?*

How long could it take to drive to a tree lot and choose a tree? William and Olivia had always accomplished the task in record ti—

Damn.

Taking a deep breath, she dropped the paper on the table. "Come on, Dog. Let's go get dressed and find something constructive to do before I decide to hide in a closet for the next month, shall we?"

Eventually, after getting dressed, pouring coffee, and poking unsuccessfully through the cupboards for food that appealed, she and Dog—the poor beast really needed a name soon, she thought, even if it was going to be temporary—ended up in Mitch's office. Together, they surveyed the disaster within.

"Wow," she said. "He wasn't kidding about falling behind, was he?"

She'd been in here before, of course. Twice. Both times, she'd been too preoccupied by other activities to pay much attention to her surroundings—first, when she'd tripped over the pile of blueprints and face-planted on the floor, and Mitch had picked her up; and then again, when Dog had tried to wreck the same blueprints.

"How about we deal with those first, to make sure they're out of our way?" Abby asked Dog. She set her coffee—which she'd poured into a sealed travel mug, just to be on the safe side—on the desk and scooped up the rolls, placing them beside the mug. Then, with Dog gnawing contentedly on a rawhide bone, she began sorting. And sorting. And sorting. By the time the garage door opened, throwing her into a state of paralysis at the thought of seeing Mitch again, she had funneled the bulk of the chaos into four tidy piles: receipts to be filed, a lot of things to ask Mitch about, junk to be recycled, and everything family to be put into the empty binder she'd found that had triggered an idea for a household how-to manual.

Dog tilted his head to one side, staring into the hallway as the garage door closed again. Then the connecting door to the laundry room opened and happy chatter spilled into the house. They were back. Christmas had arrived, and so had Mitch. Dog lurched to his feet with a happy *"Oof!"* and trotted out of the office to greet everyone, leaving Abby standing frozen by the filing cabinet, a sheaf of papers in one hand and her now cold-coffee in the other. She hadn't yet convinced her feet to move when Mitch found her a couple of minutes later.

"You're back," she said. It took every ounce of strength she possessed not to hide behind closed eyelids. She forced a smile and tried again, "Did you have fun?"

"We did. Thank you." Mitch's gaze held hers for a second, and then, blessedly, left to travel the room. Hers, however, contrarily fastened on the lips she'd kissed last night.

"You've been busy."

She blinked. "What?"

"I said, you've been busy."

"Oh. Yes." She looked away, her face fiery. "Yes," she said again. "But just sorting so far." She waved the papers in her hand, regretting the movement when his green glance returned to her. She pointed the travel mug at the stacks of paper on the bookshelves lining the wall. "I made piles," she said. "Four of them. Of papers."

The corner of Mitch's mouth twitched, and he slid his hands into his front pockets. "I can see that."

Abby's face flamed even hotter. She lowered mug and papers to her sides. Dear Lord, could she please string together just one complete sentence? Such as the most important one she needed to get out of the way?

"Mitch, about last night—"

"Daddy, did you ask her?" Kiana danced into the room, hands flapping as she bounced in circles. "Did she say yes?"

"I—" Mitch began.

"Will you, Abby?" Britt darted in after her little sister. "Please?"

Torn between being glad of the interruption and wishing she'd had a chance to get her apology over with, Abby forced a smile. "Will I what?"

"Help us decorate the tree tomorrow!" Kiana bounced some more, then stopped as Dog nudged her. She curled her fingers into the animal's wavy, rough coat.

Huh, the coherent, practical Abby thought, watching the interaction. *Would you look at that.*

And *oh, dear Lord, I can't,* screamed the panicked one, focused on the tree idea.

Two pairs of expectant eyes watched her, joined by a third when their sister walked in.

"Don't you like Christmas?" Rachel asked. "It was

our mom's favorite holiday. It's hard without her, but Daddy says we need to keep her traditions going."

Abby almost folded in two at that, blinking furiously to keep the tears at bay. She wasn't the only one facing Christmas without someone, she reminded herself. Far from it. But she *was* supposed to be the grown-up one.

"Of course I like Christmas," she said, her voice husky. "I've always loved it." That was only a small white lie, right? Because once upon a time, she had loved it very much. "I would be honored to help with the tree."

"Yay!" Kiana and Britt shouted, grabbing hands and bouncing up and down together. They released one another, seized Dog's collar, and paraded out with him, singing, "Oh Christmas tree, oh Christmas tree, how lovely are thy branches!"

"Awesome," said Rachel. "I'll see if I can find the decorations in the basement. We'll bring them up into the living room so we're ready tomorrow."

"Storage room where the furnace is," Abby called after her. "Bottom two shelves. The boxes are labeled!"

"Of course they are," Mitch said. "By the time you leave us, I have no doubt that every item we own will be sorted and labeled, at the rate you're going." He waved a hand to encompass the newly tidied office. A note of amusement underlying his words removed any sting they might have held.

Not that it mattered, because Abby still had something she wanted to say. That she had to say. "About last night—"

"Consider it forgotten," Mitch said gruffly.

"Really?"

"Really." One black brow, salted with gray, rose. "If that's what you want."

Her mouth dropped open. Of course it was what she wanted—wasn't it? Because she was only here for a short while, and Mitch was her employer, and she was still a grieving widow with no intention of changing that status, and there were three kids and a dog, and—

"Well?"

Did he have any idea what that voice of his did to her knees?

Abigail snapped her mouth closed and made herself nod. "It's what's best," she croaked.

"That's not what I asked."

This time, she did close her eyes because this—all of this—was getting way out of hand. Digging deep, she found a thread of the fine, steel-like strength that had held her together for the better part of her life. "No, but it's what I'm answering," she said, opening her eyes again. "And it's what I stand by."

The continuing chorus of "oh, Christmas tree" floated between them while Mitch watched her. At last he inclined his head. "All right, you win."

She regarded him suspiciously, waiting for the *for now* she felt certain was coming, but he only tipped his head to one side, a little like Dog, and asked instead, "You sure you're okay with this decorating thing? You looked like you wanted to turn tail and run when the girls asked. I can put them off if you'd rather not. It's supposed to be your day off tomorrow."

She was tempted. Oh, how she was tempted. With her heart bleeding all over the floor at her feet at the very thought of joining in, how could she not be? But she shook her head. If those three young girls could find the strength to celebrate Christmas in their mother's absence, then she would find the strength to help them.

"Thank you, but I'll be fine," she said.

But that evening, after dinner, she took refuge in her room rather than sitting in her usual reading spot, because the sight of the waiting tree stand and neatly stacked boxes reminded her she was anything but fine.

She just didn't know how to tell Mitch.

CHAPTER 35

They decorated the tree just after sunset the next day. It was tradition, Rachel told her, because their mother had always said that they should first see it after dark, with all its lights on, when it was at its magical best. And Abby remembered how William and Olivia had insisted on decorating in broad daylight, so they could be sure everything was in the right place and perfect—and then they'd spend the next week rearranging things to make them even more perfect, like two fussy oldsters.

"It's beautiful, isn't it?" Rachel leaned back against her father to gaze at the tree twinkling in the living room window. Abby's heart hitched a little as Mitch's arms went around his daughter and he rested his chin atop her head. With dusk falling outside and the lamps turned off, the lights from the tree glowed against their burnished skin and reflected in their eyes. Rachel had been right. It was magical. Abby returned to putting ornament cartons into their bins.

"It is," Mitch agreed softly. "Your mother would approve."

"Do you miss her?"

"Every day, sweet girl. Every day."

His voice had dropped to that gruff note again,

making Abby's breath catch and drawing his other two daughters to his side. Brittany slid her arms around his waist, and Kiana leaned against his leg. Abby closed the last of the bins and stacked it on the others.

"Can you tell us a story to help us 'member her?" Kiana asked. "A funny one."

"A funny one, huh? Let me think about that for a second." Mitch glanced toward Abigail as she tiptoed toward the hallway. She couldn't quite meet his eyes but managed a ghost of a smile and a *go on* kind of motion before she made good her escape. Mitch's voice followed her. "How about the one when I took her camping the first time, and she thought she heard a bear outside the tent and woke the whole campground with her screaming?"

Abby took refuge in the darkened kitchen, where Mitch's deep voice faded to a rumble and his words couldn't quite reach her. Standing at the sliding glass doors, she stared out into the back yard, watching night fall over the neighborhood. A light winked on in an upstairs bedroom of the house behind, and a moment later went out again. Overhead, a single bright star peeked out from the sky. Olivia had once told Abby she thought the stars were peepholes in heaven, so that the angels could watch over them. At the time, Abby had nodded and smiled at the childish earnestness, thinking the idea sweet and innocent; now, she wished with all her heart that it was true, and that she knew which peephole her daughter looked through, so she could look back.

Christmas.

Christmas without William, without Olivia, without the very things that had given her life purpose and meaning. And on this one—unlike the last one, when it had all been too new and too stark and too impossible to take in—she feared she would feel every single moment of loss. Every ache. Every hollow, fragile heartbeat.

A cold, wet nose shoved its way into her fisted hand, distracting her. Abby looked down through her tears and the shadows into mournful brown eyes. "You do have a way about you, Dog," she whispered, sniffling. The nose nudged again, and she crouched down beside the beast and wrapped her arms around his neck, burying her face in the clean fur. Already the citrus scent of the shampoo was fading and giving way to an earthy animal scent, but Abby didn't mind. "I hope you get to stay. You'd be good for them all when I'm gone, I think."

Dog's tongue swiped her earlobe in agreement, and she giggled through her tears as she ruffled his head. "Goofy mutt. How come you're in here and not with Kia?"

"I think he decided you needed him more," Mitch said.

Abby pushed upright, brushing at her cheeks. "Mitch. I didn't hear you come in."

"You seemed deep in conversation with that." He didn't turn on the lights but came to join her at the sliding doors, indicating Dog. "I didn't want to interrupt."

She wiped wet fingers against her pant leg, then rubbed the dog ear nearest her hand. "He's pretty special," she said. "And he's smart. I get the feeling someone has spent a lot of time with him."

"Someone who might be looking for him, you mean."

"I wouldn't be surprised."

Mitch's shadow nodded. "I agree. He cleaned up rather nicely after the bath you gave him, and he seems to have settled into the house well. The girls will take it pretty hard if his family does show up."

And that would be one more thing he'd have to deal with, Abby thought.

"I'll try to mitigate expectations," she said. "Lots of warnings and reminders."

He chuckled. "Thank you, but I think we're too late for that. They've decided he needs a name, even if it's just temporary, and they want you to pick it."

"Me? But—"

"They said it will help them remember you when you're gone."

The rest of Abby's words piled up in her throat, forming a lump. In the semi-gloom, Mitch pulled a face.

"I know, right? They got me with that one, too." He leaned a shoulder against the doorframe, hands in pockets. "And, apparently, it was Rachel's idea. You've worked minor wonders with that one, Abigail Jamieson. I mean, she still has a thirteen-year-old attitude, but at least she's *mostly* human again. Thank you for that."

Abby hesitated, wondering whether she should mention that the change in Rachel seemed directly correlated with a reduction of Perky Perkins' influence in the girl's life. Mitch spoke again before she'd decided.

"She was even on board with going out to the farm with us yesterday. Surprised the heck out of me."

"Farm?"

"The Christmas tree farm. It's where we've always gone, ever since Rachel was a baby and we strapped her into a sled. It takes a little longer than going to a lot, but there's something special about being able to cut down your own tree. Eve and the girls always loved it. I wasn't sure they'd want to continue without her, but I'm glad they did. We didn't have a chance to go last year." He stared out the glass door. "Eve died just after New Year's, here at home. We turned the dining room into a bedroom for her and put the bed near the door so she could see the Christmas tree and be with the kids. She didn't want them to be afraid of death or dying. She wanted them to know that it was just another part of life."

Abby stayed silent for a minute, comparing the Abrams family's experience with loss to her own. Wondering whether expecting it and being there for it had been better or worse than having a grim-faced police officer shatter her existence with a few horrific, impossible words. But, no—loss was loss, no matter how it happened. It still left an unfillable hole. Still irrevocably changed you. Still left you desperately trying to regain your footing in a world you no longer recognized. She released a long, tremulous sigh and looked up from her own loss into Mitch's. "She sounds like quite the lady," she said.

Mitch smiled. "She was," he agreed. "Quite the lady." He met her gaze in the faint light filtering into the kitchen from the hallway. "When I came into the kitchen just now—"

"Daddy, can we order pizza tonight?"

Feet thundered into the room, heralding the arrival of Britt, owner of the voice behind the interruption, and Kiana. The overhead light turned on, and Abby blinked in its sudden brilliance, even while silently blessing the girls' interruption. Dog left her side to join Kiana.

"Can we?" Britt asked. "We didn't have it on Wednesday like we usually do, and we could eat in the living room for a special treat, and then we can watch the tree."

"Why, are we expecting it to do tricks?" Mitch teased. "Is Dog going to teach it how?"

"Da-deeeeeeee." Britt rolled her eyes in a remarkable imitation of her older sister.

Her father reached out and tweaked her nose. "Yes, we can order pizza and sit in the living room," he said, taking his cell phone from its clip at his waist. "Who wants what?"

"A Christmas party," Rachel announced from the doorway.

"I don't think they deliver those, but I can ask."

Mitch's eldest frowned at him. "What?"

"We're ordering pizza," Britt told her. "You just said you wanted a Christmas party on yours."

It was Rachel's turn to roll her eyes, and Abby revised her previous thought. None of the others held a candle to that girl's mastery of that particular mannerism.

"That's so lame," Rachel said. "And I'm serious. We should have a Christmas party. We could invite all our friends, and Abby can invite her family, and—"

"Whoa there, kiddo. A party is a lot of work, and two weeks before Christmas is a little late to be organizing one. Most people are already booked up."

"Just a little one, then. Please?"

"It could be potluck," Britt suggested. "Then it's not so much work. And we can do the rest of the decorating tomorrow night. Please, Daddy?"

Kiana, who had curled up on the floor with Dog as a pillow, added her voice to the chorus. "Pretty please, Daddy?"

Mitch exhaled a long sigh as he turned to Abby. "It's a lot to ask," he said, "and I want you to say no if you'd rather not."

Abby regarded the three expectant faces. It *was* a lot to ask, but for reasons the girls didn't need to know. Not when they needed to focus on their own healing, and not when it was her job to help them do so. Oddly enough, the smile she summoned wasn't nearly as forced as she thought it would be. "I'm game if you are," she told Mitch, and the kitchen erupted into cheers, followed by a rousing chorus of *It's Beginning to Look a Lot Like Christmas* with accompaniment courtesy of Dog.

Laughing, Abby put her hands over her ears and shook her head at the entire group. The challenges to her carefully maintained hold on herself might be unending in this family, but on the bright side, she was learning she was capable of a great deal more than she had ever thought possible again. She looked up to find Mitch watching her with a half smile. He said something she couldn't hear over the din, and she shook her head and shrugged.

He leaned down and, his skin warm against hers, took one hand away from her ear. "I said, I think we've created Christmas monsters."

Abby looked back to the girls, half her heart dancing with them, and the other half holding tight to the memory of another who was forever absent. "We have," she agreed. "But this is the way it's supposed to be."

Together, they watched Rachel whirl Kiana around the room, Dog circling them. Then, his voice rough, Mitch said, "Thank you."

She shot him a surprised look. "For what?"

"For all of this," he said, his green eyes warm. "I don't know why, but I know Christmas is hard for you, Abby. And I want you to know how grateful I am for putting that aside for my daughters. I can never thank you enough."

Abby closed her eyes on a shaft of pain. She took a deep breath, striving for control. She'd been unprepared for Mitch's words, the compassion she heard behind them, and the tiny crack they had opened in her defenses. Memories of Christmases past trickled out. Olivia at two, staring up at the tree, her face alight with wonder. Olivia at six, waltzing around the great room with William, both of them singing along with Bing's *White Christmas*. Olivia at ten, handing out the gifts and watching with excitement as William opened his, so proud of the crooked scarf Abby had helped her knit for him to wear on their annual ski trip.

Last year's tree, sitting bright and merry in the window as Abby opened the door to the uniformed police officers. Turning garish as she collapsed on the floor before it. Sitting in the dark as it waited for weeks, needles dropping like tears, for the little girl who was no more. A mere skeleton by the time she hauled it to the curb, decorations and all.

"I don't know why, but I know Christmas is hard for you."

The crack opened wider, and driven by grief and the deep weariness that came from keeping secrets for too long, words forced their way out.

"She was eleven," she whispered, "Her name was Olivia, and it was two days before Christmas."

Mitch stood as if turned to stone, and one by one, as if sensing the change in energy between the adults, the girls stopped singing and dancing—Rachel first, then Britt, and finally Kiana. Even Dog stood still. Kiana sidled over to tug on Abby's sleeve.

"Are you sad again?" she asked.

Abby tried to pull a smile of reassurance from the ache, but her face refused to cooperate.

Mitch cleared his throat. "Rach? How about you use the phone in my office and order the pizza for us? Britt and Kia, you go with her, please. And take Dog."

Without so much as a murmur of disagreement, the girls filed out, shooting worried backward glances over their shoulders. And then the kitchen was empty, and Mitch's arms were around her, and Abby was sobbing her heartbreak and loss into a broad, solid chest.

CHAPTER 36

"Here." Mitch set a steaming cup on the table beside Abby and then pulled another chair close. He sat down and leaned forward to rest elbows on knees not quite touching hers. "I put a bit of brandy in it, so be careful."

Abby giggled tiredly into the soggy tissue she was using to wipe her nose yet again. "Afraid of a repeat of Friday night?" she asked, then wondered if the question was appropriate. Probably not, but she was too worn out to worry about it.

Mitch smiled. "Not exactly," he said.

She wondered a little at the oblique note in his voice, but she decided she was too tired to figure that out, too. It felt like every particle of energy had been wrung from her along with her tears, leaving her exhausted, empty, and so stuffed-up that she could scarcely breathe. As if reading her mind, Mitch plucked the used tissue from her fingers and handed her a fresh one.

"I'm so sorry I ruined your tree day," she said, looking toward the hallway. "You should go and join them."

The pizza had arrived a few minutes before, and Mitch had told the girls to start without them. But there were no happy noises coming from the living room the way there should have been, and guilt moved in to over-shadow Abby's grief.

"They're fine," Mitch said. "I'll head out in a few minutes."

"Your pizza will be cold."

"I'll pretend I'm back in college."

She gave a watery smile and blew her nose. "Thank you," she said. "For listening."

"Thank you for trusting me to."

"I haven't told anyone except Gwyn—she's my sister—and Gareth. Not since I left the group therapy thing, and I only stayed with that for a month or so."

"Not much of a group participant?"

"Not much for talking."

"Not even to friends?"

She grimaced. "William was quite a bit older than I was, and our lifestyle didn't lend itself well to me forming my own friendships. I tended toward being private."

"That sounds lonely."

"I didn't mind at the time, because I had Olivia, but yes. Now that I look back, I think it was."

"How much older was he?"

Her gaze slid away from his. "Twenty-six years. I was nineteen when I met him."

"Wow. You're right. That's quite a gap." Mitch watched her. "But you loved him."

It was more statement than question, but Abby answered anyway. "I suspect I was more *in* love with the idea of him at first. He was very handsome and very sure of himself, and I was very young. But, yes, I think I learned to love him."

"You think...?"

"He wasn't an easy man. He was set in his ways, and he could be demanding."

"You thought about leaving him."

Another statement. Another answer. "I did, but I had no money of my own and nowhere to go. And then I had Olivia, and he made it clear he would take her from me if I tried to leave."

Mitch stared down at his hands, his expression dark, and she added the same thing she'd told Gareth. "He was a good man in his own way. And a good provider. He cared about us."

"As long as you did things his way?" Mitch's voice was neutral. Too much so.

She hesitated and then sighed. "Yes."

He scowled at her. "You know there's a term for relationships like that, right?"

"Yes," she said again. "And you know how hard it is to admit you're in that kind of relationship, right?"

He held her gaze for a second, and then his shoulders sagged. "No," he admitted. "But I can imagine."

"I had a plan to leave." The admission surprised Abby as much as it seemed to surprise Mitch. She'd never told anyone that, not even Gwyn. "I opened a savings account when Olivia was six, and I tried to keep a few dollars aside every week from the household budget. I had enough for one and a half plane tickets to come here when—when—"

"Take your time." Mitch's calm, soothing voice was at stark odds with his clenched jaw.

She did, inhaling shakily before continuing. "William found out about the account, and we had a huge fight. He told me he would make certain I never saw my daughter again, and then he took her and left. He'd taken off before, when we had disagreements, so I knew he'd come back—only this time he didn't. And neither did she. There was an accident. A drunk driver, head on. The police said he didn't stand a chance of avoiding it, and..."

"And you blamed yourself," he finished softly. "Oh, Abby."

The compassion in Mitch's voice nearly broke her again. She gripped the tissue and held onto the last vestiges of her inner fortitude as, for the first time, she spoke the words that had haunted her for so long. "If I'd just been happy with what I had, she'd still be alive," she whispered. "They wouldn't have left the house. He wouldn't have taken her from me. I'd be putting up the tree with her, and wrapping her gifts, and—"

Mitch leaned forward and engulfed her hands in his work-roughened ones. "You are *not* to blame, Abigail. No one is to blame. It was an accident, and it wasn't any more your fault than Eve getting sick was mine."

"What?" The last bit shocked Abby into blinking at him. "You thought that?"

His lips pulled tight. "I did," he said. "I'd been working insane hours and leaving her to look after the house and kids pretty much solo. I knew she was exhausted. She told me so. But I thought I was too busy to change anything. So, yes. You bet I blamed myself when she was diagnosed."

"But that makes no sense."

"I know that here"—he took one hand away to touch his temple—"but things got a little confused here." His hand traveled to his heart. "Grief isn't a kind thing, Abby. And it's not particularly reasonable. The accident was *not* your fault. Sometimes bad things just happen."

"I know," she whispered. And she did, but somehow, hearing it from Mitch gave a depth and truth to the words that hadn't existed before. A truth she hadn't wanted to accept, because it meant letting go of the guilt that had anchored her for the last year. Part of her had been terrified of what would remain in its absence.

The inevitable moving forward with life.

A life without Olivia.

A life alone.

Mitch's hands returned to hold hers again, and his callused thumbs stroked gently, warm and strong and comforting.

"But good things can happen, too," he continued, "such as you being with us for Christmas. We're all hurting this year, Abby, but maybe we can be there for you the way you've been there for us. "

If it had been anything more than an offer of friendship, she wouldn't have been able to accept it, because despite her growing awareness of Mitch and her behavior on Friday night, she was in no shape to be considering anything more. Not with him; not with anyone.

Not yet.

"Well?" Mitch asked.

That's all it was. An offer of friendship and shared space for healing. Abby took a deep breath.

"I think I'd like that."

"Me, too," he said, giving her hands a little squeeze. Then he grimaced. "The girls will have questions."

Her insides froze. She hadn't thought about that yet.

"If you'd like, I can tell them about Olivia while you wash your face," he suggested, and Abby gave a little start at the sound of her daughter's name on someone else's lips. It had been a long time. Too long.

She nodded. "That works. Thank you."

Mitch stood and pushed his chair back under the table. Abby let him pull her to her feet. "I'll warm up the pizza," he said. "See you in a few minutes."

CHAPTER 37

"Is Abby okay?" Britt asked when Mitch joined them in the living room. The tree sparkled beside her, casting a warm glow over the room and its occupants—and the unopened pizza boxes. He motioned to the latter, stacked on the coffee table.

"You guys were supposed to start without us."

"We were worried about Abby," Rachel said from the floor, where she and Kia sat with Dog on his back between them, belly exposed for rubs, snoring lightly.

And Mitch had been worried about the dog's temperament.

"Abby's going to be okay," he said, lowering himself into his usual armchair, repositioned to make room for the tree. "But it turns out she's going through a rough Christmas, too. You were right about her having been married before, Rachel. Her husband and daughter died in a car accident just before Christmas last year."

"Oh my gosh," Rachel breathed the words, eyes wide with shock. "That's *awful*. I feel even more horrible for snooping in her room, now."

"You snooped in Abby's room?" Britt demanded.

"Already dealt with, Britt," said Mitch. "Let's stick to the subject at hand." He pulled Kia, who'd gotten up from the floor, onto his lap. "Abby's going to be here with us for Christmas, but I need you girls not to ask her too many questions, all right? Let's be patient with her and give her some room. In fact, let's be patient with everyone. The next couple of weeks are going to be pretty rough for all of us, and we're going to need a little extra love and understanding."

"Abby's picture should be on the mantel," Kia said, leaning back against his shoulder.

"Pardon?"

"Her picture of her little girl and her husband. It should be there"—his youngest pointed to where Eve's picture sat—"beside Mommy, where they can see the tree, too. Then they'll know that Abby is happy with us, just like Mommy knows we're happy with her."

Out of the mouths of babes...

"That's a great idea," Britt said. "Rach?"

"I agree. Daddy? Can we ask her if she wants to?"

Mitch blinked away a sheen of moisture and cleared his throat. Damn, but he was proud of these three. "I think that would be a wonderful, but let's wait for a day or two, okay? Now, is that pizza still warm, or should we heat it up?"

Rachel placed a hand on the top box. "Feels warm to me."

"Then let's dig in." Mitch set Kia on the floor again and passed out plates and napkins. By the time Abby joined them, each of the kids was halfway through their first slice, all sitting cross-legged on the floor by the tree with Dog watching them hopefully.

"Abby! Are you better now?" Kia sprang up and threw her arms, plate and all, around Abby's waist. Her pizza slid off and, before Mitch could open his mouth, disappeared down Dog's throat.

Mitch blinked at the sheer speed with which the bulk had moved.

"See? He can be useful," said Rachel, making them all laugh—including Abby, he noted.

He replaced Kia's missing pizza, then put another slice on the last free plate and set it on the coffee table for Abby. "Come and eat," he said. Then he pointed a finger at Dog. "Not you."

Dog pulled back his top lip in a grin, then curled up beside the tree again with a deep, contented sigh. Mitch echoed the sigh, but his was one of concern rather than contentment. The animal had been with them only a few days, and he already fit into the household as if he'd been with them forever. If his owners turned up, Mitch's family was in for a world of hurt—and an already battered Christmas would take another serious blow.

But one day at a time, right? Because if there was one thing Mitch had learned in the last couple of years, it was that there was no point worrying about things he couldn't control—and that life didn't come with guarantees of ease, or happiness, or forever. He'd forgotten that lately. Forgotten it for a long while, if he was being honest. He'd fallen into the trap of bouncing from one disaster to the next, always scrabbling for a handhold and trying to do more instead of recognizing what he already had. Seeing what was truly important.

Abby's story had reminded him in a big, big way.

He studied her as she sat on the loveseat nearby,

her skin so pale in the lights from the tree that she almost looked translucent. A far cry from Eve's dark coloring, which he had so loved, but beautiful in its own right—and covering a core of steel that he had only guessed at before tonight. He had no idea how she'd remained standing after what she'd endured, because just dealing with Eve's death alone had nearly felled him to his knees. If he'd lost a child at the same time...

Mitch's throat tightened, and his gaze touched fiercely on each of his daughters. Rachel, with his eyes and her mother's take-no-prisoners attitude; Britt, the family peacekeeper—and resident troublemaker, depending on her mood; Kiana, blissfully oblivious to the challenges that faced her. All so beautiful, so confident, so generous. He looked back to Abby and wondered what her daughter had been like. Had Olivia looked like her? Had she had the same wonderful laugh? The same smoky blue eyes?

"Daddy, are you even listening?" Britt asked, exasperation edging her voice.

He brought his focus to bear on his middle child. "Sorry, kiddo—I missed that."

"We're talking about the party. Abby said we should have it on the twenty-third. Can we?"

"That's not too close to Christmas for everyone?" Not to mention being the date on which Abby had said Olivia and William had died. He shot her a sharp look. "Are you sure you're up to that?"

"I think it will be fun. Especially if we go with Britt's idea of a potluck." Abby smiled at Britt, who beamed. "By the twenty-third, most people have finished their shopping, and the holiday parties are pretty much done. It's kind of like the eye of the storm."

"That wasn't what I meant."

"I know." She turned to him, still sad, but calm, too. "And yes, I'm sure. It will keep me busy, and it feels... right."

He held her gaze, then nodded. "Then that date is fine with me, too. Who are we inviting?"

"We need a list," Rachel said. "I'll get some paper."

"Top drawer of your father's desk," Abby called after her. "Pens are in the righthand drawer beside it."

Mitch sat back and laced his fingers behind his head. "You were busy in there today."

"I got a good start on it," she agreed. "But I'll need your computer password to access the financials on Monday."

He pulled a face. "Yeah... about that. I don't have them."

"Your partner does the books? That's okay. He can send the files—"

"Derek doesn't have them, either. At least, not electronically."

"You're still on a manual system?" Both of Abby's fair brows rose. "Wow."

"Tell me about it. Is that the end of our deal?"

"Not at all. I started off doing Will—William's books manually. I'm sure I remember how. Maybe you can set up a meeting with your partner for me, so I can get a handle on his system."

"That, I can do."

"I have paper!" Rachel announced, skipping back into the room. "And a pen."

Mitch couldn't help but smile. He hadn't seen his oldest move in such an undignified fashion since before her mother got sick. Whatever else Abby might do for this family in her time here, returning Rachel's childhood to her would top the list. Well, that and making sure Kiana's needs were recognized, and lifting their home out of the chaos into which it had sunk, and restoring his hope for their survival, and—damn, but he hadn't thanked the woman nearly enough for what she'd accomplished around here.

He looked across at the cascade of blond curls around the bent head as she huddled with his daughters over the guest list and, not for the first time, wondered how they would manage without her.

How *he* would manage.

And not just for practical reasons anymore.

CHAPTER 38

Abby texted her sister on Monday after she dropped off the kids at school and got the laundry started. She tried to tell herself that it was only for the girls' sake, because they wanted Gwyn and Gareth and their family to come to the party, but she had to admit that she was glad of the excuse. She'd ignored Gwyn's every-single-day texts since their blowup, but now that she had opened up to Mitch about Olivia and William, it was time she did the same with her sister. And so, taking a deep breath for courage, she typed, *Hey. It's Abby.*

She waited, but the cell phone sat unresponsive in her hand, her message showing as delivered but unread. She set it down and poured coffee into a travel mug, so that she'd be ready to head out again, then she switched off the coffee maker and waited some more. Was Gwyn maybe still in transit herself, ferrying kids to school?

The notification changed to "read," and three dots blinked in the bottom left corner to indicate typing at the other end.

Hey, came her sister's answer.

...

Sorry it took me a sec to answer.

...

I almost dropped the baby when I saw it was you.

...

I thought it was safer to put her down.

Abby caught herself rolling her eyes. Great. Rachel was contagious. *Funny,* she texted back.

...

I try. What's up?

You guys busy on the 23rd? Mitch and girls are having a party. Potluck. The girls would like all of you to come.

The message showed as read, but it took a while before the three dots appeared again.

Only the girls? Gwyn asked.

No. I'd like you to come, too.

...

Can we maybe talk while I'm there?

Deep breath. *Yes.*

...

We're in. Put me down for a pineapple ham.

Mom's recipe? Abby asked.

...

You remember it?

Abby smiled and typed, *Of course. But I haven't had it since that last family Easter.*

...

I'll bring you the recipe. What time should we be there?

It's a family thing, so we thought 4:00 would be good, Abby tapped in.

...

Perfect.

...

Abby?

What?

...

I'm glad you texted.

Me, too.

Abby turned off her phone and leaned back against the counter to consider her final response to Gwyn, surprised at how much truth was in it. And how much she was looking forward to talking to her sister. Or rather, how she wasn't dreading it anymore, the way she had been. *Maybe the whole opening-up-to-people thing gets a bit easier once you start actually doing it*, she thought. Not a lot, but a bit. It was a beginning, at least.

She glanced at the clock on the stove and screwed the lid onto the travel mug. And now she had another beginning to make, by getting the company books from Mitch's business partner. She headed into the laundry room and nudged a toe against the dog laying across the doorway to the garage.

"Come on, you big black beast. Move, so I can get out of the house."

Dog opened an eye, regarding her with a look that seemed to inquire what was in it for him. Abby took a bone-shaped dog cookie from a box on the back of the utility sink and held it up.

"Will that do?"

Heaving a sigh, Dog lumbered to his feet, daintily accepted the offering, and moved aside. He wouldn't go far, Abby suspected. He'd spent the entire day in front of the same door on Friday, waiting for Kiana to re-materialize. At most, if he gave up waiting here, he'd head upstairs to Kiana's bed, which was his second-favorite place in the house—his first being wherever Kiana herself was.

"Be good," Abby told him, patting the broad black head and edging out the door.

She arrived at the address Mitch had given her with five minutes to spare, only to find the second-floor office locked up tight. She knocked on the door that bore old-fashioned brass letters spelling out *Abrams Construction Ltd.*, with the letters for *Abrams* looking somewhat shinier than the others, and the shadow of a former, longer name underlying them that Abby couldn't quite make out. There was no answer to her summons. She stared at the door for a moment. Mitch had said 10:00, she was sure of it. Maybe Derek had run out for—

A square of paper taped to the sidelight caught her eye, and she bent closer to look at it. A terse message was scrawled across it.

Husband in hospital.
Ledgers on desk.
Mitch has key.
Questions when I'm back.

CHAPTER 39

Abby peeled the note from the glass and read it again, pondering her options. She hated to bother Mitch for the key right now. Maybe she could have him swing by to pick up the box on his way home, and then she could get a start on everything tomorrow.

The thud of booted feet on thin carpet made her turn. Mitch strode down the corridor toward her, looking apologetic—and pulse-rocketingly pleased to see her. He wore a battered, padded canvas coat, unzipped to reveal his standard garb of blue jeans and plaid work shirt—this one red and black, and unbuttoned far enough to make Abby's gaze drift down from the white flash of his smile. She wrenched her attention back to where it belonged.

"I just got Derek's text a few minutes ago," he said when he reached her. "I tried to call to tell you I'd bring the ledgers home after work tonight, but you must have been on the way already."

"You still could have called instead of coming over here. It would have been easier for me to turn around than for you to take time to meet me. You're busy, and I wouldn't have minded waiting until tonight for the books."

"It's all good. I didn't want you making the trip for

nothing, and I'm on a job site not far from here, so it wasn't any trouble." Mitch reached past her and slid a key into the deadbolt. He gave it a twist, the door swung inward, and he held a hand out in invitation. "After you."

The premises of Abrams Construction consisted of three small offices off a front reception area, and a meeting room that Abby estimated would hold ten comfortably. She looked at Mitch in surprise. "I didn't realize your company was this big."

Mitch's mouth twisted. "It isn't. Not anymore. We had to downsize quite a bit when Eve got sick. Derek doesn't have the stamina to drive around to job sites, and I didn't have the time, so we didn't take on a lot of new jobs. We let more than half our guys go, including Trevor, our office assistant, and we're just waiting for the lease to run out on this place in March so we can find something smaller and tighten our belts another notch. At least, that was the plan." He sighed and ran a hand over his head in a familiar gesture of frustration. "Now I don't know what I'm doing."

"You're letting me have the ledgers so I can help— unless you'd rather I work here?"

"No." He waved a hand. "You'll be more comfortable at ho—the house. It's warmer there, too. Derek keeps this place like an icebox. Come on, his office is this one."

Abby followed him through the door to the left. Derek Simmons's office was the antithesis of Mitch's at home—and yes, despite Mitch catching back the word himself just now, that was how she thought of it. *Home.* At least for now.

Her gaze traveled the room. Not a single thing looked out of place. All the objects were placed perpendicularly to the walls and each other, four pictures hung in an exact line across one wall and three on another, one plant stood centered on the filing cabinet, and the desktop contained a stapler and pen—both perfectly aligned with one another—and a box marked with "Abigail Jamieson" in precise lettering.

"Derek is a little... particular," Mitch said, following her gaze around the room.

"Thank heavens," Abby murmured, then smiled at his surprise. "If the books are half as precisely kept as this office, this just became the world's easiest job."

"I sincerely hope so. Derek took them over when we laid Trevor off, and I haven't looked at them myself since then. I'd hate for it to be any more trouble than it already is." Mitch swung the box under one arm. "I'll carry it down to the vehicle for you. You parked at the side?"

Much to Abby's relief, they took the stairs rather than the elevator. Mitch had been wonderfully brisk and professional since she'd cried all over him on Sunday, but a new level of awareness had opened up between them, and she hadn't quite decided what to do with it—especially when he'd greeted her with a broad smile and his shirt half unbuttoned. She would prefer neither of them acted on it, so she was grateful when he seemed to be of like mind.

Well, mostly grateful.

But perhaps a little bit wistful, too. It had been a long time since a man had held her close enough that she could hear his heart beating. A longer time since she'd felt that safe in someone's arms. And an even longer time since—

Abby stumbled on a stair and tightened her grip on the railing, flushing hot at the direction her mind had taken. *Compassion*, she reminded herself. *That's all it was. That's all you want it to be for now, because you both have a lot to work through this Christmas and*—

"You okay?" Mitch asked over his shoulder as she stumbled again.

"Fine," she said. "I'm fine."

Or she would be, once she figured out what to do with the spark that had flared inside her at the "for now" part of her thoughts.

CHAPTER 40

Dog's owner called on Wednesday.

Abby was immersed in a morass of debits and credits for the third day in a row, having discovered that Derek's penchant for extreme order in his office did not, after all, apply to his bookkeeping. The ledgers were a mess—to put it kindly—and so were the company's finances, if the emerging picture was right, so her heart was already heavy with dread when she dug for the cell phone ringing somewhere beneath the tsunami of papers on the desk. She found it on the fifth ring.

"Hello?"

"Abigail Jamieson, please," said a woman's voice.

"Speaking."

"My name is Heidi Leduc, and I got your name from the humane society. I think you may have my dog."

Abby's heart plummeted to her toes. Closing her eyes, she rested an elbow on the desk and cradled her forehead in her hand. "I—uh—we did find a dog, yes. Last Friday."

"Ours has been missing since the end of October. A big black Bouvier des Flandres, neutered, no chip."

Abby's hand found its way to her mouth, covering it, and she looked across the office to where Dog snoozed by the door, waiting for his girls to come home from school. His girls... except they weren't.

"Ms. Jamieson?"

"Hi. Yes. Yes, that sounds like Dog."

"Dog?"

"That's what the girls have been calling him until we knew for sure whether we could—" Abby stopped and took a deep breath. "You'll want to come and see for yourself if it's him."

"I can be there in twenty minutes."

"No! No, it will have to be later. After dinner, so that the girls have a chance to say goodbye, and their dad is home. Please."

"Of course."

"Can I ask—how did you lose him?"

"We were moving from Kemptville to a property in the Eastern Townships. He was traveling in the truck with us, and he slipped out when we stopped for gas in Rigaud, just outside of Montreal. My guess is that he was heading for home. We never dreamed he'd make it as far as Ottawa. I'm in town for the day and made a call to the humane society on impulse."

That would explain the worn pads on his feet and the weight loss.

"You must miss him."

"With all my heart."

Abby's own heart squeezed tight. *Devastated*, she thought. *They'll be devastated.* For a second, she considered just hanging up on Heidi Leduc, but decency and common sense prevailed—because of course the humane society had Mitch's address, and wouldn't *that* be a scene? Instead, she gave Heidi directions.

"Thank you so much, Ms. Jamieson. I'm so excited to see him—his name is Henry, by the way."

"Henry," Abby repeated, and she could have cried when Dog lifted his head at the sound of the name. She did cry when she ended the call and went to bury her face in the rough, shaggy hair, forgetting all about the strings of figures that had painted a less-than-rosy picture of Mitch's company's future.

Dinner was a somber affair that night. Kiana refused to eat and lay in a corner of the kitchen with her arms around Dog's neck and her head resting on his shoulder, and Rachel and Britt joined her there after just a few bites. Abby was next to give up, carrying her own untouched plate to the counter and putting the contents into a container for lunch the next day on the off chance she ever ate again. Mitch came over to the island as she put the container in the fridge.

"I knew it would be rough," he said, his voice a low, raw rumble, "but I didn't think it would be this bad."

"Our hopes were up," Abby replied, crossing her arms and leaning a hip against the cabinet to watch the three girls. "It's been almost a week."

Mitch braced both hands on the counter and leaned his weight onto his arms, his shoulders hunched. "Damn it to hell," he muttered. "This Christmas is rough enough without them losing someone else."

"I thought about hanging up on her," Abby admitted.

"You should have," he said, but she knew he didn't mean it.

Impulsively, she put a hand over one of his. "We'll get through it," she said. "I promise."

"I know." He sighed. "I just wish—"

The doorbell rang, and all heads turned toward the hallway. For once, Dog remained quiet, staying with the girls instead of raising his usual ruckus. Mitch's mouth pulled tight.

"It's almost as if he knows," he said. He turned his hand over beneath Abby's and gave her fingers a brief squeeze, then released her and strode down the hallway.

A moment later, Abby heard the door open, then Mitch's greeting, followed by the voice of the woman she'd spoken to earlier. Footsteps came toward the kitchen, and she braced herself and willed the girls to do the same. And then Dog was up and hurling himself at a slight, middle-aged woman with long black braids streaked with grey, and clear, bright eyes the same dark brown as his. Heidi Leduc dropped to her knees, laughing as her face received a thorough washing in between doggy wriggles of pure joy.

Abby bit her lip and looked at the girls, knowing even before she saw their devastation that they would understand what they saw: the reunification of a dog named Henry with his beloved owner. There, was no doubt. Gritting her teeth, she blinked back tears as Rachel slid her arm around Kia's shoulders. In the doorway, the woman rose to her feet, fending off Dog's continued adoration, the fringes on her sheepskin-lined jacket swinging wildly in time with his attempts to climb into her arms.

"Well," she said, humor rich in her voice, "I think we can safely say we recognize one another. I can't tell you how glad I am that you found him and took him in, and I don't even know how to start thanking you for taking such good care of him. We were offering a reward. Can I—"

"No," Mitch said. "Thank you, but we were happy to look after him."

"Are you sure? I know how much he eats, and—"

"Really." He cast a speaking look at the huddle of girls by the sliding glass doors. "I think it's best if we get this over with as quickly as possible."

"Oh." Heidi followed his gaze, and her smile faded. She looked genuinely sorry, adding, "Of course. I see what you mean, and yes, we should get going. Thank you again for everything." She walked down the hallway toward the front door, snapping her fingers, and Dog padded obediently after her.

From the corner of her eye, Abby saw Kia shrug off Rachel's arm, shaking her head. Her hands flapped at her sides, and she jiggled from foot to foot. As if sensing her distress, Dog stopped a few feet outside the kitchen and looked back over his shoulder.

"Henry, come," the woman ordered.

Dog turned his head toward her, then looked back again at Kia. A low grumble sounded in his chest. Then he sat.

Out in the hallway, Heidi retraced her steps, coming to stand in front of him. "My goodness," she said. "I've never seen him do that before." She peered at the girls, and Abby watched her gaze settle on Kia and soften. "Autism?" she murmured.

"Among other issues," Mitch said. "Dog—Henry—seemed to know."

"I trained him as a support animal," Heidi explained. "We visit nursing homes and hospitals. He likes the children's hospital best, and he's particularly good with kids who are on the spectrum." She fell silent, staring down at the dog, who stared back at her, and Abby could have sworn an entire unspoken conversation passed between them.

At last, Heidi raised an eyebrow at the creature. "You sure that's what you want?" she asked, and Dog's tail stub wiggled. She shrugged. "All right, my friend. It's your decision."

She shifted her attention to Mitch. "It looks like I've wasted your time, Mr. Abrams." Her tone was brisk. "I don't think this is him after all."

Mitch gaped at her. "But you—he—"

Heidi turned a critical eye on Dog. "Nope. Definitely not. My dog is wider between the eyes. And taller. And he's never this clean, even after I give him a bath. I'm sorry, but he's not my Henry." Her voice caught a little on the name, and she cleared her throat. "I guess you'll have to keep him."

"You—you're—" Abby exchanged looks with Mitch, who appeared as astounded by the turn of events as she was.

"Ms. Leduc," he began.

The woman held up a hand to stop him. "This dog has made his choice, Mr. Abrams. Even if he were mine, I would have to respect that."

"At least let me—"

"The dog has *chosen* you, Mr. Abrams. That is a gift, not something you pay for."

Mitch stared at her, his jaw tight. "You have no idea how much this will mean to them," he said finally.

"Oh, I think I do." Her eyes shiny with unshed tears, Heidi glanced back to Abby. "You'll need to change his name. He needs a name from this family now, to mark his belonging."

"Hope," Abigail said without hesitation. "His name is Hope." She'd been thinking about it ever since Mitch had told her the girls wanted her to name the animal, because that was what he had brought into this family, and what she herself hoped his continued presence here would remind them of when—as the girls had said—Abby was gone.

"I like it," Heidi said. "It fits him." She went down on one knee and gazed at the dog at eye level. "Do good work here, my friend," she whispered. "I'll miss you."

Dog—now Hope—lifted a giant paw and placed it gently on her bent knee, then leaned forward and swiped her cheek with his tongue, just once. Heidi stood again, wiping her eyes. "Look after him," she said to Mitch, and then, long braids hanging down a ramrod straight back and hands curled into fists at the ends of fringed sleeves, she left.

CHAPTER 41

Abby handed Mitch a mug of tea as he came back into the kitchen after tucking in the girls—and Hope. She still couldn't quite believe the evening's turn of events, and judging by Mitch's bemused expression, he felt the same.

"Well," he said, meeting her gaze.

"Well," she echoed. She raised her cup to clink against his. "Here's to miracles?"

"That's kind of what that was, wasn't it?" He shook his head in disbelief. "I still can't believe she just gave him to us like that."

"I think she saw it more as him choosing to stay."

Mitch grunted. "It did look that way when he sat down like that, didn't it? He's quite the animal. And the girls like the name you gave him, by the way. So do I. Heidi was right. It fits him—and us."

"I'm glad." Abby hesitated. After all that had happened, it didn't seem right to put a damper on things tonight, but neither did she want to sit on the information she needed to share with Mitch.

"Something on your mind?"

She sighed. The sooner he knew...

"I've been going over the books."

Mitch paused mid-sip, regarding her over the rim of

the mug. He swallowed his tea. "I'm not hearing good news in your tone."

"No. You're not," she said bluntly, because there was no gentle way to tell him. "Derek's office wasn't an indicator of his bookkeeping skills after all, Mitch. The ledgers are a mess. Half the entries are in the wrong place, and several months' worth of invoices weren't entered at all."

Mitch gaped at her.

"And that's not the worst of it," she forged on. "You've maxed out the company credit line and you're two months behind on payments, and your tax returns weren't filed last year."

Shocked disbelief stared back at her from the green eyes. "You're kidding me."

"I wish I were. But the good news is that you have enough funds in the checking account to make up the missing payments and cover about three months more, and I'm finding a lot of unpaid receivables as well. I'm just not sure it will be enough to keep you afloat long term."

"Hell," he said. "Freaking, goddamn, bloody *hell*." He set his mug on the counter and turned away to pace the kitchen, hands on hips, coming to a halt by the sliding doors.

His reflection in the glass was too dark for Abby to see his expression, but there was no mistaking the weary droop of his head or the sag of his shoulders—a far cry from the buoyant air he'd worn when he'd joined her a few minutes ago. Abby set her own cup on the counter beside his and waited, because she had no words to offer.

"How long do you think I can keep going?" he asked at last.

"Four to six months would be my guess. But you're going to need an accountant to do your taxes before you know for sure."

He blew out a long, slow breath. "When Derek said he was overwhelmed, I guess he wasn't kidding. But I had no idea know how bad it was."

"I'm guessing you did the books before?"

He snorted. "Hardly. I don't exactly get along with columns of numbers. Trevor took care of them for us, before we had to let him go six months ago."

That date dovetailed with the sudden decline in ledger-keeping that Abby had seen. She bit her bottom lip, watching Mitch's broad back. One last thing niggled at her.

"Mitch, you said you have to buy out your partner, but even if you manage to keep the company going for now, I don't think you have enough funds for that."

"Yeah. I figured as much." His mouth drew tight.

"What will you do?"

"No idea. We had an offer on the company last year that we turned down. Derek says they're still interested in buying out his share, but if we're in the condition you say, they're not going to want to pay him the original amount. That kills me," Mitch said, "because the company was Derek's retirement plan, and I was the one who talked him out of selling. I don't know what he and Paul will do, especially now that Paul is sick. Freaking *hell*."

"It's not your fault. Things—"

"Things happen. I know. But sometimes we make them happen, too, and that's what this is, Abby. This was me ignoring Derek's concerns." Mitch swiveled on his heel, hands raking over his short-cropped hair. His mouth took on a bitter twist. "Turns out that's a bit of a pattern for me, don't you think?"

"I think you're upset," she replied equably, "and not thinking clearly."

Anger flashed in the pale green depths of his eyes, reminding her that—despite their new closeness over the last few days—she was still technically his employee. She hesitated for a second, then shrugged off the misgivings and continued, "I also think you shouldn't jump into any decisions just yet. Get the taxes done—I can have the books ready for the accountant by Friday—and then figure out where to go from there. Derek gave you a month, remember?"

"Filing the taxes won't change anything. I still won't have the funds to buy him out."

"No, but your taxes will be paid, and you'll have three more weeks to explore options."

"Are you always such an optimist?"

"Are you always such a pessimist?" she countered.

Mitch scowled. Then a corner of his mouth twitched. Then he shook his head. "Fine," he said. "No hasty decisions. Happy?"

"Yes." Abby nudged his mug across the island counter. "Your tea's going cold."

He strolled back to join her, settling onto one of the stools. "Speaking of decisions and changing the subject, what about you? Have you given any thought to the university idea?"

"A little."

"But?"

"But..." Abby hesitated. An idea had been in the back of her mind for the last few days, but she hadn't stopped to examine it, and she wasn't sure she was ready to share it. On the other hand, there was no real reason not to, because it might give Mitch the breathing space he needed for the decisions he needed to make. Across the island, Mitch frowned.

"But...?" he prompted again.

She took a deep breath. "I've been thinking of extending our agreement for a few months. You have a lot on your plate right now, and you're going to have no choice but to focus on the business until you get it sorted out. Plus, if the pediatrician refers Kia for occupational therapy the way we expect, there will be extra work there, too. Appointments, practice. No matter how organized I get you here, Mitch, there just aren't going to be enough hours in a week for you to do it all. Not while you're running the business singlehandedly."

For a long moment, Mitch stared down at his tea—surely it had to be stone cold by now—and said nothing. Then he looked up to meet her gaze, but not with the enthusiasm Abby had expected. "And what about your life?" he asked. "What about whatever it was you planned to do when you left here?"

She gave a short laugh. "I have no plans for when I

leave because I have no clue what to do with my life. The three-month idea came out of sheer panic, when I didn't think I could survive caring for your children while never seeing Olivia again." Sympathy flashed across Mitch's face, and Abby waved a hand at it. "But I was wrong. Being here has been good for me. The girls have been good for me. And I really would like to help all of you get back on your feet. I just don't think it's possible in our original timeframe."

"It's a generous offer," he said. "Are you're sure it's what you want to do?"

She didn't mean to hesitate, but somehow a silence wedged itself between her and an answer. Between her and Mitch. Because there was so much more than just three children and the running of a household between them now. There were moments and touches that Abby didn't know how to interpret, and somehow an offer to stay had become entangled with all of that and more, and dear Lord, she'd *kissed* the man, and—

Mitch stood and carried his mug to the sink, dumping its contents there and then putting it into the dishwasher. After crossing the room again, he paused beside her, so close that his heat reached out to prickle along her bare forearms. So close that she had to tip her head back to meet the gaze that reflected back her own uncertainties.

"I'll give it some thought," he said. "And you should, too."

Mitch didn't have the heart to face the office after Abby's revelations about the company finances—nor did he have the brainpower after whatever the hell that had been in the kitchen—so he climbed the stairs to the second floor. He stopped at the top, hand resting on the railing, staring at the wall opposite and pondering her offer.

No. Not the offer so much as what had followed it.

Because that—whatever it had been—had given him pause.

His initial reaction had been one of overwhelming relief and gratitude, but vague reservations had almost immediately tempered it. He remembered all the times he'd noticed things about her he shouldn't have: her laugh, the crinkle of her eyes when she smiled, the way her hair cascaded around her shoulders, the curve of her hip, the soft translucence of her skin. Her unexpected, fleeting kiss. The way she fit against him when he'd held her.

Damn, how he wanted to hold her again.

Mitch exhaled a ragged breath. And therein lay his reservations, he realized.

Abby had made it clear that she regretted the kiss and that she wanted it to go no further. As much as

Mitch wanted to convince her otherwise, they both had too much at stake to treat this with anything but the utmost seriousness. Mitch had three daughters to think of, and Abby had her own life to consider... for the first time *in* her life. And Mitch was all too aware that his continued reliance on Abby put her right back where she'd been when she was married to William.

Not something he wanted to do.

Even if she'd offered.

And God knew he could use the help.

And—

He sighed.

And standing at the top of the stairs arguing with himself was getting him nowhere. He needed to get some sleep and do what he'd told Abby he would: give her idea some thought. A lot of thought. He also needed to consider what the hell he was going to do about the company, and Derek, and Kiana, and all the rest of the tangled mess his life had become.

And freaking hell, now he was thinking of his youngest as part of the "mess"? He couldn't even begin to count the shades of wrong in that.

Wearily, he dropped his hand from the railing and turned left, toward his daughters' rooms and his final check on them for the night.

In the kitchen, Abby listened to the creak of the floor above her as Mitch traveled from room to room on his nightly rounds. She still stood at the island, but only because she gripped the countertop so hard that her hands ached. It was the only way to stop herself from running after Mitch to apologize for her hesitation and to explain... what? That she wanted to stay but it was complicated? Her insides writhed at the thought. She couldn't say for certain where Mitch's thoughts had gone when she hadn't answered him, but she suspected they had followed her own. Were things as complicated for him as they were for her? The idea made her writhing insides turn molten, and she groaned into the kitchen's silence.

None of this was supposed to happen. She'd come here because she needed a job, not a man—and certainly not a man with three children and as much baggage as she carried herself. They were both still grieving, for heaven's sake. They were *all* still grieving. That was no foundation for—for whatever this was they were doing.

No, she'd been right to hesitate, and Mitch had been right to walk away. Staying wasn't the answer—not when it evoked this kind of panic in both of them. But she still wanted to help, and—

Abby caught her breath as a new idea sidled into her mind. It settled there, and she watched it unfold. She blinked at its simplicity, its absolute perfection—except for two small details. First, Mitch would never accept it, so he could never know; and second, if it was going to work at all, she would have to move fast.

She pressed her lips together and straightened her shoulders, then reached for the cell phone charging on the counter by the fridge and called her brother-in-law.

CHAPTER 43

Abby spent the next morning obsessively checking her cell phone for missed calls and messages. By 11:30, she was scowling at its lack of alerts. Had she not been clear enough in the voicemail she'd left for Gareth? What part of *important* had he not understood? Should she call again? Call Gwyn instead? Dear Lord, how hard could it be to pick up her message and call her ba—

The cell in her hand trilled, startling her into dropping it onto Mitch's desk, where she'd been pretending to work. She scrabbled to retrieve it, glanced at the display, and answered with a breathless, "Gareth —finally!"

"Is everything okay?" her brother-in-law asked. "Your message said important but not urgent, or I would have called sooner."

"No—no, everything is fine. I was just being impatient." Abby reined herself in and took a deep breath. She stood up from the desk and began pacing the room. "I've been thinking about our conversation. Does your offer still stand? Because I think I want to hire that L.A. law firm after all." Silence met her words, and she swallowed. "You changed your mind."

"I haven't changed my mind at all. In fact..." Gareth

cleared his throat at the other end of the line. "I—ah—kind of took it upon myself to get things started for you after we talked that day. I was afraid if you waited any longer, you'd be too late, and I was right. A decision was rendered on Monday."

The world rushed away in a haze of disappointment. "I missed it?" she whispered. "The money is... gone?"

"God, no. That's not what I meant at all," Gareth said cheerfully. "The estate goes to you."

She reeled under this news, too. "What, just like that? Without any kind of fight?"

"As the surviving spouse, that's the law."

"But what about William's sister? Her lawyer said—"

"Her lawyer said what lawyers are paid to say—a lot of nonsense. The court struck down her claim and signed off on probate on Monday. The law firm couriered the papers here because I didn't know if you'd told Gwyn about the estate, and I didn't want to ask her for your address and stir up more trouble between you two. As soon as they arrive, you'll need to see a lawyer here to prove your identity and have everything notarized. Then the California firm will transfer the funds to the Ottawa firm, and they'll issue you a check. Altogether, it should only take about three to five business days. If you want a good financial planner, I can give you the name of ours, by the way."

"I suppose that might be a good idea," she mumbled, still processing the *all* part of the conversation—and the part where, if Gareth hadn't gone ahead on her behalf, she would have been too late to claim anything because she'd been too blinded by grief and guilt to care.

She would have been too late to help Mitch and the girls—assuming there was even enough in the estate to do so.

Gareth snorted. "For that amount? I would think so."

Assuming there was enough to help th—

Abby's thoughts ground to a halt as Gareth's words registered. Hope had padded over to nudge a wet black nose into her hand, and absently, she patted the broad head. "What do you mean, *that* amount? What amount?"

"Oh, that's right—you thought most of the money was his family's."

"It wasn't?"

"Not by a long shot, Abby. William supported his family, not the other way around. You have a check coming for eleven million dollars. And those are U.S. dollars."

Gareth continued talking, but Abby heard nothing more than a few words amid a lot of noise.

"... multi-million-dollar corporation..."

The sound of her own heartbeat thundered in her ears.

"... offshore assets..."

Her breath caught in her throat.

"... debts paid off..."

She wanted to swallow—needed to swallow—but couldn't.

"... could be years..."

"Stop," she grated. She fumbled for the chair behind Mitch's desk and dropped into it. "Just... let me catch my breath. Please."

"Of course." Warm sympathy underlined Gareth's voice. "This must be quite a shock."

"You have no idea." Abby held her free hand in front of her and stared at its tremble, then curled it into a fist and let it drop to her lap. "*I* had no idea. William never said—he told me—I don't understand why."

"I have a theory, but it's not a nice one."

How bad could it be? "I'm listening."

"I think it was another way of controlling you. If you didn't think he had any money of his own, you wouldn't try to divorce him."

Abby considered the idea, wondering how numb she had to be that it didn't even surprise her. Hope nudged under her hand again, and she stroked the silky ears. "I think you're right," she said quietly, thinking back to how secretive William had been about money over their years together. And how angry. Had he really been so afraid of her leaving that he had pushed her away with his behavior? "How sad," she murmured.

"That's one word for it," Gareth's said, his tone hard. "I can think of others. But I don't suppose there's any point now."

"No." She leaned her head back against the chair and stared at the ceiling. "No, I don't suppose there is. So, slowly this time, tell me the details again."

Patiently, Gareth explained California's inheritance laws. He listed her late husband's assets and liabilities, naming sums that made Abby's mind boggle and her chest go tight. Then he told her that the L.A. lawyers were forwarding a complete list along with the other papers, and finally, he summed it all up.

"So, eleven million U.S. after the attorneys' fees are paid, plus the proceeds from the house in L.A., once the sister pays you for William's share. And a rather enormous weight off your shoulders when it comes to finances, I suspect."

"Rather."

"Do you want the name of the financial planner now, or would you like some time to absorb everything? I imagine it's a lot to take in."

"It is a lot," Abby agreed. Then she sat up straight in the chair, remembering her reason for calling Gareth in the first place last night—and for waiting so impatiently for his return call. Because while her own life-planning could wait, that of Mitch and his daughters could not. "But I need the name of a good lawyer here in town, first," she told her brother-in-law. "I want to make a business investment."

"You should have told me about the finances." Mitch tried to keep the accusation from his voice, but the silence on the other end of the call told him he might not have succeeded. He pinched the bridge of his nose between the thumb and fingers of his free hand and closed his eyes, slumping against the door of his pickup. Outside, the snow fell thick and fast. At this rate, they'd break their winter average before Christmas. Right about the time he had to pull the plug on the company. He made a concerted effort to unlock his jaw.

He'd pulled off the highway and into a parking lot to take Derek's call, and he'd promised himself he'd ask about Paul before he launched into Abby's findings. He tried again.

"Sorry. I have a lot on my mind right now. How's Paul doing?"

"Resting. He has pneumonia, so they've delayed his first treatment until the new year. And I'm sorry about the books, Mitch. I know I should have said something, but you were already dealing with so much, and I fell behind, and..." Derek trailed off, sounding old and tired, and Mitch's gut twisted. The older man had been nothing but good to him throughout Eve's illness, taking on far more than he'd signed on for with their partnership, despite his own declining health. He deserved the same consideration from Mitch, now that the tables were turned.

Mitch tipped his head from side to side, trying to ease the tension in his neck and shoulders. It didn't work. He sighed. "It's all good," he said. "Abby's working through the books this week, and I'm turning them over to the accountant on Friday for the taxes. I'll figure things out."

"Taxes..." Derek mumbled. "Hell. I forgot about those."

Mitch winced at the admission and set his jaw again to keep the words locked in.

"I think I forgot to make the payment on the line of credit this month, too," Derek continued. "You might want to have her check that."

Mitch breathed in deeply through his nose. "Yeah. She mentioned it."

"How bad?" Derek asked heavily. "Be honest."

If Mitch could have found a way to lie, or seen a point in doing so, he might have tried. But Derek's hiding things from him was what had gotten them into this mess, at least partly, and Mitch would be doing neither of them any favors by perpetuating the habit.

"It's bad," he said. "We're behind on payments and taxes, and we're maxed out the line of credit. Abby says that at this rate, I've got another four to six months left before I have to shut down completely."

"God, Mitch. *That* bad?"

"Yep."

"There's no way you can buy me out."

"Nope."

"I'm so sorry."

"I know." And he did know. Deep, deep, deep down. He just had one or two things of his own to worry about at the moment, such as keeping a roof over his kids' heads and continuing to feed them. "I know," he said again. "And I meant what I said. I'll figure it out. But you need to worry about you and Paul, my friend, so I want you to call Alex Peterson and offer him your share of the company. Things may be a bit rocky right now, but the Abrams Construction name is still worth a lot in this town, so don't let him talk you down from last year's offer. Promise me."

"Mitch, I—"

"Promise."

"I promise."

"Good man. Now go make that husband of yours a cup of tea or something, and tell him I said hi. Oh, and if you guys aren't doing anything on the twenty-third, the girls are planning a Christmas party and they'd like you to come. It's a potluck."

"I think that's an excellent idea, if Paul's up to it. Will we get to meet that miracle worker you hired?"

"Abby?" In spite of himself, Mitch smiled at the very apt description. "Yes, she'll be there."

"You tell your daughters I said we'll be there. I'll get Paul to make his famous chili."

Mitch ended the call and sat with cell phone in hand, staring at the windshield now covered in snow. Telling Derek to go ahead and call Peterson had been tough, but not nearly as tough as he'd expected, given he'd been up most of the night worrying about it. It actually felt pretty good, like a load had been lifted from him. Like he was finally getting himself organized and on the right track—even if it did mean giving up some of the control he'd fought so hard to keep.

Now if he could only manage to get his family on their right track, too.

And Abby on hers.

He dropped the cell phone onto the passenger seat, started the truck, turned on the wipers, and then pulled out into traffic, hands clenched around the steering wheel. He'd start by refusing her offer to stay longer.

Even if it meant lying to her about the reasons.

For her sake.

Soon.

CHAPTER 44

The next week passed in a blur for Abby. In between tackling the usual household chores and finishing the books for the accountant, she made treats for three separate class Christmas parties and a costume for Kiana's part in the school concert, fielded multiple phone calls and meetings with the local lawyer Gareth had recommended, made appointments for the girls with their dentist and optometrist, and slowly pieced together the family binder she'd started for Mitch.

Before she knew it, it was Friday again, and the binder sat on the desk before her in all its organized glory. It was a masterpiece, even if she did say so herself, containing everything Mitch could possibly need to help him look after his house and family, with half the binder devoted to each. Under family, there was a section for health with all of their records, contact names, and a schedule of upcoming appointments; another section for school records and extracurricular activities; and yet another for the dog. Under house, she had filed all the instruction manuals and warranties, along with the home maintenance schedule she'd found in the back of a filing drawer, in handwriting Abby assumed to have been Eve's. She'd also found a file of paint chips labeled by room, and that information had gone in as well.

It was the kind of thing she imagined Eve would have approved of and would probably have done herself, if she'd had the time. A labor of love for a family who needed all the help they could get.

Within its pages, Abby had answered every possible question and covered every contingency she could think of—and now she had no idea what to do with it. She rested an elbow on the chair's armrest, fingertips against her lips, and stared at the four-inch binder. Should she present it to Mitch now, in an offhand, oh-by-the-way manner? Leave it on the desk for him to find? Give it to him along with the keys to the house and SUV when she departed?

It should have been easy.

"Mitch, I made this to help you out once I'm gone."

But it wasn't, and for the life of her, Abby couldn't figure out why.

"Problems?" Mitch's voice asked. She looked up to find him in the office doorway, buttoning up the sleeve on a pale blue dress shirt, tie looped over his shoulders. Instant befuddlement settled into her brain, rendering her speechless because, wow, he cleaned up nicely. Through the fog, she tried to string her thoughts back together. Tie. Dress shirt. There was a reason for those, but darned if she could remember—

Mitch frowned. "You're not ready. Did you change your mind?"

Had she changed her mind about wha—

Her eyes widened in horror. "Kiana's school concert!" she exclaimed. "I totally forgot."

"You really don't have to do this, if you'd rather not." Mitch did up his other sleeve. "It's been a long week for you—and a tough time. Kia will understand."

To her shame, Abby considered the out he offered. It *had* been a long week—made longer by Mitch's renewed habit of not coming home until the kids were in bed—and they were only one day from the party. The date had loomed bigger and darker in her mind the closer it got, while she had steadily become more and more regretful that she'd agreed to it. What in heaven's name had she been—

Kia twirled past Mitch into the office. "Daddy, Daddy! Look how pretty I am!" She did another pirouette and stopped in front of him. "See? I'm all white and silver and sparkly like the snow." She pointed to her white tights and silver tulle skirt, dotted with the snowflakes Abby had stitched onto it, then to the white sweatshirt embellished with another glittering, slightly lopsided snowflake. "And Abby let me help paint the snowflake on the front of me, too."

Not waiting for him to confirm the costume's beauty, she did three more spins and staggered to another halt, this time in front of the desk. She took in Abby's appearance, and her face fell. "You're not ready," she echoed her father's words. "Aren't you coming?"

And that answered the question of whether Abby could skip out on the evening.

"Of course I'm coming," she assured the little girl,

who rewarded her with another beaming smile. "I just finished in here, and it will take me two minutes to change. I'll even bet I'm ready before you get your boots and coat on."

"A race?" Kia beamed brighter. "On your mark, get set, go!" She turned and ran from the office, yelling to her sisters that it was time to go, and at Hope to move out of the way.

Mitch grinned and shook his head. "I didn't even get a word in edgewise," he said. "But she's right. She looks beautiful. You put in a lot of work on that costume."

Abby shrugged and leaned down to open the bottom desk drawer. "It wasn't as complicated as it looks. Just a bit finicky getting the snowflakes onto the skirt." Aware of his gaze tracking her, she slid the binder into the drawer and closed it again, making a mental note to retrieve it before bed and put it somewhere safer until she'd made up her mind about it. Then she stood and headed for the door, stopping when Mitch didn't give way. "Umm..."

"Are you sure you're up to this?" he asked, studying her face while he adjusted the tie and expertly knotted it.

"I promised the girls I'd go."

"And they will understand if you can't. I'll talk to them. The accident anniversary is tomorrow, Abby, and the party, too. If you go to the concert tonight..." A gentle hand lifted her chin until she had no choice but to meet the concern in his eyes. "You need time for you."

"I've had plenty of that in the evenings all week, while having tea by myself." The words slipped out before she could think better of them. She pulled away from Mitch's hand and stared at his shoulder. "I'm sorry. I have no right to—"

"You have every right." He sighed. "And I'm the one who should be apologizing. The truth is, I've been avoiding you—and the conversation we need to have."

She knew, then. Knew why he'd taken to working late and skipping dinner with them. And why giving him the family binder was so hard. He was going to decline her offer to stay—and she didn't want to go. The realization slid down her throat to land like a boulder in the pit of her stomach. How? How had that happened? At first, she hadn't wanted to stay at all, and now she didn't want to leave. Not the girls, not the house she'd come to think of as home, and not Mitch.

Mitch. Her view of his shoulder blurred. Tall, strong, compassionate Mitch. Mitch reading stories to his youngest daughter, helping his older ones with their homework, quietly allowing Hope onto Kia's bed, holding Abby tight when her story spilled from her.

Air. She needed air.

Breathe, Abigail.

She did, inhaling just enough to croak, "I should get ready."

The concert was a smash hit—at least, Abby assumed it was, from all the laughter and applause that surrounded her, because she didn't take in much of it herself. Oh, sure, she laughed and clapped along with the rest of the audience, and she even kept her eyes trained on the stage, but she saw nothing of what happened there. Instead, her gaze was turned inward, focused on memories of past school concerts, the brush of Mitch's suit jacket sleeve against her arm, the turmoil in her heart, and that one nagging question: How?

How had she managed to do this to herself? How, amid all the chaos and darkness in her life, had she managed to find a light as bright as the Abrams family, only to stand on the verge of losing them, too? How had she let her defenses slip that much? And, above all else, how would she ever manage to walk away?

"Kia's up," Mitch murmured in her ear, and she yanked her attention back to the stage, where a beaming little snowflake flapped her hands in excitement and bounced in a circle.

Abby forced a smile and raised a hand in the promised wave so Kiana could see where she and Mitch were seated with Rachel and Britt. The little girl and her classmates all blurred around the edges a bit, and Abby drew a shaky breath. Beside her, Mitch leaned in again as the first chords of "Frosty the Snowman" tinkled cheerily from the piano.

"You okay?"

She nodded, not even trying for a voice while snowflakes twirled and spiraled onstage, and children wearing scarves and hats paraded behind a giant, crooked snowman that swayed perilously from side to side. According to the program, this was the final performance of the evening. When it ended, everyone would go home, and she and Mitch would have the conversation he'd asked for, and she would...

She had no idea what she would do. Grit her teeth and pretend it didn't matter? Beg him to reconsider? Tell him how she felt? The last option made her swallow a snort, given that she hadn't fully sorted it out for herself.

Liar, her inner voice whispered. *You know exactly how you feel. You just don't want to admit it.*

Applause broke out around her, making her jump. Mitch and the girls stood up and others in the audience followed suit, giving a standing ovation to the beaming performers returning to the stage. And then kids were swarming the floor, and parents were swarming the stage, and merry mayhem ensued amid holiday wishes and farewells that seemed to last forever and end all too soon.

The girls chattered nonstop as they trooped out to the SUV with Mitch, all vying for his attention. Abby trailed them, watching her breath fog in the cold night air and peering up at the star-studded velvet sky beyond the parking lot lights. She picked out the Big Dipper, searched for Cassiopeia, and wondered again which pinpoint of light marked her daughter's peephole.

A small, mittened hand slipped into hers halfway to the vehicle.

"Did you know that stars are angel lights?" Kia asked, turning her face toward the heavens. "The angels make them so we know they're watching us. That one"—her other mitten pointed upward—"is Mommy's light. Which one is Olivia's?"

Abby cleared the lump out of her throat. "I'm not sure," she said. "I don't know how to find her."

"Hm." Kia pulled her to a stop and studied the sky with a frown. Then her brow cleared and she smiled her satisfaction. "There," she said, pointing again. "The little one beside Mommy. And the one on the other side of her is her daddy. They're keeping each other company so they don't get lonely without us."

Crouching beside her, Abby followed the line of Kia's arm to where three stars seemed isolated from the others around them, sitting in a crooked line, the middle one smaller than its companions. She smiled. "I do believe you're right, darling girl. Should we wave?"

"We should blow kisses."

And they did, three each at Kia's insistence. "Because we're all family now," she explained, and Abby very nearly shattered on the spot. She scraped herself together the best she could and stood again.

"Come on," she told the little girl. "I'll race you to the car."

CHAPTER 45

Mitch circled his office, waiting for Abby to say good-night to the girls and come downstairs again. He'd wanted to put their conversation off until after Christmas, but given the palpable tension between them all evening and the way she'd jolted every time his sleeve brushed her bare arm, it seemed sooner would be better. For both their sakes, he had to tell her that he wasn't accepting her offer to stay longer. That he had to let her go.

Even if it damn near killed him just to think it.

He pulled the chair away from his desk and dropped into it, tipping back to stare at the ceiling and trying to imagine the house without her in it. All he could summon was a sense of emptiness. Abigail Jamieson had only been here a month and a half, and already she belonged in a way he'd never thought another woman could belong.

And yet, she didn't.

Because she deserved more than to move from the life she'd had with William to a life that paralleled it in far too many ways—and not good ones. She deserved to go to school and make her own friends and do what *she* wanted for once. If she stayed here, with him and his girls, she wouldn't have those opportunities. Oh, they might start off with good intentions, but with his business already struggling and Kia's needs and the girls already depending on her so heavily, it would be just a matter of time before their intentions fell by the wayside and Abby disappeared beneath the household responsibilities, the way she once had with William. And the way Eve had with Mitch.

He cringed at the memory, then set his jaw.

Nope. No way he'd do that to another woman. And no way he'd set that example for his daughters, either.

At his waist, his cell phone vibrated. He unclipped it and saw Derek's name on the screen. His thumb hovered over the "Decline" button, but he hesitated. Derek never called this late at night. What if it was an emergency? Something with Paul? He sighed and hit "Accept."

"Hey," he said. "Everything okay?"

"Better than okay," Derek replied, sounding happier—and younger—than he had in months. Maybe years. "Didn't you get any of my voicemail messages? I've been calling since three this afternoon."

"Sorry. It was Kia's school Christmas concert this evening. I haven't checked my messages."

"Never mind. Doesn't matter. Are you sitting down?" Derek didn't wait for an answer. "I sold the shares, Mitch. Signed the papers this afternoon. I'm done. Out. Finished."

Mitch's stomach hit the floor. He leaned an elbow on his desk, cradled his forehead in his free hand, and closed his eyes. Digging deep, he summoned what he hoped sounded like happiness for his partner. "That's great," he said. "Seriously. I'm happy for you, Derek. Did Peterson give you what you were asking for?"

"It wasn't Peterson."

Mitch's head came up and his eyes snapped open. "What do you mean, it wasn't Peterson? Who was it?" *And why do you sound positively gleeful?*

"No idea. I got a call from a lawyer on Monday with an offer twice what I was hoping for. The investor wants to remain anonymous, so all there is on the papers is a numbered company."

The blood in Mitch's veins ran cold, and he lunged upward from the chair. "Wait, so you're saying some stranger now owns half my damned company?" His voice had risen several decibels by the last word, and he made a concerted effort to bring it under control. "You've got to be kidding me, Derek. Why would you do that without consulting me?"

"Could you have matched the offer?"

Mitch didn't respond.

"That's why," Derek said. "But don't get your knickers in a twist, because I also retain a ten percent share in the company, so whoever is behind this only has forty. That makes him a silent partner. A silent partner with deep pockets and an awfully wide streak of generosity, I might add. You'll want to sit down again."

How had he—? Mitch waved away the suggestion. "Go on."

"The line of credit has been paid in full."

Mitch nearly dropped the phone. He sat. "Excuse me?"

"You heard me. And there's been a deposit made to our operating budget. Fifty grand. Enough to bring back Trevor to run the office. I already called him, and he says he can start after Christmas. And you can hire some new guys for the extra jobs you'll be able to take on again. Before you know it, you'll be back up to where we used to be."

Mitch opened his mouth. Shut it. Opened it again. Then he shook his head in numbed silence. Nope. He had nothing. No words. No reaction. Nothing.

"I know, right?" Derek said, his voice carrying a gratitude Mitch was too shocked to summon himself. "I have no idea who your guardian angel is, Mitch Abrams, but you just got a whole new lease on that company's life. I have to go now—Paul's waiting for me to watch a movie with him—but I wanted to make sure I gave you the news tonight. I'll see you tomorrow for the party, and we can talk more then. In the meantime, go pour yourself a stiff drink and give yourself time to let everything sink in, okay?"

The connection went dead.

For long minutes, Mitch sat without moving, trying —as Derek suggested—to absorb everything. But he couldn't. It was simply too big. Too much. Just last week, he'd taken the books in to the accountant and told her that, in addition to having the taxes done, he needed an honest look at the company's viability... and her recommendation for a bankruptcy trustee, if necessary. Now, the company was debt free and had enough to hire staff again, and Derek had retired. Comfortably.

The floor overhead creaked as Abby moved down the hall between his girls' bedrooms.

Abby.

Mitch's pulse gave a sudden jolt.

Abby. If the business was doing better and she didn't have to take on the office end of things, maybe they could figure things out. Maybe she could find time to go to school and have a life of her own and still be a part of theirs. Of his. Maybe he could make sure he took on enough of the family load to give her the space she needed. Maybe they could make this work. Maybe—

Maybe that's an awful lot of maybes, Abrams.

Freaking hell. He scowled at the desktop. Could there not be *any* easy answers in his life? Did everything need to be this damned complicated all the time? His gaze drifted down and came to rest on the bottom drawer, where Abby had put that binder she'd been looking at earlier. He hesitated, then pulled the drawer open and stared at the binder's bright blue cover. Its block title, hand lettered by Abby, made a corner of his mouth lift: *The All-You-Need-to-Know Abrams Household Guide.* He lifted the binder from the drawer's confines, set it on the desk, and flipped it open to a table of contents, color coded to match the index tabs running down the side and listing everything from medical and school information for each child to appliance warranties and paint colors—by room, no less. Everything Eve had known about and taken care of; everything Abby had found and sorted into one place;

everything Mitch had never even thought to track or handle.

Even the dog had his own section, with vaccine and sterilization certificates pre-dating his arrival. Heidi Leduc must have sent them, and Abby had looked after that, too. Seamlessly, effortlessly. The way she took care of a thousand other daily details that never disturbed his own life.

It was a lot.

An awful lot.

He flipped through the last pages to the end of the binder. Just inside the back cover, he found the university calendar he'd brought home for her. It had been folded back to the page for an undergraduate Bachelor of Science degree in psychology, with half the first-year compulsory courses circled. In the back of his mind, he heard again Abby's offer to stay longer—and her telling silence when he'd asked if she was sure it was what she wanted to do.

In the doorway, Abby cleared her throat. Mitch replaced the course calendar and closed the binder. Then, steeling himself, he raised his gaze to hers.

"I can't stay," she said.

"I know," he replied.

She hovered in the doorway for a few seconds, her face pale but set, and then ventured into the room and sat opposite him in a chair he'd forgotten he owned, because it had been buried for so long beneath months' worth of stuff. He still couldn't get over how much she'd done to get them—him—organized in the few weeks she'd been here. And he still didn't want to think about how he would manage when she was gone.

But the time for that discussion had come.

Abby sat ramrod straight on the edge of the chair, linked her fingers in her lap, and lifted her gaze to meet his. "I know I said I'd be here for Christmas, but I'm going to ask Gwyn if I can stay with her and Gareth," she said. "This Christmas is important for you and the girls as a family, and I don't belong here."

Mitch clamped his teeth together to keep from objecting. Whatever her reasons for coming to that conclusion, it mattered only that she had, and that her decision to leave meshed with the one he had made. He leaned back in his chair. "Will you be coming back?" he asked.

The hands in her lap twisted together. "If you need me to, I will. But it would be better for the girls if I didn't."

So that was it. "Kia?" he hazarded.

Abby's gaze slid away for a second. Her effort to make it return to him was visible. "She's young," she said. "And I'm not sure she understands the meaning of *temporary*. After the concert tonight, she said—" Abby's voice wobbled. "She said we were all family now."

Silently, Mitch extended a hand across the desk to her, palm up. She shook her head.

"Don't," she whispered. "I don't think I can handle sympathy right now." Her hands became fists, pressing into her thighs, and she took a deep breath. "I'm afraid that the longer I'm here, the more attached she'll become. And I can't stay."

"I know," he said again, withdrawing his hand. "When...?"

"Tomorrow after the party, if it's all right with Gwyn and Gareth."

He took a deep breath of his own, tucking away the emptiness invoked by her words. Reminding himself that this was what he had wanted. Well, maybe not *wanted*. But Abby was right. It was best. He curled his own hands into fists beneath the desk, out of view.

"We can cancel the party. People will understand."

"I thought about it," she admitted, "but the girls have talked about it nonstop all week. It would crush them."

Not nearly as much as losing Abby would, he thought, but he nodded his agreement. "I'll tell the girls in the morning before I leave," he said. "But if it's all right, I won't say that you're not coming back. Not until Christmas is past."

"Of course. And you can tell them that I can still come and visit."

"Of course."

"And at least they have Hope to look after now. He'll be good for them."

"He will."

"And you have the binder." She nodded at his desk. "I put everything in there that I could think of, but you can call me if you have questions. And the schedule of optometrist and dentist appointments is in the front."

"I saw." And with a mysterious silent partner behind the company, he'd be able to hire the staff he needed to let him keep those appointments, too. Funny how things had worked out so well after all those months of chaos. Well, most things.

They sat in silence for moment, and then Abby stood and smoothed down the creases on the front of her pant legs. "Well," she said. "I should get to bed. Tomorrow will be a long day."

Mitch watched her walk to the door. He knew he should say something, but the words that piled up on his tongue had nothing to do with *thank you* and *goodnight*, and everything to do with *stay*. So he pressed his lips together, swiveled the chair around, and stared out the window into the darkness. Not until he heard the tread of her feet going up the stairs did he remember the reason tomorrow would be particularly long for her.

Olivia.

Damn.

CHAPTER 46

Abby woke the next morning with thoughts of Olivia heavy on her mind, but the girls were electric with excitement from the moment they hit the floor, providing a distraction for which she could not have been more grateful. As promised, Mitch had spoken to them before he headed out the door to meet a client and hand off the keys for the house his team had just finished, but after a moment of disappointment, the girls had recovered and thrown themselves into party preparation. Abby was grateful for that, too.

No amount of gratitude or distraction could entirely make up for the loss that lay beneath the excitement, however, and all day long, through all of the supervising and the party preparations, the words from her conversation with Mitch the night before followed her around like a pall, tangling with the pain of others already contained in the date.

"I have to go... I know... I'm sorry, ma'am, but your husband and daughter have been in an accident. There were no survivors... I have to go..."

"I finished dusting." Britt's voice wrenched her back to the present and to the party just around the corner. "And Rachel is cleaning the bathroom, and it's almost three o'clock, and people will be here in an hour. *Now* can we set the table?"

Abby forced a smile. "How about you get yourself all fancied up first? That way, you'll be clean before you set out the dishes, and if anyone gets here early, you'll be ready."

As anxious as Britt was to get the "fun stuff" under-way, she was equally thrilled about getting dressed up. Mitch had taken all three girls shopping the Sunday before, and each had a new outfit for the occasion: dresses for Rachel and Kiana, and a tuxedo-like affair for Britt—complete with sparkly white shirt and a red bow tie. Abby's suggestion, therefore, met with a whoop of joy, and Britt galloped down the hall and up the stairs to tell her sisters it was time to change. Abby took a moment to center herself, then went back to laying out a charcuterie board, the family's contribution to the potluck, under the watchful eye of Hope, who had apparently decided the kitchen needed his supervision more than Kia did for the moment.

The rumble of the garage door heralded Mitch's arrival as she unwrapped the brie and set it into an empty space on the charcuterie board. Her heart gave an unwelcome sideways skitter as Hope trotted away to the mudroom, leaving a nerve-wracked Abby to clear a space in the fridge for her creation.

"I have to go... I know..."

The door from the garage to the laundry room slammed, Mitch's deep voice greeted Hope, and then his footsteps came toward the kitchen. Abby closed the fridge to find him in the doorway, one hand scratching the dog's head, the other in his pocket, his expression as carefully neutral as she was trying to keep hers.

"Sorry I'm so late," he said. "The walk-through took longer than I expected. How are things coming along?"

Casual conversation for one more day, Abby. You can do it.

"We're just about ready. The girls are getting dressed, and then they'll put out napkins and dishes, and that's the last of it."

"And the other?" he asked. "You okay?"

The air left Abby's lungs in a little whoosh. *Which other?* she wondered. *Because they're both killing me... Olivia...leaving you and the girls...*

"I'm fine," she managed to say. His eyes told her he knew otherwise, but as the girls' feet thundered down the stairs, he nodded acceptance of her lie—yet one more thing for which to be grateful—and gave Hope a final pat on the head before going to admire his daughters and follow their instructions to hurry up and change.

Then Britt and Kia bounded into the kitchen in all their party finery, and Abby dug deep for the strength that would let her pretend everything was normal.

She'd survived losing her entire family once, she reminded herself.

Somehow, she would find a way to survive losing another.

Gwyn and Gareth were first to arrive, with four kids in tow and apologies from Gareth's daughter Amy for not joining them. Rachel and Britt hung coats and placed boots in the closet Abby had cleared out, Gareth solemnly shook hands with a giggling Kiana-Fred, and Abby made introductions between Mitch and her sister and brother-in-law. They hadn't even cleared the front entry when the doorbell announced the arrival of Derek and his husband, closely followed by Mitch's next-door neighbors. Before Abby knew it, the gathering was in full swing.

She smiled and chatted her way through the first hour before her sister cornered her in the kitchen, as Abby was refilling the charcuterie board with more sausage and crackers.

"Hey," Gwyn said, her voice soft and her blue eyes sympathetic. Abby's own eyes promptly filled with tears.

Gwyn pulled a tissue from the box on the island and handed it to her. "Would a hug make it better or worse?"

"Worse," Abby whispered. "Definitely worse." She dabbed at her eyes, blew her nose, and gritted her teeth behind a tight smile.

"I didn't put two and two together when you told me the date of the party. Christmas is a bit of a blur around our—" Gwyn broke off with a grimace, seeming to realize the insensitivity of her words. She waved an encompassing hand. "Why...?"

"Why this and why today? It seemed like a good idea at the time," Abby said, trying for a light tone, but her forced smile wavered. She had to pause to shore it up before she shrugged and said, "It's the girls' first

Christmas without their mom, and I wanted to give them some good memories to replace the other ones."

Good memories like having their nanny desert them? her inner voice wanted to know. Abby told it to shut up.

"And what about you?" Gwyn asked. "What about your memories?"

Abby's mouth twisted. "All very much still intact, trust me."

A shadow passed over Gwyn's face. "Oh, Abby."

Oh-Abby flapped her hands at her eyes and blinked rapidly, willing back more tears. She scowled at her sister. "Sympathy is *not* helping, f.y.i."

"I'm sorry, but seeing you like this—"

"Mom! Nicholas is eating all the shrimp!" the voice of Abby's niece preceded her into the kitchen.

Her nephew followed in full denial. "Am not! I only had six!"

"You wrapped the other tails in a napkin," Katie accused. "I saw you, and Mom said—"

"Out." Gwyn pointed at the door through which they'd come. "Mom said out. And Nicholas, no more shrimp."

Still bickering, Katie and Nicholas departed, and Gwyn heaved a sigh. "We're not going to have a chance to talk today, are we?"

Abby gave a small laugh. "Not likely, no."

"But soon? Can we maybe even set a date? We could meet for coffee or—"

"How's tonight?" Abby interrupted. "After I clean up here."

"Well, sure," Gwyn said, blinking a little at the suggestion, "but won't that be a bit late for going out? You'll be tired, and—"

"I could stay over at your place."

"You—I—" Gwyn stared at her, a furrow between her brows. "Abby? What's going on?"

"I—Mitch and I—the girls—" Abby bit her lip, not knowing how to explain. She shook her head. "I need somewhere to stay, Gwyn. It will only be for a few days, until I get my own place. If it's a problem, I can stay in a hotel instead."

"It's Christmas. You're not staying in a hotel."

Abby nodded acceptance of the statement. Then she warned, "But I can't answer questions. Not about this."

Gwyn came around the island and wrapped her in a brief, fierce hug. "Then I won't ask any," she promised. She released her hold and turned to pick up the refilled charcuterie board. "You take your time and catch your breath. I'll put this back on the table and try to keep everyone clear of here for a few minutes." She stopped in the doorway to look back. "Will you need a ride?"

Abby hadn't thought that far ahead. She'd gotten used to having the SUV at her disposal, but she'd be leaving that behind, and she supposed she'd need to buy a vehicle now, too. At some point. But for now...

"I'll take a cab," she said.

CHAPTER 47

"Penny for them," Derek offered, handing Mitch a glass of amber liquid. "Oh, wait, I can afford more now that I've been bought out. How does a whole dollar sound?"

He chuckled at his own joke, and Mitch shook his head. "I'll miss your sense of humor," he said. "You were a good partner."

"I was," Derek agreed. "The best you had. Except when it came to bookkeeping."

"You were the only partner I had, and don't remind me. I think I died a thousand deaths when I realized how bad things were."

Derek shrugged beefy shoulders. "Meh. All's well that ends well, my friend. And you"—he raised his glass to Mitch—"are ending well indeed. New partner, Trevor back in charge of the office, no debts—I'd say that things are looking way up, and I couldn't be happier for you."

"Speaking of new partner, can you tell me *anything* about this investor?"

"I wish I could, but the lawyer's mouth was sewn up as tight as—" Derek looked around, seeming to remember he was in polite company. "Well, let's just say he wasn't talking."

Mitch scowled into the glass Derek had given him.

"Who does that?" he muttered. "What kind of investor pays better than market value for shares in a company that's up to its ass in alligators, clears its debts, and gives it a load of cash to top it off?"

"I told you—the guardian angel kind." Derek frowned at him, his bushy white brows meeting in the middle of his forehead. "Seriously, Mitch, stop knocking this. You've been given a *gift*. Accept it. Enjoy it. Make the most out of it. If not for yourself, then for those three little girls of yours. Hell, even if whoever's behind this turns around and sells the shares again, no one can move on you because you're still the majority shareholder. The company is yours, and it's safe."

"I suppose." Mitch sighed, met Derek's glower, and held up a hand to ward off more argument. "Fine," he said. "No more lectures. I'll relax."

"That's better." Derek held his glass aloft. "Here's to new challenges and adventures for both of us."

Mitch tipped his glass to clink against his former partner's and took a sip of the whisky, frowning as the round fullness of his best Scotch settled over his tongue. He shot a sharp look at Derek, who had turned and wandered off, sending him a sly grin over his shoulder.

"You should have known better than to show me where you keep the good stuff, Abrams," he called back with a chuckle. "And you need a new bottle, by the way."

Wonderful, Mitch thought. Just wonderful.

The rest of the party slid past in a haze for Abby. The

guest count swelled to at least thirty, including kids, and she stayed busy fetching and carrying, keeping an eye on Hope's predilection for snagging snacks off plates whose owners were distracted, smiling and laughing in all the right places, and chatting with everyone—including Jessica Perkins, who popped up at Abby's shoulder shortly after her arrival.

"You look like you could use this." Perky held out a glass of red wine to her.

Abby took the glass from her. She wasn't drinking today—alcohol and melancholy were a bad combination for her—but it seemed easier not to explain. "Thank you."

"You're welcome." Perky studied her for a moment. "Can I ask you a question?"

"Umm..."

"Why am I not picking up Rachel and Britt for school anymore?"

Maybe a little wine wouldn't hurt after all. Abby took a sip, let the wine swirl over her tongue while she debated a response, and then swallowed. "Why did you tell them women like me take jobs as nannies so that we can get married?"

"What?" Perky blinked at her, stepping to one side as a child hurtled by in pursuit of another—Abby had lost track of names, there were so many at the party. Perky stepped back again. "Who on earth told you—oh, God." She put one hand, fingernails painted the same bright red as her sequined camisole, to her mouth. "Is that—hell, no wonder—I—" She stopped, took Abby's arm, and towed her from the crowded living room to the slightly quieter front hallway.

Then she released her hold and faced Abby squarely. "First, I would never speak that way about another woman. Ever. God knows we have a hard enough time in this world without stabbing one another in the back. Second, if that's what you heard, I don't blame you for thinking the worst. And third, what you heard is *not* what I said." She shook her head, scowling. "Those two," she muttered, and Abby assumed she meant Mandy and Rachel, "can get things *so* twisted up in their heads."

"Right," she continued. "So here's what I *actually* said. After you arrived, the two of them asked me if I was serious about helping out Mitch with the house and stuff. I said of course, and they said wouldn't it be cool if the two of you—me and Mitch, I mean—got married. I just about killed myself laughing at that, because as much as I'd like to get into Mitch's pants, I am *not* the marrying kind. I told them it was far more likely that you and he would get hitched, because given that you were a nanny, you were almost certainly more nurturing than I would ever be, and men tended to like nurturing. Not that I think you're a pushover or anything," she hastened to add, "but you just have that air about you, you know?"

Abby gaped at her. "So they...?"

"Behaved like typical thirteen-year-olds and jumped to all kinds of conclusions."

"But—but things with Rachel got so much better after she and Britt stopped riding with you."

Amusement danced in Perky's eyes. "And did you stop to think it might be because Rachel had the chance to get to know you better and decided you weren't the threat she thought?"

"Well, I..." Abby put one hand to a hot cheek. "Lord," she whispered. "I am so, *so* sorry, Jessica."

"Meh." Jessica—not Perky—shrugged a shoulder. "I'm a divorcée and I'm not shy about going after what I want. You're not the first to consider me a threat, and I doubt you'll be the last. But if you're worried," she added with a sly smile, "you don't need to be. I promise to behave myself where Mitch is concerned. I've seen how he looks at you, and I know when to admit defeat. I'll be setting my sights elsewhere."

"I—I don't—" Abby stammered. But she didn't know how to finish—how to explain.

"So, can I start taking the girls to school for you again after the holidays?"

Abby nodded. "That would be great," she whispered, because it would be. For Mitch.

"Excellent." Jessica held up her glass and *tinked* it against Abby's. "Happy holidays, Abigail."

Before Abby could summon a response, the other woman was already back in circulation, sidestepping children, weaving her way back into the thick of things, stopping to tip her glass against others and bestow the customary kisses on cheeks. Abby watched her for a few moments, and then, almost without thinking, she glanced around the room in search of Mitch. He was standing with Gareth and one of the neighbors, Kia in his arms, his head thrown back and teeth flashing white in laughter. As if sensing her gaze on him, his laugh faded, and he turned to look at her through a gap in the gathering.

"*I have to go,*" her heart whispered.

"*I know,*" his pale green eyes said.

"Are we sure Abby can't have Christmas with us?" Kia asked, standing with Hope beside Abby's luggage in the front entry.

Mitch uncrossed one arm from the other and reached out to tweak one of his daughter's ponytails. "We're sure," he said, his voice gruff. "Abby has her own family, and they decided they want to see her, remember?"

"Well, they could have decided that *before* we got all excited," grumbled Brittany. "We got her a present and everything."

"And I'm sure she'll love it just as much when she opens it at Gwyn and Gareth's." Mitch glanced over his shoulder as Abby came out of the hallway from the laundry room with her coat and scarf over one arm and her ridiculously fuzzy boots in her other hand. She'd changed from the dress she'd worn for the party into her usual jeans and a turtleneck that molded itself to all the body parts Mitch still wasn't supposed to notice... but did. He cleared his throat.

"All set?" he asked.

She nodded, the ache in her expression making his heart hurt. For the thousandth time that day, he battled the urge to ask her to stay. He was certain she would.

He'd seen the answer in her eyes every time he'd looked her way, saw it now in the pale set of her face and the way her gaze lingered on each of the girls in turn, as if trying to memorize every detail. He would ask, and she would stay, and she would love them and care for them as Eve had done—and she would be lost in that love, as Eve had been lost.

"The cab is here," Rachel said from living room.

"That's my cue to get a move on," Abby said. She set the boots on the floor and stepped into them, then shrugged into her jacket and looped the scarf around her neck. Then, being Abby, she turned to the practicalities. "I've left everything you need for Christmas dinner in the fridge," she told Mitch. "All you need to do is roast the turkey—instructions are on the counter by the stove—and reheat the vegetables in the microwave. They'll keep warm in the oven while you carve the turkey and put everything together. Oh, and there's a gravy base in the fridge, too. You'll need to add some of the turkey drippings to it. If you have any questions—"

"I have your number," Mitch said, but they both knew he wouldn't call.

The doorbell rang, and Mitch held Hope back while Abby opened the door to the cab driver. The stocky man on the porch greeted them warmly, giving Kia a little wave as he took Abby's largest suitcase from her. He trundled it down the snow-covered sidewalk, and Abby turned back to face them. Taking a deep breath, she held her arms wide.

"All right, everyone," she said. "Line up for Christmas hugs!"

There was a flurry of activity as three bodies pressed in on her for individual hugs and then a giant group one, while Mitch held back on the pretext of controlling placid Hope. Then Abby was looking across at him and whispering goodbye, and the last two suitcases were disappearing out into the night with her, and Mitch was closing the door, and—

She was gone.

Mitch stared at his hand against the door for a long moment before he dropped it and turned back to the house—only to find his daughters lined up across the hallway with hands on hips and accusatory gazes fastened on him.

"We have a question," Rachel said with a scowl. "Exactly why does Abby need all her luggage for a couple of days with her sister?"

CHAPTER 48

"What do you mean, she's not coming back?" Rachel demanded. Her arms were crossed, now, and her scowl had deepened to a glower. Her sisters, one on either side, copied the stance—and the expression. Mitch might have smiled if the matter wasn't so serious.

Life-cripplingly serious.

"It was time for her to go," he said, wishing yet again that this conversation could have waited until after Christmas. But his daughters clearly would not be put off by excuses. "Abby did what she came here to do, and now she's finished. The house is clean and organized, she made us a binder that has everything we need to know in it, you girls are doing great, and I have a plan for keeping us all on track. All we need is someone to be here after school for you girls, and then we're ready to look after ourselves."

"What does *that* have to do with anything?" Brittany asked. "We like her. And she likes us."

"I know, sweetheart, but we knew this was temporary, remember? It's time for Abby to move on to her own life."

"Didn't she like looking after us?" Kiana asked, uncrossing her arms to wrap them around Hope's neck instead.

"Of course she did. But she has other things she likes to do, too. Such as going to university, and making her own friends, and—"

"So you're saying this was just a job for her," said Rachel.

"Well, yes. That's what we agreed it would be."

"If you married her, it wouldn't *be* just a job. We know you like her that way. Everyone knows. Mandy even heard Jessica tell Abby she was setting her sights elsewhere."

Jessica was giving up her pursuit? Well, at least that was one small candle in the current blackout. Mitch leaned his shoulder against the wall and stuck his hands in his pockets. "It's not that simple, Rach. Marriage is a really big step, and things are... complicated with Abby."

"Complicated how? You like her, she likes you. I'm not seeing complicated here."

Freaking hell. She wasn't going to let it go without an explanation, was she? Mitch regarded his eldest with a mix of exasperation and admiration, choosing his words carefully. "Abby's husband was a very controlling man, sweetheart. Mr. Jamieson liked things to be a certain way, and he expected her to stay home and look after him and Olivia and the house. He didn't let Abby have any of her own money, so she never had the chance to go to school or make her own friends. As much as we might love her, I'm afraid that if she stays with us, she'll end up doing more of the same things she did for her first family. You saw how hard she worked around here. I want her to have the chance to do more than just cook meals and clean house. I want her to have the chance to be just Abby, without having all these responsibilities. Do you understand?"

The green eyes narrowed. "You let Mom do all those things."

"And I'm sorry for that," Mitch replied, making a mental note to remove the knife from his heart later. "I made a lot of mistakes with your mom, and I want to learn from those and not make the same ones."

"Hm," said Rachel. Then, clearly pulling from her critical-thinking class at school, she added, "It sounds reasonable, but I think your logic is faulty. I can't figure out where, right now, but I'll let you know when I do."

Mitch swallowed a smile. "You do that. In the meantime, are we good? You guys will pitch in and help me run this place?"

"Of course. We want it to be tidy when Abby comes back." And with that, Rachel turned on her heel, summoned her sisters, and marched upstairs with them, Hope trotting behind.

CHAPTER 49

"We're calling a family meeting," Kiana announced from Mitch's office doorway. "In the kitchen. Rachel says now."

Mitch looked up from the estimate he'd been staring at for the last hour and eyed his youngest, who stood with the fingers of one hand wound into the shaggy coat of her ever-present companion. "She does, does she? Can I finish this first?"

Kia shook her head. "It's important."

"Did you guys decide on someone for after school?" He'd called Estelle Gagnon at Nannies to Go that morning, relieved to find her in the office so soon after Christmas, and she'd already emailed five resumés for part-time help. Mitch had particularly liked the look of one of them, but he'd learned his lesson and decided to solicit the girls' input this time around. He'd left the information on the island for them to review.

"We're not getting someone." Kia's eyes widened, and she slapped a hand over her mouth.

Mitch narrowed his eyes. "What do you mean, we're not getting someone?" he asked. "We've already discussed this. Someone has to be here for you girls after school."

Kia shook her head, removed her hand long enough

to say, "Can't say!" and then slapped it back in place and turned to go. Untangling her other hand from Hope's back, she beckoned Mitch to follow.

Mitch hesitated, then stood. It wasn't like he was getting any work done anyway. He'd been staring at the same column of numbers for an hour now, and he still hadn't come up with a tally. Besides, even without the ironclad family rule about attending meetings no matter who called them, curiosity would have driven him out of his chair and down the hall behind Kia.

In the kitchen, he stepped over a sprawled-out Hope and sat down on a stool at the island. "Thank you for clearing up the dinner dishes," he said, thinking he'd start things off on a positive note rather than demanding an explanation. "You guys are a great help at keeping us on track. "

"We told you, we're keeping things clean for Abby," Britt said.

Right. Mitch grimaced. So much for positive. He moved on. "So, what's this I hear about us not getting a housekeeper?"

"That's not what this meeting is about," Rachel said, looking smug. "I've figured out the problem with your logic."

"What logic?"

His eldest crossed her arms and scowled. "Your Abby logic."

Her *duh* hung in the air unspoken, but only barely.

Hell. Mitch leaned an elbow on the counter and braced a hand beneath his head, thumb resting on his cheekbone and fingers against his temple. How much longer could they keep up their bring-Abby-home efforts? For four days straight, from Christmas Eve until now, they had reminded him at every opportunity that they only did things so the house would be in good shape when Abby returned. They'd refused to open the gifts she'd left for them until then, too. Sighing, he wondered how much longer he could hold onto his own equilibrium in the face of their efforts, because God, he missed her, too. He missed her calm presence in the house, her smile, her laugh, the expression he saw in those smoky blue eyes when he caught her looking at him with her guard down, the faint scent of strawberries that tickled his nose when he stood close...

In a nutshell, everything. He missed everything, and he'd been second-guessing his decision to let her go ever since she'd walked out that door. And third-guessing it, and fourth-guessing, and—

"But first," Rachel continued, jarring him back to the kitchen, "we have a question. You know all those times you've told us women should make our own decisions in life? That we shouldn't let a man tell us what to do?"

"Unless it's a police officer or a doctor or something and he's trying to help us," Kiana added.

The corner of Mitch's mouth twitched as Rachel predictably rolled her eyes. "Yes, except those times," she agreed. "But do you remember, Daddy?"

"I remember."

"Were you lying to us?"

Mitch frowned at her. "Why would you say that? Of course I'm not lying. I absolutely believe women should make their own decisions. Your mother and I both did, and—where is this going?"

"Bear with me." Rachel locked her hands behind her back and paced the length of the island on the other side, watching him. "Do you also remember telling us that Abby's husband wouldn't let her do what she wanted, only what he wanted, and you didn't want that to happen to her anymore?"

"Yes, of course. But why—"

"Uh uh." Rachel held up an imperious hand. "Wait, please. One more question."

"That makes three, you know," he said dryly. "You said *a* question when we started."

Rachel ignored him, not even bothering to roll her eyes this time. "When you say *you* don't want Abby to have to clean house and look after us, and *you* want her to go to school and make friends and have her own life, doesn't that mean *you're* telling her what to do, too? Just like her husband did? Shouldn't you ask *her* what she wants and let her make her own decision about whether she stays with us or not?"

"It's hardly that simple, Rach."

"Why not?"

"Well, because you—how—but—" Mitch broke off and replayed Rachel's words in his head—twice. Freaking hell. *Was* it that simple? Had he really been so blinded by his good intentions that he'd taken Abby's decision-making capacity from her? He stared at Rachel as her truth sank in. He had. And his thirteen-year-old daughter had nailed it. She had discovered the flaw in his logic, which meant—

It meant nothing, because as wise as Rach's words might be, the decision to leave had been Abby's as well as his, and he couldn't dismiss the world of hurt he'd seen in her eyes when she'd sat across from him in his office after Kiana's concert and spoke those words. *"I can't stay...I'm afraid that the longer I'm here, the more attached she'll become. They all will. And I can't stay."*

"You make a good point," he allowed. "But"—this as a triumphant grin spread across her face—"that still doesn't change anything. Abby..." He trailed off and motioned for Rachel to join him on his side of the island. When she did, her smile fading, he took her hands in his and, looking at each of three girls, said, "Abby has been through a lot. Losing her husband and daughter at the same time was incredibly hard on her, and she's still healing from it. She's afraid of getting too close to other people in case she loses them, too, and that's why she wanted to leave. Why she had to leave."

The girls stayed silent for a moment, and Mitch held his breath, hoping he'd finally found the words to convince them she wasn't coming back, so they could start healing in her absence—him included, because seeing his daughters hurt all over again was killing him.

"But if we're not there and she's not here," Kiana said gravely, "doesn't that mean she's lost us already?"

"Well, yes," Mitch allowed, struggling for words, "I suppose it does, in a way, but she's trying to protect you girls, too. Because she knew how much you were starting to love her, and—"

"And now we've lost her already, too." Leaning her elbows on the island counter and cupping her face in her hands, Britt scowled at him. "Why do grownups have to make everything so complicated?"

Mitch tried to rein in his frustration. Love and loss at the level of Abby's were experiences that came with adulthood, he reminded himself, and he couldn't expect the girls to understand those experiences—or the sense of responsibility that came with them. He reached across with one hand and gave her arm a little squeeze. "Because sometimes being a grownup *is* complicated, sweetheart."

"Did you at least ask her to stay?" Rachel asked.

"No, but—"

"Didn't you want her to?"

"Well, yes, but—"

Rachel pulled from his grasp and held up both hands. "*You* want her to stay"—she ticked off the point on one finger—"*we* want her to stay"—another tick—"but we have no idea what *she* wants, because you didn't give her a choice." She shook her head. "I'm sorry, Daddy, but I really don't see the complicated part of that."

As if by some prearranged signal, all three of Mitch's daughters turned and headed for the kitchen door, where Britt paused and looked back to shake her head sadly before following the others down the hall. Mitch stared after them, then dropped his gaze to Hope.

The dog, while undoubtedly devoted first and foremost to Kia, had an intuitive ability to seek out and offer comfort to the person most in need of emotional support, and it spoke volumes that he'd chosen now to remain with Mitch, looking up at him with those intelligent, too-understanding brown eyes.

"Well, damn," Mitch said to him. "Now what?"

"You sure you won't come join us for a movie? Sean and Grace and the kids are here, and they'd love to see you."

Abby looked up from the couch and the magazine she wasn't really reading and summoned a not-really-smiling smile in response to Gwyn's query—and her concern. "Honestly, I think I'd rather just sit back here." She gestured at the sitting room addition her architect sister had designed. "It's peaceful."

And it didn't contain a pile of children that made her ache for the ones she'd left behind. Lord, but she missed those girls more than she'd expected. She still hadn't been able to bring herself to open the gift they'd sent with her. It was already two days past Christmas, and the brightly wrapped package still sat on the desk in Katie's room where she was once again ensconced, silently chastising her for her cowardly departure every time she looked at it.

Gwyn surveyed her with pursed lips and furrowed brow. "I'm worried about you," she announced.

"Don't be. I'm fine. And I promise I'll be out of your hair sooner rather than later this time. I already have three places lined up for viewing this weekend, and today's only the day after Boxing Day. You watch— another week, and I'll be gone."

"That's not what worries me." Gwyn stepped down into the sunken room and made a shooing motion at

Abby's feet. Abby drew her pajama-clad knees up to her chest, and her sister plunked down beside her. "You've just been so quiet since you came back here, Ab. You're like a shadow, the way you move from room to room. You barely touch your food, and you're with us, but you're not. Honestly? It's as bad as it was when you arrived here from L.A. *That* is what worries me."

That bad? So much for thinking she was putting on a brave face. She'd have to try harder.

"Well, you can stop worrying, because I'm all right. Really." Abby reached over and squeezed Gwyn's hand. "I'm not saying I haven't been through a lot, because I know I have. But I'm tougher than you think, Gwyn. Heck, I'm tougher than *I* think, most days. I just need a little time to get my feet back under me is all. And look at this." She reached over to the oversized trunk that served as a coffee table and retrieved a stack of papers, which she dropped in Gwyn's lap. Distraction time.

Gwyn leafed through them. "University course descriptions?"

Abby nodded. "Mitch—" Her voice wobbled on the name, but she shored herself up and continued, "Mitch brought home a course catalog for me a couple of weeks ago, and it got me thinking about going back to do that psychology degree. I'm not sure yet if I can get into the winter term, but at least it's a start. And I have the money for it now."

"You do," Gwyn agreed, her eyes turning suspiciously bright.

"Stop that," Abby ordered. "Or you'll get me going, too."

Her sister sniffled. "It's just—when I think of everything you went through, first with William and then losing your family, and me not being there for you, and then you finding and losing *another* family—"

"Hey." Abby put down her magazine and shuffled along the couch until she could give Gwyn a one-armed hug. "You're here for me now, remember? You and Gareth and your entire brood—you're my family now. And that's more than enough."

Gwyn looked sideways at her. "You're a terrible liar, Abigail Jamieson."

"Yeah," Abby said, resting her head on her sister's shoulder. "I know."

They both fell silent, and Abby felt the slight rise and fall of Gwyn's breathing in the shoulder beneath her cheek. There was a pause. Then a deep exhale.

"Can I ask you a question?" Gwyn asked, then proceeded without waiting for permission. "Why didn't you just stay? I mean, I know all the excuses you gave me about the girls getting too attached, but if you stayed, that wouldn't be a problem, right? You and Mitch—it's pretty obvious there are some feelings between the two of you..."

Abby closed her eyes.

"*I have to leave.*"

"*I know.*"

"Abby?" her sister prompted. "Why didn't you stay?"

Abby let out a tremulous sigh. "He didn't ask," she said simply.

There was another long pause, and then Gwyn's

arm went around her. She dropped a kiss into Abby's hair. "I'm sorry, sweetie."

"Me, too. But I'm still going to be okay."

"Yeah," said Gwyn. "I know."

With a last hug, Gwyn went to join her family for their movie, leaving Abby to her magazine, her memories, and her absolute determination to never, ever again attempt a Christmas that even resembled a traditional one.

"No tree," she muttered, flipping a page. "No lights. No ornaments. No turkey. No—"

The tumult of voices coming from the end of the hall died down as the strains of the theme song from *The Grinch* floated through air, and Abby's thoughts stopped dead at the sheer irony. In spite of herself, she felt the corner of her mouth twitch. Then she snorted. Then she lifted her gaze ceilingward.

"Touché, universe," she said. "Touché."

And she wondered again how Rachel and Britt and Kia—and Mitch—were faring with their holidays.

CHAPTER 50

Mitch plugged in the kettle and took the makings for tea out of the cupboard, going over the "family meeting" in his head for the hundredth time. The girls had made some excellent points, but so had he—and nothing had changed. Whether he had asked her to stay or not, Abigail's decision to leave had been her own.

Hadn't it?

Except a few days ago, she offered to stay longer, too.

He scowled at the lazy spiral of steam drifting upward from the kettle spout. She might have offered to stay longer, but she'd also hesitated about it. And then she'd changed her mind. "*I have to go.*"

Her words, not his.

But he hadn't disagreed.

Because I knew it was best.

But Rachel was right. He hadn't asked her, and he hadn't given her a choice, and he'd made the decision for her, and damn it to hell, what if he asked now and she said yes and then it didn't work out? If she left, how would his kids cope with the loss of someone else? How would *he* cope? Losing Eve had damn near killed him, and losing Abby might well finish the job. Except Britt was right about *that*, too. If he didn't make an effort, if he didn't at least try, then they'd have lost her already.

The kettle reached a full boil and switched itself off with a loud click in the otherwise silent kitchen. Mitch reached for it, then paused as he looked at the two cups he'd set out beside it, one with a chamomile tea bag for him, and the other with peppermint... for Abby. He looked down at the dog still sprawled on the floor watching him.

"Well, damn," he said again. "I guess that kind of answers my question about what to do, doesn't it?"

Hope yawned loudly, heaved himself to his feet, and padded from the room, nails tapping on the floor. Mitch watched him leave, yet again both impressed and somewhat unsettled by the dog's uncanny ability to know where he was most needed in the house—and when he was not. Then he roused himself, unplugged the kettle, and followed in the dog's wake.

"Girls!" he called as he headed for the living room to turn off the tree lights. "Get your coats and boots on! We're going to see Abb—"

He stopped in his tracks. His three daughters were squished together on the loveseat with their coats, hats, and boots already on.

"Took you long enough," Rachel said, standing and pulling Kia up with her. "We're boiling!"

Thank God for technology, Mitch thought as he retraced Abby's route to her sister's house using the vehicle's GPS history.

"Are we there, yet?" Kia asked from the back seat.

Mitch glanced at the moving blue dot that was their SUV on the GPS display, then at the estimated travel time ticking down at the bottom. "Ten more minutes, sweetie," he said. He did a rear-view mirror check on his two youngest, but the streetlights lining the bridge they crossed weren't strong enough to penetrate the shadows. The remnants of an unease he'd been unable to shake stirred in his chest. This could still go so, so wrong.

He looked sideways at Rachel and cleared his throat. "So. We're clear on there being no guarantees about this, right? Abby might not—"

"We *know*, Daddy. She might not want to come home with us. You've told us a bajillion times since we left the house."

"And you're sure you're okay with taking that chance?" Another sidelong look.

"We're sure it's better than not asking at all," she retorted. "And we've told you *that* a bajillion times, too. Can you please just stop worrying?"

Easier said than done, sweetie, Mitch thought, tightening his grip on the steering wheel and focusing his attention on the road. *So much easier said than done with this much at stake.*

Abby made it to the halfway point of the movie before the merriment coming down the hall from the living room drove her out of the sitting room and upstairs to her—Katie's—room. There, with the door closed and a pillow pulled over her head, the sound was muted enough that she could hardly tell who was laughing anymore. It didn't help.

Neither did not being able to breathe.

She shoved the pillow off in exasperation and stared at the ceiling. *Why* was this so difficult? She'd already lost a husband and a child, hadn't she? That was way worse than walking away from Mitch and the kids, right? A hundred thousand times worse, in fact. At least.

So why did leaving the Abrams still make her feel as though a knife had wedged itself between her ribs at just the right angle to scrape her heart raw with every beat? Why—

She turned her head toward the package still sitting on the desk. It was wrapped in paper covered with snowmen wearing red scarves and black top hats, and an enormous bow sat crookedly atop it, the way Kiana's poof ponytails always seemed...the knife scraped again.

Abby sat up on the bed. Dear heavens. She blinked at the gift. That was it, wasn't it? She wasn't hurting because she'd lost Mitch and the girls, but because she *hadn't* lost them. She'd walked away from them. Left *them* instead of the other way around—and on purpose, no less. And all because Mitch hadn't asked her to stay, just as she hadn't asked him if she could, and neither one of them had a clue how the other felt.

And they never would, if they didn't talk. And then the choice she'd made to leave would be permanent, and she really *would* have lost them, and—

The very possibility made her want to fold in on

herself, but instead she scrambled off the bed and fumbled out of her pajama top. No. No way would she lose another family. Not without one heck of a fight, because no one knew better than she did how very short life could be—or how precious the people in it. She tugged on her sports bra and snatched up the thin cotton turtleneck she'd dropped on the chair back earlier. She'd seen how Mitch looked at her. Heck, Gwyn and Perk—Jessica had both commented on it. That meant *something* was there, right? And if something was there, then—finished with the turtleneck, she hopped around on one foot, trying to slide the other into her jeans—then there was a chance. She needed to *give* it a chance.

She wiggled the denim over her hips and then paused with the zip half done up.

But what if Mitch didn't want to? What if the reason he'd responded to her *I need to go* with his own *I know* had been his way of saying he wasn't ready...or interested...or—

Abby turned her head toward her reflection in the mirror hanging on the back of Katie's door and stared herself in the eye. She could go around in circles on this for the rest of her life, wondering *what if*, she told herself firmly, or she could just talk to him and find out. At least if she took the latter route, she would know one way or the other, and that had to be better than continuing to wallow in angst the way she'd been doing.

Talking it would be.

Decision made, she finished dressing, grabbed her handbag off the dresser, and ran down the stairs.

Halfway there, she turned and ran back up again to collect her unopened gift from the girls. That definitely needed to go with her. Then she retraced her steps downstairs, arriving in the living room as the Grinch's heart was about to grow three sizes that day.

"I need to borrow a vehicle," she announced breathlessly.

All heads turned toward her, and Gareth pointed the remote control at the television. The Grinch paused mid heart-growth.

Belatedly, Abby looked around the crowded room at the kids sprawled on the floor and the adults wedged together on the sofa. She hadn't even come out to say hello to Grace and Sean and their brood when they'd arrived. "Hey," she said to them now. "Sorry for the interruption, but I just"—her gaze returned to rest on her sister and she clutched the wrapped gift against her chest—"I need to see Mitch and the girls. Can I please borrow a vehicle?"

"It's about blasted time," Gareth said, his mouth quirking with more smirk than smile. "You can take mine; Gwyn's resembles a fast-food restaurant gone wrong at the moment. The keys are in my coat pocket in the closet, tank is full, and there's no need to get it back to me tonight."

Abby's face turned hot at the underlying meaning behind her brother-in-law's words. She hadn't got as far as that idea, and she didn't dare stop to address it now. Summoning every ounce of bravado she possessed, she nodded her thanks, shoved her feet into her boots, collected her coat and Gareth's keys from the closet, and opened the front door.

"Abby!" squealed a child's voice, and a small shadow hurtled across the porch and launched itself at her.

CHAPTER 51

Abby staggered under the impact and grabbed for the doorframe so they didn't both tumble backwards into Gwyn's front hall. "Kia?" she wheezed. "What are you doing here?"

"We came to get you!" The little girl beamed up at her, arms still fastened around her waist. "We missed you, and we've been keeping the house really really clean so you won't have too much work to do when you come home again, and Hope says he misses you, too, and..."

Across the porch, Mitch stepped into the light, tall and broad-shouldered and utterly gorgeous. Abby lifted her gaze to his, and Kia's words faded into the background. "You came...to get me?" she whispered.

Mitch grimaced. "Nothing that presumptuous, but I did come to talk." He gestured at the coat she held. "You're going somewhere?"

"I was coming to see you. To talk."

"I see," he said. He cleared his throat, and his eyes crinkled at the corners as he gave her a half-smile. "Then I suppose we should. Talk, I mean. Is there somewhere...?"

"Use the sitting room!" Gwyn called from within the house. "The kids can hang out with us here."

Kids, plural? Abby pulled her gaze from Mitch and saw Rachel and Britt peering out from behind him on either side. Rachel gave her a little wave; Britt, a big grin. Then, before she could react, Gwyn was behind her, urging everyone inside and taking coats. She pointed Mitch toward the back of the house, plucked Abby's coat and gift away from her, and gave her a little shove between her shoulder blades in Mitch's direction.

"No need to rush," she said. "I'll make sure the girls are looked after, and we have popcorn and drinks here, so you won't have any interruptions."

Leaving her sister to supervise the rearranging of the bodies on the living room floor to accommodate the newcomers, Abby tried to concentrate on putting one foot in front of the other as she followed the broad, strong shoulders down the hall toward the kitchen and sitting room. She wasn't terribly successful. Mitch was wearing one of those long-sleeved t-shirts that molded itself to his every muscle—and there were a lot of those. Hard to the touch, she remembered from her brief encounters with them, but warm and—

She put her hands up to her cheeks. *Talk*, he'd said. He'd come here to talk. That was what she wanted to do, too, and—Mitch stopped abruptly in front of her and she skidded to a breathless halt, just shy of running into him. He glanced over his shoulder, one eyebrow raised.

"Did she mean to send us to the kitchen?"

Abby opened her mouth to respond, decided she didn't trust her voice while standing this close to him, and edged past him to flip on a light switch. Two lamps came on, illuminating the sitting room that had been in deep shadow beyond the brightly lit kitchen, and Mitch's gaze turned to it.

"Nice," he murmured.

Abby seized on his admiration, relieved to have a neutral topic of discussion. "It's my favorite room in the house. Gwyn designed it herself—she's an architect. She's very good. She does mostly houses, but I think she's done small offices and other—"

"Abby."

She snapped her mouth shut and wrapped her arms around herself, then gave a rueful grimace. "I'm babbling, aren't I?"

"Maybe a little." Laughter danced in Mitch's eyes, the kind of warm, gentle teasing that made Abby's toes curl against the cool ceramic tile. "Come on," he said, tipping his head toward the sitting room. "Let's sit."

She led the way across the kitchen and down the single step, but she didn't try to sit. She didn't think she could, given how rigid her body had become. She hugged herself tighter.

"So," she said.

"So," said Mitch at the same time.

They both stopped. Abby stared at the floor. Mitch, she was sure, stared at her. She felt his gaze as if it were a physical touch on the top of her bent head.

"I'll go first," he said. "Abby, I know you're still grieving William and Olivia, and I won't try to tell you that the girls and I have recovered from losing Eve, because we haven't. But something happened to all of us when you came into the house—into the family.

Something good. The girls are happier and more settled. *I'm* happier and more settled. And you...you smile a lot more now than you did when you came to us. And yes, some of it has to do with being more organized and having routines and schedules, but I think it's more than that. At least, for me it is, and—"

"You didn't ask me to stay." Her interruption dropped between them, bald and blunt. She raised her gaze to his. "That's why I left," she said. "Because you didn't ask me to stay."

"I know. And believe it or not, I did it for you. Letting you leave, I mean. I thought it was the right thing to do because—" Mitch broke off and turned to pace the floor near the Palladian windows. He shoved his hands into his pockets, his forearms corded with tension. "I didn't want to be another William in your life, expecting you to stay home and look after the house and the kids and me. And I didn't want you to be another Eve in mine. I have so many regrets about not giving her the chance to have her own life outside of being a wife and mother, I can't even begin to list them. I wanted you to have more. I *want* you to have more. I want you to go to school, and to have that independence you're trying to achieve, and—"

"You know she stayed home because she wanted to, right?"

Mitch stopped pacing. "What?"

"Eve. She stayed home because she wanted to. She looked after the girls and the house and you because that's what *she* wanted to do."

His jaw went tight. "You don't know that."

"But I do. I know it because you're not another William, Mitch. You're not anything like him. You never took choices away from Eve. She did what she wanted to do. And when I offered to stay longer to help you out, that was what *I* wanted to do."

"But you hesitated."

"Because of what—because of—because..." She trailed off and looked away, unable to give voice to the tiny flare of hope that resided just beneath her ribs.

"Because you felt something between us?" His voice took on the husky note that made her knees want to dissolve. "I felt it, too, Abby. I still do. I'm just not sure what..."

"To do about it?" She swallowed a slightly hysterical giggle at how they were finishing each other's sentences. "Me, either."

"The girls and I know there are no guarantees this will work out," he said, "and there's a lot to lose, for all of us."

She nodded. "I know."

"But as Britt pointed out to me, we've already lost if we don't at least try."

"Your daughters are wise girls."

Mitch gave a snort of laughter and said, "You have no idea," but he didn't explain. Instead, he strolled toward her and stopped a few inches away, close enough that she had to tip her head back to look at him. Close enough that his warmth reached out to mingle with hers. His gaze turned serious and searching.

"*Will* you give it a try, Abigail Jamieson?" he asked. "Will you come home with us and see where this goes, whatever it is? We'll take it slow, and we'll get help so you can still do what *you* want—I saw the classes you circled in the course catalog—so after-school help, a housekeeper, whatever works for you. And I'll make sure I take Kia to her appointments, and—"

"Yes," Abby said.

He stared at her, then exhaled a long, slow breath. "It won't be easy," he cautioned. "We both come with a lot of baggage, and we're going to need to be honest with one another. No holding back secrets in an effort not to hurt the other's feelings."

Abby thought about her role as investor in his company, decided it wasn't the kind of secret he meant, and tucked away the revelation for later. "Agreed."

"Well, then." He regarded her across the space separating them, and Abby's stomach did a queer little flip-flop as she met the banked, slumbering heat of his gaze. "Well, then," he said again. "I'm sure the girls would like to know you're coming home—"

Home. Abby's heart swelled at the thought.

"—but first," Mitch continued in that low rumble she loved so much, "if it's okay with you, there's something I've been wanting to do for a while."

"There—there is?"

"Mm." He reached out and traced a thumb over the swell of her bottom lip. "Even before you beat me to it, in fact."

Beat him—Abby felt the heat rise in her cheeks. Oh. He was talking about the time she'd so brazenly kissed him.

Oh. He's talking about kissing.

"May I?" he asked huskily, his gaze searching.

Every atom of air left Abby's lungs in a hiss, rendering her incapable of voicing the *yes, please* that sprang to her mind in answer. But she nodded, and Mitch stepped forward, closing the gap between them, and his hands cupped her face, and finally—*finally*—his lips touched hers and—

"They're kissing! Everything's okay, everyone!" a boy's voice yelled, and Abby's eyes shot open to find her nephew grinning at them over the railing behind the couch.

"Nicholas!" Gareth's voice bellowed from the other end of the house.

Her nephew heaved a sigh and scuffed a toe against the floor. "Oh, man! I always have to miss the good stuff." He slouched across the kitchen toward the hallway, turning at the doorway. "You can go back to kissing now. Sorry I interrupted you."

"*NI-CHO-LAS!*"

"Coming!" Nicholas thundered down the hall, leaving silence in his wake, but not for long, because almost immediately, more footsteps thundered in the opposite direction, followed by a chorus of voices calling out Kiana's name—presumably to no avail, given their increasing volume.

Mitch's wry gaze met Abby's. "Well," he said. "So much for that idea. Is he always like that?"

"Gwyn can tell you stories that will give you nightmares," Abby replied. "Let's just say her and Gareth's courtship was... challenging."

"I can imagine. And I suspect we'll have a few challenges of our own." Mitch tipped his head in the direction of the little body hurtling across the kitchen toward them, followed closely by Rachel and Britt, who were still trying to recall their baby sister. "You're okay with that?"

"I'm fine with it." Abby smiled up at him, her heart doing its own private little dance at the idea of a courtship with this amazing man.

And then Kiana wedged herself between them, and Rachel and Britt joined them, and a babble of voices vied to be heard, and the warmest, most comfortable glow Abby had ever experienced enveloped her in a bubble that radiated outward to include Mitch and his daughters—all wrapped up in the bittersweet memory of Olivia. She was absolutely fine with challenges, she thought as she watched Kiana bounce and flap, then raised her gaze to meet the answering glow in Mitch's eyes.

And she would be eternally grateful for the chance to have them, too.

About the Author

Like all romance writers, Linda Poitevin is a firm believer in happy-ever-afters, but she also knows how hard you have to work at relationships sometimes. She tries to reflect that in stories about people who live, laugh, cry, and love just as hard as they can in this crazy life we all share—people who are as real to her as she hopes they'll be to you.

Linda lives outside Ottawa, Canada's capital, where (in her other-than-writing life) she is a wife, mom, friend, avid gardener, walker of a giant dog, and keeper of many (many!) pets. She also writes dark urban fantasy under the name of Lydia M. Hawke.

You can find Linda on her website at Linda-Poitevin.com (sign up for her newsletter there to get book updates!) or shoot her an email (she loves to hear from readers!) at info@LindaPoitevin.com.

OTHER BOOKS BY LINDA POITEVIN

Gwynneth Ever After

Forever After

Forever Grace

Always and Forever

Shadow of Doubt

Writing as Lydia M. Hawke

Sins of the Angels

Sins of the Son

Sins of the Lost

Sins of the Warrior

www.ingramcontent.com/pod-product-compliance
Lightning Source LLC
Chambersburg PA
CBHW061301190726
48288CB00002B/303